D1553447

Bad JuJu in Cleveland

By Karl Bort with
Thekla Madsen

Madsen Communications, Inc. ·
River Falls, Wis.

ADVANCE PRAISE FOR "BAD JUJU IN CLEVELAND"

"There very well may be BAD JuJu in Cleveland, but Bort and Madsen have conspired to write a very, very GOOD novel, which will please hardcore police procedural fans and general readers alike."

– Dave Wood, past vice president National Book Critic Circle, syndicated author of "Dave Wood's Book Report"

BAD JUJU IN CLEVELAND

Copyright Karl Bort with Thekla Madsen, 2014

Madsen Communications, Inc.
River Falls, Wisconsin 54022
www.bortmadsen.com

ISBN-13:978-0-692-22837-1

Cover design by Chris Cheetham |
chrischeetham@att.net
Website design by Donald Bort |
donaldbort@gmail.com
Formatting by Rob Bignell, Inventing Reality Editing Service |
http://inventingreality.4t.com/editingservices.html

Manufactured in the United States of America
First printing May 2014

Dedicated to the men and women of the Cleveland, Ohio Police Department

Local police forces and their federal counterparts work hard every day to make the streets safer for everyone, often at great sacrifices to their families and themselves. For every bad event that is publicized, there are many more good things police officers are doing that never make the news. The central crime of the book actually did occur and was used as the basis for this work of fiction. While selected locations, businesses, and characters may be real or have a factual basis, they are portrayed fictionally in this novel. Any resemblance to actual persons, places, or situations (current or historical) is unintentional.

Acknowledgements

Special thanks to those who allowed their real names to be used (you know who you are!), Thekla Madsen for co-writing this book, Rob Bignell for his e-publishing expertise, and Chris Cheetham for the "killer" cover!
– Karl Bort

Prologue

Cleveland Police Detective Nicholas Silvano, Badge #124, lounged on the rear deck of his twenty-eight foot Rinker cruiser and stared out over Lake Erie. Nick and his good buddy Jack Daniels had been hanging out since his Narcotics Unit shift ended – seven hours ago. At 3 a.m. the Great Lake's waters were calm and a slight breeze kept the humidity level manageable.

His six-foot-two-inch frame was a solid presence in the ephemeral pre-dawn hours and filled the deck chair without spilling over, thanks to regular workouts at the police gym that held his weight at 220 pounds. You didn't have to know his last name to peg him as Italian. His ancestry was reflected in the tanned complexion, distinctive cheekbones, dark eyes, and wavy, slate-colored hair he controlled with a short haircut and gel.

He watched a mosquito land on his exposed arm. *Could a mosquito get drunk by sucking blood from a drunk?* He decided it didn't matter and swatted it dead. The hypnotic sway of the boat and the whiskey's influence lulled him back in time. Twenty-one years ago he was a rookie fresh out of the Police Academy when he was "officially" welcomed to the job.

"There are four stages to being a cop, Kid," a grizzled

veteran told him. "The first is Rookie stage. You always wear your hat when you get out of the car. You have clean underwear on in case you get shot, stabbed, or end up in a hospital emergency room. Next is Cowboy Cop. You drink to excess. If you're married, you'll probably get divorced. You get a military buzz haircut, probably a couple tattoos, work out constantly, wear black fingerless gloves, and pound the piss out of anybody who challenges your authority.

"Helpless and Hopeless mode hits around year fifteen. Much of your time is spent in Federal Court defending yourself against lawsuits filed by the people you pounded the piss out of during your Cowboy Cop years. You probably get a part-time job to keep up with child support and alimony payments. You'll be lucky if alcohol is your only vice. But you hang on because now you're vested in your pension.

"The last stage is Auto Pilot. You try to make it to retirement without being too big of a drunk. You'll put in transfer requests to any inside job that will take you off the streets and wonder if your liver will last long enough for you to get that first pension check. And even that may not amount to much after the ex-wife, or ex-wives, get their cut."

The old-timer had looked him straight in the eyes then with an expression that was half pity and half humor. "It happens to everyone; you can't escape it. Welcome to the job, Kid!"

At the time it sounded like a load of bullshit, but now it seemed prophetic. Nick thought he was entering

Auto Pilot stage. He took another pull from the bottle. *Empty.*

Chapter 1

One last squinting glance in the rented Dodge Caravan's rear-view mirror confirmed the two Jamaican accomplices, Dion and Tarik, were in position a few car lengths behind. JuJu's gaze returned to the windshield before his two passengers registered there might be something of interest behind them, then turned into the narrow driveway and put the van in Park. Despite the windshield wipers' valiant efforts to defend the view, the mid-day July thunderstorm made it seem like he was peering through wavy block glass.

He turned the ignition off and the wipers ceased their battle, causing the two-story house in front of them to waver like a mirage in the desert. The only sound was the muted thudding of the rain bouncing off the roof of the van. While the conditions were not ideal for driving, they were perfect for murder.

JuJu twisted slightly to the right and unbuckled his seat belt. The movement caused a corresponding nudge in his side from the knife sheath attached to his belt. The van's passengers unbuckled their seat belts and one of the men hoisted a black duffel bag onto his lap. The passengers were couriers, employees of a Mexican drug cartel, who traveled 1,200 miles non-stop from Miami to Cleveland with a load of cocaine.

Just twenty minutes earlier JuJu had picked them up in the parking lot of the Independence Inn Hotel and brought them to their destination on Dickens Avenue. As the Cartel's Protector, it was JuJu's job to ensure the deal was completed without any complications. So much could go wrong. Prior successes had earned him a cautious degree of trust from his employers. A trust that would soon be betrayed. Today, JuJu was only protecting himself.

"Ogun - may your warrior spirit protect and guide me," JuJu mumbled the familiar mantra under his breath, instantly feeling the electric tingle of Ogun's power in his veins as he and the two passengers exited the van. Despite the noise created by the heavy downpour, one of the passengers nodded in JuJu's direction as if acknowledging a silent instruction from the large man charged with protecting the drug exchange.

The three men climbed the dilapidated steps of the tired looking house. The front door opened quickly and a diminutive black man motioned them inside. In those few seconds, JuJu both assessed and dismissed him as a threat. The man's dove grey suit was elegantly tailored in a way that suggested a wiry strength despite the slim stature, but he was no match for JuJu.

Sylvester "Pookie" Ashford stepped aside, allowing the new arrivals to enter. JuJu noticed another black man standing in the opening between the front room and the dining area about four feet in front of where he stood. Definitely the muscle. His alert eyes swept over both men looking for weapons.

"Right on time," Pookie said. "I like that."

The group stood quietly for a moment, taking measure of each other. Drug deals this large had inherent risks but yielded vast rewards.

JuJu spoke first. "My associates," he nodded toward the Mexicans, "don't speak much English. I will conduct this transaction. Do you have the money?" he asked Pookie.

"Yeah," Pookie said, turning toward the other man in room. JuJu pegged him as "Track Suit" since he was dressed in matching navy sweat pants, T-shirt and jacket. The man was tall and looked like he could block an elephant. A dark blue duffel bag hung by his side suspended from a hand that could cover a basketball.

JuJu eyed the partially zipped nylon jacket and saw the familiar bulge of a weapon. *I'll have to take care of him first.*

Pookie turned back to JuJu. "Let me see the product."

JuJu nodded and one of the couriers stepped up and placed his duffel bag on the battered coffee table top and unzipped it, revealing white, tightly wrapped bricks of cocaine. Pookie removed one of the bricks and turned it over in his hand as if to gauge its weight. Then he performed a careful count of the number of white bricks in the bag, turned to Track Suit and nodded. Track Suit set his duffel full of cash next to the black bag and backed away. JuJu kept his eyes on Pookie and Track Suit while one of the Mexicans counted the bundles of hundred dollar bills. With everyone focused on the money, nobody noticed as JuJu stealthily faded back from the assembled group.

The front door flew open and the two Jamaicans rushed in, brandishing Mini-Mac 10 machine guns. "What the hell!" Pookie yelled, looking to JuJu for reassurance. JuJu held his gaze for a moment, then calmly looked away.

"What the fuck!" one of the couriers shouted, frantically reaching for his gun only to remember it was back in Mexico. They traveled without weapons in case they became the subject of a traffic stop.

"On your knees," JuJu calmly instructed the group. "All of you," he said, including the couriers in his command. He was in charge now.

The four men did as ordered. Pookie's mouth tried to form words but there was no sound to support them. In that instant, Track Suit reached for his weapon. Before he could remove it, JuJu sprung with a rattlesnake's deadly accuracy, jumping over the coffee table at his prey. With one slashing strike, Track Suit's neck split open and his body jerked violently.

JuJu held Track Suit's eyes with his own, forcing the dying man to his knees, his hands clawing desperately as if to close the hole at his throat. "I knew you were the one to watch," he hissed, "but my power is stronger!" The man's blood pooled warmly over JuJu's forearms, then wrists, then hands, before finally breaking off onto the tributaries of his fingers.

"Ogun shoro shoro, eyebale kawo!" JuJu roared, abandoning his usual formal style of speaking in the frenzy of the moment. The Jamaicans kept their weapons trained on the Mexicans, but the men didn't move. Even if escape were possible, their days would be numbered. Returning to Mexico without the cartel's money was the same as a death sentence; they would be burned alive. Better to die here with some measure of honor.

JuJu approached the couriers. Even in the face of death, their eyes met his as if acknowledging they had been a part of his plan all along. "For Ogun!" he screamed. The bloody knife easily passed through skin, cartilage, and sinew of the first courier's neck. He turned to the courier's partner.

"For Ogun!" Again, the knife performed the task for which it was created.

The drug couriers' bodies slumped and folded over themselves onto the bare wooden floor, their blood and breath mixing to create red bubbles still laboring to escape through the smiling holes in their throats.

"Don't do this man!" Pookie pleaded, finally finding his voice. He scrambled toward the front door, his feet trying to propel his body out of the room like a long jumper. "I can get more money!" He didn't make it. Tion hit him in the head with the gun and he crumpled to the floor. JuJu picked Pookie up by the back of his suit coat and enfolded him in a violent embrace. The Obeah Man would make sure his warrior god Ogun would not be denied his sacrifices. Almost unconsciously, his arm moved against Pookie's neck and it was over. He watched, fascinated, as the soft grey material of Pookie's lapels darkened to a hellish maroon. Using the back of Pookie's suit coat as a rag, he wiped the knife clean. *It is done.* The Jamaicans stared, mesmerized at the carnage brought by the Obeah Man. If only they could have played too! But the big man's orders were clear - this time, it was hands off.

"Give me the bag!" JuJu demanded. Darik removed the brown leather messenger bag that had been slung over his shoulder and handed it to the man who had just killed four people in a matter of minutes. JuJu removed a small iron cauldron containing an eleke necklace of green and black beads with white shells and placed it in the middle of the obscene square created by the four bodies.

"This is my offering to you, Ogun," he spoke loudly, wearing a wild look of exhilaration mixed with pride. One-by-one, he positioned each body on its back and using the knife, cut each of the men's blood-soaked shirts open, exposing their chests. He extracted a glass jar containing black paint from the bag and dipped his index finger into the mix, then like an artist wielding a paintbrush, drew a black cross onto each man's chest. When he was done, he wiped his finger clean on one of the courier's legs.

"We must leave now," he said, standing quickly. He caught Tion frisking Track Suit's body. "Leave them!" JuJu roared, just as Tion removed a 9mm Smith and Wesson. "You two don't need a gun! Anything that exposes you will expose me as well." He pointed to the duffel bags. "Take a bag!" he commanded. Regretfully, the Jamaicans left the bodies as they were, picked up the bags, and headed for the door. The pair weren't accustomed to merely being spectators where violence was concerned. JuJu looked at the dead bodies one more time, and then followed the Jamaicans out the door.

"What did you say to them?" Darik asked as he and Tion dropped the duffel bags in the backseat of the van. "I've never heard that language before."

"It is the language of my ancestors, the Lucumi," JuJu answered, then translated, "Ogun speaks loudly, blood sacrifice - observe what the Gods have decreed!"

Chapter 2

The Homicide Detectives and blue uniformed Cleveland Police patrol officers mingled at the crime scene house on Cleveland's east side. Two white, windowless Cuyahoga County Coroner vans were parked at the curb. Four attendants loitered outside by the vans, waiting for permission to collect the bodies.

A couple of the Zone Cars parked on Dickens Avenue still had their overhead lights on, illuminating the onlookers and news media people in flashes of red, white, and blue as they stood behind the yellow tape designating the area as a crime scene. Most of the gawkers wore clothing fitting of the hot, humid July night; as little as possible. Kids ran around and played like it was some sort of neighborhood party, and in a way, it was. The inner city streets had their own rules. If only Police cars were out, you stayed inside your house. The bad guys might still be around and you didn't want to catch a bullet from the cops or a crook if gunfire broke out. If the police and the news media were there, it was safe to come outside. The newsies wouldn't be there if bullets were flying.

From their side of the crime scene tape, reporters from several local stations elbowed each other for position and thrust their microphones toward the yard, frantically competing for comments, or better yet, a live interview from one of the cops standing outside. When it was apparent they were being ignored, they turned their attention to the crowd. But not everyone wanted their face on the Channel 19 evening news. You might as well stand in the street holding a sign saying, "Shoot me, I'm a snitch!" Even if it was to mug for the camera, you didn't want the neighborhood gangbangers tracking you down later.

The air was still oppressively hot and the lack of any breeze had the summer bugs buzzing in large swarms around the lone working streetlight. While the city did what it could to keep the lights on, it was like chasing the tide. As soon as a disabled light was replaced, the gangs or some other drunken idiot with a gun would come along and shoot it out.

The Dickens Avenue address was a double home, typical of the kind built in the 1930s when the city's east side neighborhoods were thriving, not yet infested with crime and gangs. These dwellings had identical floor plans up and down with two entrance doors on the front porch and a single side door entering into a shared hallway for access to the basement and the stairway to the upper floor.

"Damn," Narcotics Unit Detective Nick Silvano uttered as he maneuvered the beat up, unmarked, blue Ford Taurus through the crowd looking for a place to park.

A uniformed cop jumped in front of the car waving

his arms and shouting, "Where do you think you assholes are going?"

Nick braked to avoid running the cop over and slammed the gearshift into Park. He stuck his arm out the window and waved his gold Detective badge. "Us assholes are the cops you dumb shit! Don't you recognize a cop car when you see one?"

The uniformed officer stammered an apology. "Sorry Detective, we got a lot of news people trying to slip by and all these fuckin' little kids running around like they're at a birthday party – it's been a zoo! Go ahead on."

"Thanks," replied Nick. This guy had to be a rookie. If kids had him coming apart, he didn't want to be around when the real shit started. Nick parked the Taurus on the dirt lawn in front of the house, using the yellow DO NOT CROSS tape as a parking line. "Show time!" he told his two partners.

Nick and Detectives Frank Hartness and Lenny Moore had been partners for over three years and each knew their place in the triangle of the job they performed. Nick had seniority in the unit and handled most of the undercover operations. Frank had typing and organizational skills, and Lenny prioritized assignments as they came in from the bosses upstairs. Frank came on the job the same time as Nick and had two extra years on his partner. He still pursued sports with the zeal of his younger years and said his graying hair actually gave him an advantage as people underestimated his abilities on the basketball court.

Lenny was ten years younger with a slight build and a full head of blonde hair. His youthful look was an advantage in undercover operations; he could easily pass as a college student looking for a high or a down-and-out player looking to make a big score. Cleveland narcotics detectives generally traveled in threes. The extra body functioned as two more eyes for surveillance and protection.

The three detectives dodged the mud and puddles as best they could. The previous day's rain had left a sludgy mess. Nick spotted Homicide Lieutenant Jonathon Fratello standing on the home's sloping front porch, smoking a cigarette. He and Fratello had been Police Academy classmates and graduated together. Although they had never been partners, they played together on Police softball teams along with the current Chief of Police, Robert Marinik. Eleven years ago when Nick was new to the Narc Squad, Fratello had uncovered a plot by a crazed junkie to 'take Nick out'. While it was uncommon for a cop to be targeted, Nick often wondered if he would still be here today if his friend had not revealed the plan and stopped the junkie. Their wives became best friends. Fratello was still married to the same woman; Nick and his wife, Cheryl, split up after six years of intermittent disputes and trial separations.

Nick ducked under more yellow tape and walked up the splintered wooden front porch taking care to avoid the missing top step. "What brings the Homicide Commander out on such a glorious Cleveland night?"

he asked his friend.

"Sorry to bother you Nick, but I think this one is in your wheelhouse," Fratello said.

"What have you got, Jon?"

"Four dead bodies in the house, all with their throats cut and black crosses painted on their bare chests."

"Holy shit," Nick muttered.

"That's not all," continued Fratello. "There's a metal bowl with some beads and other stuff on the dining room floor. I have no idea if it means anything at all. A ritual? A warning? We're pretty sure it's a dope house; we got scales and baggies, but no dope! We got a Smith 9 off one of the bodies, still in his pants and not fired."

"Who called it in?"

"Some burglar looking to steal the copper plumbing came in and found more than he bargained for. Lucky for us, he called it in but didn't stick around. He even left the big screen television."

"He really must have been spooked," Nick agreed. "Anyone else see anything?"

"Nobody is coming forward, and with all the rain we had this afternoon, there weren't many people out. We are being told that the house has been abandoned for months with both the upstairs and lower units uninhabited. There just isn't much to go on."

"It's early," Nick offered.

"The Chief doesn't see it that way. He's already on my ass from that Imperial Avenue case a couple months back where that mental giant raped and killed eleven women and buried them all over his property. We got him in custody but Chief Marinik doesn't want this case to go nuclear like that one did. The national news reporters are still in a feeding frenzy and the recent discovery of those women being found alive after they were held captive ten years on the west side is giving us a lot of attention. The Feds are still looking to see where we screwed up, like we actually knew what that dickhead was doing. I thought maybe you and your guys could keep your eyes and ears open. Something might jump out on the streets about this case."

"We'll do our best," Nick assured his friend. "Like I said, it's early."

"I got two years to go and I want to retire out of Homicide. If this case blows up, the Chief will have no choice but to get someone else to do my job."

Fratello was right. Chief Marinik was a pretty good guy but he trumped Fratello. The Chief's favorite saying was, "shit flows downhill". If these killings weren't solved quickly, Fratello's chances of remaining Commander were slim to none.

Nick left his friend on the porch and walked into the house. Frank and Lenny were already working the scene. Anything drug related was placed into plastic evidence bags and sealed with red evidence tape to prevent tampering until they were reopened by the lab. The pair took great care during their search to avoid being impaled by unseen needles. Too often a cop stuck his hand under a couch cushion or into a pocket or purse only to come out with a used needle sticking out of his finger. The possibility of becoming infected with hepatitis or AIDS was very real...and in some cases, deadly. Fratello was right in describing the scene as a typical dope house. Any carpeting had long been torn up; the rooms were bare floored, old blankets hung over dirty windows. The front room where Nick stood was furnished with a torn up brown couch missing one cushion. A beat up wooden coffee table held a hubcap full of menthol cigarette butts. Empty fast food bags littered the floor. But in a corner next to a crumbling brick fireplace stood a new 60-inch plasma television, still turned on with a Cleveland Indians baseball game being broadcast from the West Coast. The Indians were ahead of the California Angels by a score of 5 to 2 in the seventh inning. The uniformed cops in the room were watching the game, oblivious to the dead men on the floor. "We gotta take this game," one of the cops remarked. "We're only four games behind the Tigers."

How the dope boys could get cable TV running without owning the home or even having any right to be there always amazed Nick. The adjoining dining room had no furnishings except for twin ornate leaded glass cupboards built into the back wall with a window seat between them. A hanging chandelier looked eerily out of place with only two of the five light bulbs still glowing. "It's been a long time since anyone used this room for its real purpose," Nick said.

A stamping of footprints trailed out from the blood pool. "I hope those aren't from the cops," he thought. Nine times out of ten, that was the case. When a call comes in, Police Radio assigns the closest available Zone Car in the area. When the uniformed cops arrive, they make sure the scene is clear of any bad guys. They're not thinking of protecting a crime scene. They're thinking of protecting their own asses, especially in a situation where they come across four dead bodies. After the area is cleared of danger and no citizens are in further harm's way, the call goes out to "send us a boss". The Boss then requests Homicide, who calls for the Crime Scene Investigation Unit, who calls for the coroner to pick up the bodies. And that's the chain of command, all nice and tidy.

The violence was limited to the living room; the victims' bodies arranged to form a macabre square on the floor. Flies crawled over the bodies, feasting on the still-warm blood and gore of exposed veins, skin, and other soft tissue. Although body temperatures would help pinpoint the time of death, Nick estimated the killer, or killers, had been there within the last twelve hours.

The kitchen was void of any cooking items except for an unplugged refrigerator and a working gas stove. The sink was crammed with garbage. An adjacent counter top held scales used to weigh dope and a box of small baggies next to it. But no dope. Just like Jon said. Nick doubted there would be much of anything to analyze from the counter tops.

A familiar voice raised in anger drew him to the living room where Frank was toe-to-toe with Homicide Detective Richie Allen. "You Narcs can't just come in here and start to search the place without a warrant or permission from the owner," Allen yelled. "You'll fuck this case up and we'll never get a conviction!"

Frank wagged his finger at the young detective. "Lookee here asshole, don't start no shit and there will be no shit! Your boss called us here. Believe me, we got plenty to do without bailing your ass out. So stop bitchin' and help me out here! Now tell me, who do you think was in charge of this house?"

"Probably that dude right there," Detective Allen said, pointing at Pookie's body. "He had the keys to the front door in his pocket."

Frank walked over to the body Allen indicated, stooped down and grabbed the man's head between his hands. "Sir," he started speaking to the corpse, "is it okay if we search your house for drugs?" Frank then shook the man's head back and forth in an affirmative manner as if he were nodding yes and granting permission.

"There, the owner just gave us permission to search the premises. We all saw it, right guys?" Frank looked at the astonished homicide detective and the laughing SWAT team cops assembled in the room.

Allen just stood there, unsure how to respond to the Narc's actions. "Hartness, you're one hot mess, you know that?"

Fratello entered the room to see what was going on. "Richie! Come with me!" he called for his young detective to join him in the kitchen. After some muttered conversation, Fratello came out alone and addressed Nick. "Sorry about that. Richie's new and just trying to do the right thing. You and your guys do whatever you have to do."

Nick and his partners continued to scour the scene for evidence while the Crime Scene Investigators dusted for prints and snapped photos. When CSI was done, they would authorize the coroner's people to come in, collect the bodies, and transport them to the morgue. Then the official cause of death would be determined, even though it was obvious to everyone present that their demise was caused by lack of oxygen due to slashed throats.

Detective Moore bent down for a closer look at the bodies. "Son of a bitch!" he exclaimed. "Frank, how did you miss this?" he asked, pointing at the man that had "granted" them permission to search.

Nick and Frank moved closer and looked where Lenny was pointing.

"Jesus!" Nick exclaimed. "Is that Pookie?"

Frank answered Nick's question with one of his own. "What the hell is Sylvester Ashford doing ending up dead in this shithole?"

Chapter 3

Pookie dealt cocaine by the pound. He supplied street-level gang bangers and, rumor had it, several people in City Hall.

Many of Cleveland's powerful politicians and business leaders were among Pookie's friends, including former Mayor Alex Brown. Both men were from the same neighborhood and their relationship grew closer after Brown was elected a Councilman in Pookie's ward. Brown was rumored to have told the now-deceased drug dealer, "You want to do business in my ward, you got to see me first!" When a certain construction company owner wanted to get a state highway contract, Pookie made it happen. In return, the grateful contractor gave Pookie a year's lease on a water-front condo in the flats, which he in turn presented to Mayor Brown, who needed a place to meet his mistress.

In order to maintain an aura of respectability, Pookie's underlings conducted the actual deals; he rarely handled the product. Despite this precaution, his rep for being involved in illegal drugs and bribery activity grew. When the former Mayor Brown made a sudden decision to leave office, the political rats and nervous businessmen saw the signs and deserted the sinking ship, leaving Pookie at the helm. He'd made himself a very rich man while the ship was sinking, but everybody in Cleveland knew it was only a matter of time before investigations and grand juries would intervene and stop the current regime's corruption. For a while, things would settle down. Then the favors and bribes would start up again. Although the players changed, the game was the same. The cops knew this and the citizens of Cleveland knew this; it was business as usual.

Nick found Fratello standing on the front porch bumming a smoke from one of the uniforms. "Find anything?" Fratello asked his friend.

"You were right, Jon," Nick confirmed. "No dope. But we know one of the dead guys is a player you might be very interested in."

As Nick and Fratello discussed the ramifications of Pookie's presence at the murder scene, a black SUV arrived, causing several onlookers to jump back before they were hit. Four men in suits got out of the car, ignoring the spectators' jeers.

"Aw shit!" Nick recognized Special Agent James Reis of the Cleveland Office of the FBI leading the way. Reis was a thorn in the side of the local cops in general and Nick personally. The man always found a way to interfere in local investigations, making half-assed accusations against other law enforcement agencies including the Cleveland Police, DEA, and the ATF.

"I smell shit," Nick said loudly, addressing Fratello but fixing a glare at the FBI agent.

The Fed ignored Nick's comment and addressed Fratello. "We heard you have some dead Mexicans here. You need any help?"

"Naw," Fratello answered nonchalantly. "We pretty much have it under control and are close to wrapping it up here." He didn't need this pompous prick and his dim-witted crew sticking their noses into his sandbox. Fratello got along very well with all other government agencies, but Reis had a habit of glory-holing himself into other peoples' business for the sole purpose of furthering his own personal agenda. At the same time, Fratello knew that dismissing the FBI would have repercussions of a political nature; he was screwed either way.

The lights of the Zone Cars illuminated the scene and Fratello could see one side of the agent's mouth turn up in a grimace. Agent Reis looked perturbed. "Do you mind if we take a quick look around anyway? Maybe we can see something your guys missed," he said, emphasizing the last word while looking at Nick.

Great. Just what I need. Fratello didn't want to play referee to the grudge match of the century between the stubborn detective and the power-hungry FBI agent. "Sure, go ahead," he told Reis. The Feds went into the house leaving Fratello and Nick alone on the porch. The last thing he needed now was for the Reis/Silvano feud to break out and alert the news cameras positioned just beyond the yellow tape. Those guys lived for stuff like this. A feud between two cops? It would be breaking news on Channel 19 for sure. Fratello flipped the borrowed cigarette into the dirt and moved to go back inside.

"What gives between you and Reis, anyway?" he asked quietly.

"It's a long story," Nick said wearily. "I'll fill you in later," he said, then followed Fratello back into the murder house.

They both watched as the Feds checked the dead mens' fingerprints with a portable scanner while the Cleveland CSI looked on enviously. The city didn't have the level of scientific equipment the Feds had. Cleveland, like most major cities, was flat broke.

Reis talked quietly to his counterparts then turned to face Fratello. "You got two locals here and two Mexicans," he said in a superior air. "All four are in our database and the Mexicans are coming back to a known drug cartel. They most likely muled a load of drugs here and were robbed and killed for it."

"You come up with that all by yourself?" Nick asked sarcastically. "No wonder you're the FBI's Golden Child."

Commander Fratello glared at both men. "Let's keep our remarks professional. I want see both of you in Chief Marinik's office. Tomorrow. Let's say eleven a.m. so we can all get a couple hours' sleep. Now if that's all," he paused, looking from the detective to the FBI agent, "let's all go and let the coroner's people do their job."

Fratello herded the FBI agents out of the house. Frank and Lenny pulled Nick off to the side just inside the front door. "Look, Nicky," Frank said. "Lenny and I know you and Fratello are tight and everybody in the world knows Reis is a big dickhead, but we don't want to be in the middle of this shit."

Nick was about to protest when Lenny chimed in. "We could give a shit if fifty dope heads get killed. Reis gets off on screwing with local cops and you know we got enough to do without getting involved in this and a feud besides! We've got your back but please, keep us out of your mess, okay?"

"Yeah," Nick acknowledged. "We'll stick to the drug aspects of this case but we still got a job to do, you guys got that?" he said, injecting his seniority into the situation. Both men nodded. Behind them, the coroner's assistants were wrestling the bodies into the thick black body bags when a woman's shriek pierced the air, startling everyone still alive in the house.

"I know that mark!" an assistant moaned in a thick Jamaican accent while pointing at the black drawing on the chest of one of the victims. "That's bad juju mon, vera bad!" She ran out of the house, leaving the other two assistants and some of the cops standing there speechless.

"What the hell was that?" Frank exclaimed.

"I don't know," answered Lenny, "but I'm going to if I can console her. She's pretty hot!"

Nick shook his head. "Fuckin' Lenny!"

Chapter 4

The man known as the drug cartel's Protector felt refreshed after twelve hours of uninterrupted sleep following the Dickens Avenue killing spree and extremely lucrative business deal "completed" with Pookie and the Mexicans.

JuJu sat at the curved end of the Clevelander Hotel Bar on the ground floor of Cleveland's Public Square. Tall windows faced Superior Avenue and looked over the steadily increasing pedestrian traffic trekking to the Horseshoe Casino located adjacent to the hotel. The sunlight moved behind the tall buildings. The earlier adrenaline high was gone. Now he was just another businessman waiting to get a drink.

This bar was typical of other big city hotel bars; dark wood with a massive bar back and huge mirrors looking back at the customers to make the room look larger than it really was. JuJu was the only person sitting at the bar. Other customers sat at small tables, their heads bowed, engrossed in their laptop computers and wondering how many drinks they could put on their bar tabs before the corporate bean counters took notice.

JuJu turned his attention from the bar patrons to the swarthy, brushy-haired Greek bartender wiping wine glasses with a white rag. After wiping a glass, he held it up to the light, twisting and turning it just so, looking for any lingering lipstick marks or fingerprints before hanging it in the wooden glass rack over the top of the back bar.

"What will you have, Sir?" asked the bartender as he placed a bowl of nuts in front of JuJu.

"A spiced rum and Coke," replied JuJu. He watched as the bartender expertly mixed his drink and placed it in front of him, all within a few seconds.

"You want to start a tab, Sir?"

"No," JuJu said, pushing a twenty dollar bill across the bar. "Keep the change."

"Thank you, Sir."

JuJu leaned back in his barstool. He'd come a long way from his youthful years in the streets of Trinidad-Tobago, he reflected. Trinidad was discovered by Christopher Columbus, who had served himself as much as he'd served Queen Isabella. Maybe he had the same spirit. JuJu's mother had given all of her children celestial names, a reflection of her high hopes for their futures. His given name was Lusa Tomari DeBoissiere which translated to "Sun" after the African God of the Sun. He was seldom called Lusa. The name "JuJu" had been bestowed on him after his aunties and uncles warned his mother that he was "bad juju" for her.

It was in Trinidad, the home of the Carnival, birthplace of steel pan music and the limbo, where JuJu committed his first robbery at the age of nine. As he got older, his methodical determination to dominate steadily developed until murder was almost a way of life for him. He had killed more than twenty people before he himself reached that numbered birthday, and gained the reputation of being a very dangerous man. His physical appearance alone caused people to give him wide berth. At six foot four inches tall and 260 pounds, he was a rough muscled man. He kept his head shaved bald and ear lobes decorated with solid gold loop earrings. He was obsessed with the practice of voodoo and held an unshakable belief that he was an Obeah Man who could empower spells for witchcraft and communicate with the Gods.

His grandmother raised him in the Baptist Orisha religion with blood-offerings and animal sacrifices of goats and chickens. Although his Spiritual Baptist religion in Trinidad-Tobago had its roots in Christianity, he felt closer to the black magic practices of the Obeah and voodoo of his African forefathers. Obeah provided the basic ethic which translated into "The work of the wand and the sword." He believed in the spiritual powers of the Loas, and regularly appealed to the spiritual guardians much as devout Catholics petitioned the Saints. JuJu appealed to the loa Legba for strength and power over his enemies; Legba was considered the most powerful of the spirits and the guardian of the gate between the spiritual and material planes.

Legba's symbol was the black cross which he painted onto his victims; his way of further honoring the loas. The medicine bag, or Oanga, he carried contained the sacrificial items to honor Ogun, the warrior spirit he worshipped and assumed as part of his own spirit.

JuJu bounced between South Florida and the Caribbean Islands doing small drug deals and ripping off drug dealers and their customers until at the age of thirty-four, he fell in with Mexican cartel members who admired his capacity for violence. He graduated from courier to protector for the larger drug deliveries and gained a reputation for successfully completing transactions without any mishaps from the police or rival dealers. In turn, he gained intelligence on the internal business activities of his Mexican benefactors. When the opportunity arose to protect this current drug shipment, JuJu was ready; he would take both the drugs and money for himself. He had never been to Cleveland but the job was perfect for his break-out move. His chance to be rich!

His older brother Moon DeBoissiere lived in Toronto, Canada, but died a few months back after finding himself at the wrong end of a gun in a drug deal. JuJu attended Moon's funeral in Toronto and under the pretext of handling his affairs, managed to steal his dead brother's passport, Canadian driver's license, and American Express Gold Card. His physical appearance was close enough to Moon's that when he was asked for photo ID, he was not questioned. But just to be safe, he used it only when necessary. He paid cash for everything he could but car and hotel rentals could only be accomplished with credit cards and photo identification. Then he became Moon.

He finished his first drink and ordered another from the bartender, who smiled broadly as he accepted another twenty dollar bill for the nine dollar cocktail.

JuJu took a deep swallow of the spiced rum drink and called forward the shining memory of his recent accomplishment. Before sending Darik and Tion on their way, JuJu rewarded them with a bundle of bills and a cut off a cocaine brick, using the same knife that had severed four windpipes only moments earlier. He instructed them to return to their hotel and wait for his call. "Do not get into any trouble, do you understand me?" No further comment was needed.

The Jamaicans didn't flinch at murder; they were notorious for their own brand of crazy, usually directed at a coveted sexual organ. JuJu discovered the pair in Miami while protecting one of the cartel's drug deliveries. They didn't make any attempts to extort outrageous percentages from JuJu and he overlooked their sexual proclivities. Their interests centered on getting high and performing sex acts. This knowledge was also useful to him.

And they were afraid of the big man who practiced voodoo. Placing the black cross mark of Legba on the chests of the four men he had killed while speaking in the tongue of his ancestors had solidified their fear. He also knew their loyalty would last only as long as they continued to be paid and, more importantly, continued to be afraid of him.

JuJu returned the rental van back to the parking garage of the Clevelander Hotel where he had registered two days earlier using his dead brother's identification. He left the two duffel bags with the cocaine and money on the van's floor and covered them with newspapers and a blanket. JuJu was a thinking man's thief and had learned long ago in his native Trinidad-Tobago that sometimes what was not hidden was the most invisible. He was gambling that the duffel-bagged cache of drugs and money would remain undetected in the van until he could plan his next move. Who'd break into a van to take a gym bag that most likely contained smelly clothes?

Murdering the four men had been surprisingly easy; he had expected a little more resistance, especially from the Mexicans. He walked away with two million in cash, another two million in packaged cocaine, and not a scratch on him. Yes, Ogun was watching over him and clearing the way before him; his magic was strong. The irony that Ogun was also the protector of police officers was lost on JuJu. He viewed the Orisha faith through his own warped lens of personal gain, just as men had twisted religion to fit their own needs since the beginning of time.

Three more rum and Cokes later, JuJu was at Morton's Steak house adjacent to the hotel consuming a twenty-four ounce porterhouse steak with potatoes, creamed spinach, and an iceberg wedge salad. He ordered his steak rare and watched, fascinated, as the meat's red juices mingled with the white potatoes on his plate just as the blood from his knife had mingled with the cocaine from yesterday's murders. After he paid the bill, in cash, he dialed the phone number of the prepaid cell phone he had given the Jamaicans. One of them answered; he never knew which one. Their voices had a similar high register and almost feminine quality. He ordered them to pick him up in front of the Horseshoe Casino on Public Square in twenty minutes.

With his physical hunger satisfied, he felt the need to satisfy a hunger of a different kind that only female companionship and the comforting warmth of powdered heroin could provide. He had a lot to celebrate and his two accomplices, while only being in Cleveland for a few days, were quick to learn the darker aspects of their surroundings and would be able to find the means to satisfy both his urges.

The black Focus pulled up to the curb. Darik rolled the window down. "How ya doin', mon?"

A uniformed traffic controller strode briskly toward them, alternately blowing her whistle and yelling, "There's no parking here, keep it moving!"

JuJu climbed into the back seat. "Drive!" he ordered.

"What we doin' now?" Tion asked in his musical island dialect. "We gonna go out and do some stuff like last night? You see the news, mon? We all over it."

"No," answered JuJu. "No more killing for now," he stated almost regretfully. "I want you to find me a woman and a hotel room. I want a high class woman, not some meth-head. I also want heroin, the best you can find. Get enough to last a while, not a couple dime bags," he instructed. JuJu needed to make sure he had enough of the heroin to serve his desires. He didn't know how much longer he would have his helpers around.

"You got it boss," said Tion. JuJu never used cocaine himself and long ago had given up the use of all hallucinogens. They took away his edge. He had seen too many idiots lose their lives and money while high on those chemicals; many of those lives taken by his own hands. Heroin was his drug of choice and he used it only when he was not involved with any business.

Even though they had just got into town, the homosexual duo had already plugged into Cleveland's underground scene. The cocaine had helped them gain entry last night, but they agreed that JuJu didn't need to know of their activities after they parted ways following the murders.

Must be some sort of secret society that only they know, JuJu mused. No matter where the Jamaicans went, they fit right into their surroundings. He gave them a wad of hundred dollar bills along with instructions to call his cell number when their tasks were completed. They dropped him off at Public Square and he returned to the hotel bar to wait for their call. The same Greek bartender was still on duty and before JuJu had even sat down and ordered, a rum and Coke appeared on the bar before him. Big tips bring good service as well as privacy. He was glad the bartender did not feel the need to have small talk with his customers.

The television behind the bar flashed "Special News Update" and showed the Mayor and Chief of Police standing on Cleveland's City Hall steps talking to news reporters. Film footage showed the front of the house where the four dead bodies were discovered. The sound of the TV was muted and he briefly thought about asking the bartender to turn it up but decided against it. He didn't want anybody to remember the "big black dude" who seemed interested in the murders. The screen flashed to a commercial and JuJu returned to his drink and watched the Greek wipe the same glasses over and over again, and wondered what his name was. *Probably Niko or George. All those Greeks are named Niko or George!*

Chapter 5

It was dark when JuJu's cell phone rang. The Jamaicans were successful in their mission and made arrangements to collect JuJu in front of Public Square. The trio drove a short distance and entered the Cleveland Interstate Inn parking garage off east 9th Street and Lakeside Avenue. "Wait," Darik said. He got out of the car and went through a steel door marked Lobby. JuJu felt exposed and vulnerable until Darik returned, grinning. "Here you go, mon," he said, and dropped a small envelope containing a hotel card key in JuJu's hand. "Room number is on the envelope," he said. "All paid for."

"Stay straight. Wait for my call," JuJu told the pair. He found the room without any difficulty and put the card key into the required slot in the door. The light flashed green and he heard a click as the lock released, allowing him to push the door open and enter the room. A bottle of rum and a six pack of cola occupied a table next to the window. The drapes were open and he could just make out the dark shape of Lake Erie. He pulled the curtains closed, adjusted the room's air conditioner to High, and hoped it could keep up; it was about to get hot.

There was a short rap on the door. JuJu glanced

through the peephole, saw two women and opened the door. One of the women was tall, black, with breasts barely contained in a purple stretch tank top, its gold threads making a sunset design on the taut fabric. Her hair was a mass of brilliant red curls that bounced against the plane of her shoulders when she moved her head. Her companion was a petite white girl with blonde straight hair and blue eyes. Virtual opposites. The redhead radiated a confidence lacking in the blonde girl, but both radiated the palatable aura that surrounded those who made their living on the streets. Others of their kind recognized the vibe when they saw it. The white girl looked at JuJu and a glimmer of fear passed over her face. She looked down at her feet.

The redhead smiled at JuJu and strode quickly into the hotel room, grabbing her companion's wrist and dragging her along like a dog on a leash. After JuJu closed the door behind them, the woman placed her hands on her hips and tossed her head, causing a tidal wave of bobbing red curls. "You like what you see?"

"That depends," he answered. "I was expecting only one woman."

"Double your pleasure—double your fun," she answered. "I'm Sydney and my friend here is Brandi. Your friend already paid up front like we asked him to so you got us for the night or whenever you are finished with us. Just so you know, we don't do any weird shit, just straight up lays, but we can do each other if you want to watch us in action." Her hands waved through the air while she spoke and he saw she had extremely long fingernails, each painted a different shade of reds and purples that matched her clothes and hair. While most women in her profession wore wigs, Sydney took extreme pride in her hair; it was her signature look.

The Jamaicans might be more useful than I thought, especially if they kept producing results like this. He pointed to the king-size bed, and then moved over to the couch and sat down. Taking their cue, the women started their opening act, with the bed as their stage. JuJu took a small envelope out of his pocket and set it on the coffee table in front of him. Despite the show now being performed for his benefit, he was more focused on the little package than what was happening in the bed.

He unfolded the paper envelope carefully, like it was a package from Tiffany's, spread some of the white powder onto the cover of *Cleveland Magazine*, then arranged the powder into thin lines using the hotel room card key. He pulled a hundred dollar bill from the wad he had in his front pocket, rolled it into a tight straw, and snorted a line of the heroin up his nose. He leaned back in the cushioned couch and closed his eyes. The high was immediate and warm. Just like the first time his brother taught him how to use the drug when he was a teenager in Trinidad. "It's better than sex, little brother," Moon had said, laughing at his little brother's reaction.

JuJu was careful to limit his use of the drug for special times, like now, although more frequently of late he had been using the drug to calm his nerves, rather than just for pleasure. Still, he considered himself to be in control. If he really was a hard core user, he theorized, he'd use a needle and shoot it directly into his veins. But he didn't want the tell-tale tracks on his arms so it was a tradeoff. He'd still get the high he wanted. *I control the drug – the drug does not control me!*

Usually the "Sydney & Brandi Show" was played out in front of an appreciative audience. While this customer had bought a ticket, he seemed more interested in the drug than the two naked women writhing on the bed. Seeing they were losing their audience's attention, Sydney pushed Brandi away, hopped off the bed, breasts and curls bouncing, and moved to the couch. *No sense in wasting time. I might as well get some of this action.* "Can I have some of that?" she whispered.

"Sure," JuJu said. "Maybe it will do all of us some good." With a long, purple, pinkie fingernail, Sydney scooped a pinch of heroin, brought it to her nostril and sniffed it up her nose in one easy motion. JuJu watched her intently as she fell back into the brown cushions of the couch.

"Wow, that's some good shit!" she breathed, then closed her eyes allowing the powder to take hold of the pleasure senses in her brain.

Brandi got on her knees in front of both of them and did a line using JuJu's hundred dollar bill as a straw. JuJu rose in front of her then and unzipped his pants. His meaning was clear and Brandi eagerly complied.

The effects of heroin and sex put JuJu into a relaxed state and after a while, the three people became a blur on the bed, and on the floor, until dawn's early light creeped through the edges of the heavy curtains that had held the world at bay.

JuJu was exhausted. "It's time for you to leave," he commanded. Brandi furtively reached for the package holding the remaining powder.

"Leave it alone!" Sydney admonished sharply. "Control yourself, Brandi or someday you're gonna die from that stuff!" The track marks on Brandi's fragile arms revealed that she was much more than an occasional user; JuJu decided then and there that while he liked the redhead, he didn't want the skinny, white junkie around him. She'd be nothing but trouble. Brandi went into the bathroom while Sydney got dressed. She pointed to the package of powder and asked JuJu, "What are you going to do with the rest of that?"

"You can have it," he told her. "But you are to never say anything about me, you understand? Sydney stowed the "gift" in her Coach purse while Brandi was still in the bathroom.

"Sure, Sugar...um-m...you want us to come back tonight?"

"I like your company," JuJu said, the message clear. "How can I contact you?"

The toilet flushed in the background and Brandi came out of the bathroom and went out into the hallway, leaving Sydney and JuJu alone. Sydney pressed a business card in JuJu's hand.

"A whore with a business card?" he remarked, with the beginning of a small smile.

"Sugar, I'm on Facebook and Craigslist too. Just give me a call?" She paused, "What's your name?"

JuJu's amused smile ran away from his face and his eyes grew cold. Maybe names weren't so important, she decided.

"Keep your phone on, but leave that junkie bitch behind," he said, his meaning clear. "I'll let you know when I want to see you again. Next time, I may have you get the heroin. Can you do that?"

"Yeah," answered Sydney. "But if you want good shit, it'll cost you."

"Money is no problem. Just make sure you deliver exactly what I want," he said, catching and holding her gaze.

Sydney tried to hold his stare but almost involuntarily felt her eyes drop until she realized she was now looking at her purple-painted toe nails peeping out from her sandals. With every fiber of her street radar, she knew this man was dangerous. But, she reasoned, cash and drugs could turn any devil into a darling!

After checking the hallways for hotel security, the girls left. This particular hotel used off-duty Cleveland cops and specifically Narcs, when the hotel could get them. While Sydney knew most of the cops working the hotel, she still preferred not to bring attention to her presence. It would only invite questions and maybe even an arrest. Sometimes, she and Brandi would go out and score some dope for Detective Silvano, which was the first step for the Narcs to find out what kind of drugs and how much was being sold on the streets of Cleveland. Following the initial buy, the Narcs would try to introduce one of their own in an undercover role to negotiate a series of buys that would lead to a bust. In exchange for the girls' obtaining this information, the Narcs allowed them a pinkie fingernail full of the contraband drugs for their own consumption if the bag was big enough. It was incentive to make the buys. Plus, it gave them a "get out of jail free" card for future troubles.

Sydney wondered where JuJu got his shit 'cause it was real good, and she was still feeling the high it gave her. *Much better stuff than I can afford.* They were barely out the hotel's front door when Brandi started badgering her. "C'mon Sydney, gimme some of that stuff! I know you got some from the man."

Sydney roughly grabbed Brandi's pockmarked arm when they reached her car. "Stop it girl, you got to maintain yourself!" But deep down she knew Brandi's need was total and had been for a couple of months now. She remembered what Detective Silvano had told her when they first met several years ago. "Heroin has no holidays," Nick told her. "Every day you use is another day closer to death. It never lets you take a day off, it never leaves your mind. It will consume you until you are all used up and then go looking for another victim to kill!" Sydney knew Brandi's days were numbered. Brandi didn't have the willpower to manage it – not like Sydney did.

As soon as the women were gone, JuJu moved around the room, towel in hand, wiping down all of the smooth surfaces to erase any fingerprints he and his female companions had touched; a glass, soda can, the coffee table, knobs on the air conditioner. In the bathroom he even wiped the flush handle on the toilet and the faucet handles. This cleaning ritual was second nature and he performed it without even thinking.

Last, he wiped the plastic card key, set it on the table, and left the room. He walked the seven blocks back to his hotel instead of calling the Jamaicans for a ride. They didn't need to know his every move.

His route took him past the Federal Building and as he looked up at the tall, gray building, he wondered what the FBI would think if they knew he was literally right under their noses. All they had to do was look out the window and see him walking in the crowd of people. He could see the Rock-n-Roll Hall of Fame from where he stood on East 9th Street and Lakeside Avenue and looked out over Lake Erie. *I wonder how far it is to Canada from where I'm standing?* He kept walking. If he could get into Canada with the drugs and money, he might have a better chance of getting back to his native Trinidad unnoticed. No, he concluded. *There's no way to move that much cocaine between the two countries on my own.* He would have to try and unload it in Cleveland. His options were limited: find a buyer for the entire twenty kilos of coke or piece it off a little at a time. Either way, it was a big chance to take. If the Mexican cartel heard about somebody selling weight he was dead for sure. He could hold his own in any type of street fight but the cartel was a different battle. Their eyes and ears were everywhere.

By now they will have figured out that he was alive and also the most likely candidate to be in the possession of their money and drugs. They probably already had people in Cleveland looking for him or maybe they would look elsewhere—after all, who would be dumb enough to stay in the city after ripping off one of the most dangerous drug organizations in the world?

No question, both the cartel and the cops were out in force searching for him. Of the two, it would be better if the cops found him. If the Mexicans found him first, there'd be nothing left for anybody else to find. *I am an Obeah man,* he reminded himself. *The spirits of my ancestors will protect me.* All the same, it wouldn't hurt to lay low in Cleveland for a while and let the heat die down a bit. Besides, it was nice here in the summer. He continued his walk back to the Clevelander, still thinking how he could get rid of a big bag of cocaine without getting killed or arrested. Maybe the Jamaicans were the key? They had proven themselves resourceful and useful so far.

He passed a building with an imposing black pipe structure looming in front of it with the words "Justice Center" affixed over large, glass entrance doors. Black and white Police Cruisers ringed the building. Here he was, right outside their front door and his rental van was just one block away with two million in cash and twenty more kilos of coke stashed inside. *Yes, my magic is strong!*

After a long shower, a nap, and a room service meal, JuJu went downstairs to the hotel bar for a drink, timing his arrival to mix in with the other business travelers looking for a stress reliever following a long day of meetings and sales calls. The Greek was behind the bar.

"Hello Niko," JuJu said.

"How are you today, Sir?" the bartender responded.

I'll be damned. This fucker's name really is Niko!

Chapter 6

Nick woke as the sun rose over Lake Erie. He peeked out of the boat's oval moisture-streaked portside window to see what the weather was like. The morning dew was already evaporating off the hulls of the more than two hundred boats tied to the floating wooden docks. All manner of cruisers and sailboats rose and fell gently with the passing of outbound vessels cruising toward the expanse of Lake Erie. The occasional rumble of an engine sounded as the die-hard fishermen left the marina for the open water beyond the granite break wall, careful to observe the no wake rules strictly enforced by the water cops.

Seagulls squawked loudly as they circled the East 55th Marina, darting between the tall sailboat masts to the murky waters below in search of breakfast. Nick watched one bird break rank and pluck a fish from the water, then return to the air with breakfast clenched in its beak while the other birds chased after, trying to steal the fish for their own meal. *Just like some people I know.*

"Rats with wings," Nick muttered as he made his morning coffee in the Gun's 'n Hoses small cabin using his miniature designer-brew coffee machine. He poured a generous glob of Baileys Irish Cream into the blue CPD cup he had earned from the last Police Olympics, then filled it the rest of the way with the strong breakfast blend. With only four hours sleep the night before, he needed the caffeine jolt.

He had kept his summer boat home at the Marina's D Dock after he and Cheryl had divorced fifteen years ago. Cheryl released the boat to Nick willingly. She wanted no part of the money involved with boating, dock fees, marine gas, or insurance. With no children in their lives, it was a fairly routine divorce, according to the lawyers. Nick was too "complicated" for her, or so she had told her friends. While she still cared for him, she knew he would never change his ways. He loved the job more than he would ever love her. At least that's what she told herself. She was remarried now to another Cleveland Detective who was "much more stable and reliable". He came home every night...sober.

According to his veteran mentor, that happened during the Cowboy Cop phase. Cheryl had always hated the boat insisting it was "just another excuse to party with your asshole friends." At that point in his career, it was probably true, he grudgingly admitted.

The boat had always been his refuge, a place where he and his buddies could get off the street, relax, and pretend the job didn't really hold them captive 24/7. He had always thought it funny that the word "job" had a special meaning for the police. "On the Job" was a term used by cops to describe their occupation and also a way for them to identify each other without announcing, "I'm a Police Officer" out loud to the unsuspecting public.

Nick liked the solitude the boat afforded. Unlike a house, there was no parking in front of a yard that needed mowing, no doors to answer, no snow to shovel. Just hose it down every once in a while and check the oil. No alarm system needed. Any unwanted intruders would give themselves away the minute the deck felt the full weight of their step.

And besides, it was close to the Captain's Quarters Bar and Kat Westerly, the blonde barmaid he was seeing. Kat was beautiful, smart, and working her way through Case Western University in pursuit of a Master's Degree in psychology. The Captain's Quarters was just as good a classroom as any, she had explained to him, and she didn't seem to mind fending off drunken boaters. Nick was the exception –she didn't want to fend him off. "I like it when you show up, Nicky," she'd told him. "It keeps the assholes away from me since everybody's afraid to mess with you!"

When the weather turned cold and the fresh water of Lake Erie began to freeze over, he put his prized boat into dry dock and moved to his one room apartment on Lorain Avenue above Betty's Café on the west side of Cleveland. He figured it was only a matter of time before a drunken bar patron fired a shot into the ceiling and killed him while he slept in the futon bed that doubled as his couch. Every year he vowed to find another place to winter over, but three years later, he was still there.

Nick rinsed out his coffee cup in the small galley,

grabbed a gym bag with his shower kit and clothes then hopped off the boat. He walked the length of the wooden dock to the parking lot where a grey cinderblock building housed the bathrooms and showers. It reminded him of the Air Force barracks he used to call home as an enlisted man. He showered, dressed in tan Dockers and a maroon button-down shirt, then removed his Apple Smartphone from the front pocket of his gym bag and called the Narcotics Unit.

"Detective Nick Silvano, checking in," he said.

"Yeah, Silvano," the office man said. "Call Lieutenant Fratello as soon as possible."

Nick dialed Jon's cell number. It was answered on the second ring.

"You up and ready to go Nick?"

"Yeah Jon, what's up?"

"Meet me at Slyman's for breakfast and I'll fill you in," Fratello said. "The Chief already called me and said your FBI Agent friend and his goons want to meet in his office. We don't have any tips yet. Nothing in to Homicide or Crime Stoppers. Not even the usual crazies calling in – kinda surprising if you ask me. Reis is already starting his shit so you and me have to be on the same page - you okay for that?"

"Sure," Nick answered. "See you in ten."

Famous for its corn beef sandwiches, Slyman's Diner was a Cleveland institution drawing both blue collar workers and suited businessmen to rub elbows over scarred Formica countertops. Even President George W. Bush and Chef Rachael Ray had lunched at Slyman's.

There was a steady line outside the door when Nick pulled up and parked his civilian Honda Civic on the side street in front of the No Parking Anytime sign.

Spotting Jon at a booth in the back, he walked past the waiting customers and slid into the red vinyl-covered seat across from the Homicide Commander. "I already ordered your corn beef and eggs, Nick. Over easy with no tears in their eyes," Fratello said, referring to Nick's disdain for runny egg whites.

"Just what I would have ordered," Nick said. "You know me better than I know myself."

"That's why we got to talk before we meet the Chief and Reis."

"Look Jon, I'm sorry about last night," Nick started in a somber voice. "I already had a long crappy day and Reis was not quite the cherry on top I had in mind."

"What is it between you two?" asked Fratello, failing to disguise his frustration.

"Alright Jon, here's the story," Nick relented. "Do you remember last fall when Reis got assigned to Cleveland after being transferred from the Chicago FBI office?"

"Yeah, so?"

"Right after he got here he started to interfere with our drug cases. Sticking his nose into DEA and ATF cases here and in Akron where it didn't belong. He began looking into a local drug ring run by a guy named Angelo Zaccaro. Reis learned that Zaccaro and me grew up in the same neighborhood. We went to school together at Wilbur Wright Junior High, were on the West Tech wrestling team and were even in each other's weddings! But that was before I became a cop and he got involved in the local mob. So even though Angelo and I hadn't seen or spoken to each other in over ten years, Reis determined that I must be a dirty cop because I knew him. He started telling people this brilliant theory of his and it got back to me from the Agent-in-Charge of the Cleveland DEA, Charley Goetz."

Nick paused while the waitress stopped at their booth to refill their coffee. Fratello took a sip of the hot brew and waited for Nick to continue.

"One night, when I was on a stakeout with Lenny and Frank, Police Radio told us to 'meet a man' on the west side in the Sears parking lot at West 110th and Lorain. When we arrived, Reis was there with the night Chief and some deputy sheriffs waiting for us - well, me in particular. He pulled out a search warrant for Angelo's house and told everybody that I was to ride with him, the implication being that I would somehow warn Zaccaro.

"Man, I was mad and embarrassed, but did it because I knew I had nothing to worry about. I hadn't done anything wrong. Later, I found out there were some grounds for Reis' thinking, but he had it all wrong."

They paused again as another waitress set their breakfast plates in front of them.

After arranging their meals, and between bites, Nick continued. "Anyway, Reis briefed everybody in the parking lot that Zaccaro had guard dogs, a six-foot fence around his property, and might even have armed bodyguards. We drove to Angelo's house with a caravan of cops and sheriffs. I didn't even know where Zaccaro lived! When we got there, Reis drove his FBI car into the driveway, and trying to be some sort of super cop, he jumped onto the hood of the car, grabbed the top of the driveway gate fence, and tried to launch himself over the top."

Nick chuckled. "Well, the gate wasn't locked and there he was, swinging around and hanging on for dear life when the gate slammed into the side of the house! He fell on the concrete driveway and dropped his gun into the bushes. When he got up he had a big rip in his pants and a bloody gash on his knee. He started fumbling around in the bushes to find his lost gun while the SWAT guys and sheriffs laughed their asses off at the dick-head trying to be the hero because most of them knew he was an asshole already."

"Are you kidding?" Fratello asked incredulously as he paused with his fork full of corned beef in midair.

"That's exactly what happened. Angelo's wife heard the commotion outside and opened the front door before the entry team even had a chance to announce themselves. She wanted to know what was going on and Reis handed her the search warrant while trying to dodge the poodle guard dog nipping at his ankles.

"Reis ordered me to stand just inside the front door. A couple of Feds ran by me, through the house, and out the back door. It was only a couple of minutes later, minutes mind you, that you could hear the FBI guys yelling, 'We got it! Found it buried in the yard!' They came back into the house waving a clear baggie they said had cocaine in it. Do you get the picture? They went through the house, into the back yard, down a hill into a wooded area and dug up a bag of cocaine...all in less than five minutes!"

Fratello shook his head. "Sounds like a setup."

"Sure it was," said Nick. "We found out later Reis had threatened some punk dopehead with jail if he didn't plant the drugs in Angelo's yard. Long story short, the U.S. Attorney's office informed Reis that the dope was buried on a neighbor's property behind Zaccaro's and no charges could be brought against him or his wife. Angelo wasn't even at home. We found out later that he was in Florida, probably making a dope deal. He had an airtight alibi. It was a big waste of time," Nick concluded as he stabbed the last piece of egg with his fork.

He looked straight at Fratello then. "Reis is upset because me and my partners found the dope boy he threatened and got a statement from him describing what Reis told him to do. We took that statement straight to his boss at the FBI. That fucker threw it away and denied he ever got it. Later, we found the dope boy again. Reis must have got to him because he clammed up and denied everything."

"You better watch your ass, Nick," Fratello cautioned. "If he did all that, it shows the lengths he will go to frame somebody, especially you for trying to expose him."

"Yeah, well now you know. He hates local cops because he tried, not once but twice, to get on the job in Chicago but he was turned down both times for psychological reasons. I guess he had vendettas against the Chicago cops too because they were the ones who called our CPPA Union and warned us about him before he even got here."

"What did you mean when you said he had 'some grounds' to think you were a dirty cop?" asked Fratello.

"Frank, Lenny and me were hearing some street talk that a couple of guys were shaking down dope houses and claiming to be us. We started asking around and it turned out to be true! And it was a couple of cops we knew. When they found out we were onto them, one of the assholes called and begged me not to say anything and promised they'd stop."

"Jesus," exclaimed Fratello, astounded by what he was hearing.

"Those two cops started this whole thing. The FBI was going to start a case on me but they found out I was in West Virginia testifying in a DEA court case at the time I was supposed to be in Cleveland shaking down dope houses. Shows you what great investigators Reis and his people were!

"I probably should have called Internal Affairs and told them about the cop that called me, but I liked him better than the FBI, so there you have it. I still worry about what those cops did. But that's the job. When you're in the middle of money and dope, false accusations are easily made."

Fratello stood up and counted out money on the table for the bill and tip. "After all that – breakfast is on me.

Now I understand why you hate Reis so much. But do me a favor?"

"What's that?"

"Please try to keep your cool in the Chief's office today."

As the two cops exited Slyman's, Nick took Fratello by the arm and said, "Thanks for breakfast Jon, but I can't and won't guarantee anything where that prick is concerned!"

Fratello exhaled wearily. That was pretty much what he expected Nick to say, but one could always hope.

Chapter 7

Detective Nick Silvano and Commander Jon Fratello were ushered into Chief Robert Marinik's ninth floor corner office in the Cleveland Police Justice Center at exactly 1100 hours as ordered.

Special Agent James Reis of the FBI's Cleveland office occupied the brown leather couch by the large windows overlooking the city and the Cuyahoga County Jail. Nick assumed the other two "suits" standing in the Chief's office were Feds too. He didn't recognize either of them.

Without acknowledging their presence, Nick strode past the FBI agents to Chief Marinik, nodded, and shook his hand before sitting down in a matching brown leather chair opposite the Chief's desk. Commander Fratello followed his lead. "Men," said the Chief while looking directly at Agent Reis, "I have a problem that only those in this room can solve." He turned his gaze away from Reis and scanned the room, his eyes resting briefly on each man before he continued.

"Four murders on Dickens Avenue and I have nothing to tell the Mayor or the news media. Nothing!" he repeated. "Our friends at the FBI claim that two of the deceased are known Mexican drug cartel couriers.

"They're ready to take over the case.

"Since the murders happened in my city of Cleveland and two of the men killed were citizens of my city, not the best of citizens, but nevertheless, they are ours, I want to know - does anyone have any updates?"

Agent Reis stood and walked to the side of the Chief's desk. "We have some early leads and the scientific skills and resources to take point in this case." Reis paused then to look at Nick. "We will get things done faster if we do it ourselves."

Fratello responded coolly to the FBI Agent. "It's the Cleveland Homicide Unit's job to clear this case. If you have any information to share, we'd be happy to listen, Agent Reis." Fratello paused to glance at Silvano, hoping that his even tone and demeanor would set an example for his friend.

Fratello continued, "This is the first we've heard of any leads from the FBI. As of this moment, it is more important for the Cleveland Police to solve this case quickly, so if you continue to insist on being involved in the investigation, it has to be in cooperation with us."

Agent Reis huffed and retorted, "Here we go again." He shot a quick glance at Silvano before focusing on Fratello. "Detective Silvano has poisoned my well with you guys, hasn't he?"

Try as he might to stay silent, Nick could not resist the bait. Before Fratello could raise an arm to stop him, Nick jumped to his feet so he was face-to-face with Reis and growled, "What have you ever done but screw with us Reis? You are a piece of shit!"

Surprised by the outburst, the agent quickly backed up and stumbled, dropping back to the couch. His crimson face couldn't begin to disguise his anger, and a neck vein visibly throbbed.

The detective was no pushover in the tough cop department. Nick had spent many hours in the 5th floor Police Gym in this very building and had won several medals for power lifting in the Police Olympics. He wouldn't hesitate to take a dispute out into the street; bad guy or another cop; it made no difference to him.

Chief Marinik was familiar with Nick's temper and of Agent Reis' attempt to frame Nick as a dirty cop. He also knew the men, from his department no less, who had posed as Nick and his partners to steal drugs and money from the dope dealers. But until Nick or his partners lodged an official complaint, it never happened. Ironically, by not reporting the dirty cops, the whole department was saved from a public relations nightmare, the Chief acknowledged. He had enough of those as it was. But that didn't mean he would let Nick get away with any crap now.

"Boys," the Chief said loudly, asserting his authority before the disruption could continue. "Stop the infighting and let's set some ground rules here. Agent Reis, I spoke to the U.S. Attorney and to your boss this morning. We came to the understanding that my Homicide Commander will hold lead with you assisting."

The Chief turned to Fratello and Nick. "You will give

top priority to this case until I get some answers. Turns out that our dead Pookie Ashford had political friends on high from his numerous and generous donations. I'm getting heat so I am putting some of the heat on you guys. I'm expecting answers from you two," he said. He turned to Reis next. "Your bosses told me that you will not be a problem...I hope that's all I need to say on the subject."

Fratello and Nick both gave their Chief a nod while Reis suddenly became fixated with the patterns on the ceiling tiles. He picked up his briefcase and answered with a surly, "Yeah, I get it," and strode stiffly out of the office, his two silent counterparts following quickly behind him.

Chief Marinik stared after Reis' retreating figure. "I know that prick was wearing a wire!" The Chief picked up the phone on his desk and barked into the receiver, "Send Sobieski in!"

Lieutenant David Sobieski from the Cleveland Police Intelligence Unit walked into the Chief's office carrying a manila folder under his left arm. After a few pleasantries, he got down to business. "You were right, Chief. Reis was wired. My guys were in the lobby and had him pegged for the wire as soon as he came into your office."

"I knew it!" Marinik said, slapping a fist on his desktop.

Sobieski walked over to a potted plant next to the couch and pulled out a small black box. "Here's the bug you wanted, Chief, so the Feds can't dispute what just happened," he said, setting the box on the Chief's desk as if it was a trophy. "My guys will have the recording later today."

The Chief walked around to the front of his desk and addressed Fratello and Nick. "Lieutenant Sobieski has an open case on our dead Pookie Ashford and Cleveland City Hall. Tell them what you got, Dave, and don't leave anything out."

The Lieutenant laid the contents of the folder onto the large dark wood conference table. After spreading the papers out, he looked intently at the two officers. "I am going to trust you both, not because I want to, but because I have to."

Nick and Fratello nodded their heads in assent.

"Sylvester 'Pookie' Ashford has been paying off the Assistant Safety Director in exchange for information to protect his drug operations," Sobieski said. "The Assistant Director, William Cussins, has direct access to Narcotics Unit duty reports. Those reports identify informants, surveillance activity, and suspects being investigated. Needless to say, this privileged information has been detrimental to our efforts to suppress drug activity in Cleveland and the surrounding community. The other person killed with Pookie was our informant, who was acting as Pookie's body guard."

"The big guy in the jogging suit?" Silvano asked.

"Yes. He was going to testify in front of a special grand jury next week. He couldn't wear a wire so when he was killed, our case died with him. If anything turns up in your investigation relating to Cussins or City Hall, treat it as confidential and relay it to Chief Marinik or me. Nobody else, okay?"

Fratello spoke first, directing his answer to Marinik, "You got it Chief," he said and thinking only a fucking miracle would keep him as Homicide Commander long enough to retire.

Before they could leave, Sobieski pulled Nick aside and out of earshot of the Chief and Fratello. "Detective Silvano," he whispered earnestly, "Internal Affairs used my guys to pick up on a telephone call from a dirty cop pretending to be you in dope shakedowns. Just say the word and tell me who he is and I can clear your name and prosecute the officer and his cohorts, but you will have to testify in court. They need more information before they can pursue the case."

"Lieutenant Sobieski," Nick said, looking the man right in the eye. "I don't have a clue as to what you are talking about."

"All right, I get it," answered Sobieski. He put the folder under his arm and left the 9th floor office with thoughts of his own. *The Thin Blue Line remains in place.*

Marinik dismissed Fratello while motioning for Nick to sit down in front of his desk. After the two were alone, Marinik spoke, carefully choosing his words. "We go back a long way Nick, you and me. We played on the same ball teams, drank together at the CPPA Union Bar and although we never partnered up, I trust you, and I hope I have earned your trust in return."

"Sure, Chief," said Nick. "I feel the same. But why do I get the feeling that something else is on your mind other than this Dickens Avenue case?"

"I know all about Reis and his false accusations, Nick. I got a call from my counterpart, the Chief of the Chicago Police, warning me about that asshole before he even got here. I know your CPPA Union guys got the same warning too. I need you to keep your temper in check. Just do your job and I got your back. Only a bombing or some other major catastrophe is going to keep this case out of the news and Mayor Somerville is counting on me to resolve it. Let's keep our lines of communication open with no obstacles like Reis or that other thing with the crooked cops pretending to be you and your partners."

"You know about that too?" Nick asked.

"Nick, as the Chief of the largest police department in Ohio, I am supposed to know it all. We've got to keep a low profile on any distractions and keep City Hall out of trouble. Mayor Somerville is our only friend right now. Can I count on you?"

"Chief, I assure you this situation will be resolved."

He'd make sure of it.

Chapter 8

Nick spent the remaining hours of his shift at the Narcotics Unit office on paperwork and a brief grand jury appearance. He had to convince the civilian members of the sequestered men and women to return a secret indictment for Sales of a Controlled Substance – specifically heroin - by members of a local street gang, The Cedar Avenue Kings, to his Confidential Informants. A dubious female grand jury member wanted to know exactly who the informants were, but Nick never divulged information that could jeopardize the safety of the people he used to get drugs off the street. Never.

Those people on the grand jury were only here for a couple of months. The CIs in this case, two prostitutes named Sydney and Brandi, could be killed if information ever left the grand jury room.

Nick had his subpoena signed at the Clerk's Office and left the Justice Center. He found the undercover car assigned to him had another parking ticket stuffed under the passenger wiper blade and threw it in the glove compartment along with several others he'd accumulated over the past months. *Some day they are going to tow this car away.* But he couldn't park inside 'cause the dopers watched the Police Garage for cars that might be used for undercover operations. They recorded the plate numbers and took photos that were then dispersed to the gang member lookouts. Regular detectives they were.

"I need a drink," he said to no one. The nearest cop bar was the Cockroach Inn on Lakeside Avenue on the east side. The Roach, as it was called, was owned by a retired Cleveland cop by the name of Willy-the-Couch. Willy figured using the word cockroach in the bar's title ensured that no civilians would enter his establishment, but the reverse turned out to be true. Civilian cop groupies flocked to the bar to rub elbows with Cleveland's Finest.

Nick and Willy went way back. They had grown up together on the playgrounds of the west side and attended the same schools. As kids, when they had gone to Willy's house and asked his mother if Willy was home, she would say, "Yeah, he's here on the couch," and the name Willy-the-Couch was born.

The Roach was half full of off-duty cops and a couple of Mounties still in uniform waiting to report off duty with their horses tied up behind the one-story bar that used to be a house. No signs adorned the white clap-boarded building. The route to the Mounted Unit barn from downtown took the stately horses and their riders down Lakeside Avenue, right past the Roach. It was only logical that the riders often stopped in to avail themselves of some liquid refreshment, as did the Motorcycle Unit cops. The horses knew the route so well that one stubborn mount, weary of waiting for his rider, pulled free of his tether and returned to the barn by himself - some fifteen blocks away!

Willy liked to tell the story of the time the traffic cops, after an evening Cleveland Browns football game, parked their bikes inside the bar so their boss couldn't find them. The Mounties thought that was a good idea and two of them encouraged their horses to enter the bar also. "I walked into my bar and saw three motorcycles parked and two police horses standing next to the pool table drinking beer out of pitchers," Willy explained. He panicked because the bar had an old wood floor and was sagging under the extra weight. "A freaking miracle the place didn't collapse!" Horses and motorcycles were kicked out. "For days, all I smelled was exhaust fumes and horseshit."

Willy waved Nick to the far end of the scarred wooden bar and pointed to an empty bar stool next to Nick's partner Frank. "What's up Nicky?" he asked while grabbing a Bud Light and a shot of Jack Daniels for his childhood friend.

"Not much," replied Nick not wanting to share what happened earlier in the Chief's office.

Nick downed the shot with one swallow and placed the rock glass to be refilled by the day barmaid, German Annie. Annie was hired for her two greatest assets, her double D breasts! Willy knew the cops couldn't resist checking out the merchandise on new bar material. Her real name was Gertrude but Willy changed it to Annie since as he said, "Nobody wants to see a Gertrude with big tits!" Her accent was thick but nobody cared, least of all Annie since the tips were good.

"The New York cops are on their way in," Willy told the group assembled at the bar. "There's a Safety Forces Softball tournament at Gordon Park this weekend."

Nick knew a lot of the New York officers from their frequent visits to Cleveland. They came mostly just to see Willy and drink at the Cleveland Police Patrolmen's Association bar, aptly named the Zone Car Lounge.

The association between the two cities had formed when some of the New York detectives had investigated the shooting death of a Cleveland Police detective killed in a robbery in New York City. The detective had gone to follow up on a suspect living in New York wanted for a shooting in Cleveland and was killed in a street robbery.

"New York's Finest" had put the full weight of their manpower behind solving the case and the detective's killer was jailed and convicted in an astonishingly short time. A type of Blue Bond prevailed between the two forces from that case and lifelong friendships were formed. Nick was in school when that happened but the New York Cops still came to Cleveland and they never forgot about the Cleveland Cop who was gunned down in their city.

As more cops came into the Roach the war stories began to be tossed about as only cops can tell them. The job that cops are charged to do can be unbelievable - the outlandish becomes normal. Nick's partner, Frank, tossed down a shot of whiskey, then turned to Nick and asked if he recalled their first run out of the Academy in the Fourth District on Cleveland's east side. "Remember the dead body on the third floor, partner?"

Nick smiled in spite of himself. "You bet I do! We both thought we were going to get fired over that one." The group of cops and German Annie begged for Frank to continue. He motioned to his glass for a refill and obliged.

"Me and Nick were both raw rookies on the night shift in the Fourth District and we weren't supposed to be working together but the Desk Sergeant had no choice. I think his name was Ronnie Welch, right Nicky?" he asked without waiting for the answer before pausing to down the shot. "The Narcs had pulled off a big raid and the druggies had locked themselves into an apartment down in the Garden Valley projects," he said, setting the scene for his audience.

"A large crowd was at the dope house with the Narcs and all the available uniforms were needed for crowd control. Nick was assigned to the office with Sergeant Welch and I was in the lobby taking walk-up reports. Police Radio called the Sarge and was begging for anybody available to take some assignments 'cause they were four hours behind on answering the runs. Welch kept telling them no, but finally relented after the Captain in Radio assured him that we would only get the report runs and no investigations or dealings with the public or arrests. Me and Nick grabbed the keys to Car 412 and hit the streets, ready for some action. I think we were only in the District four or five days, right Nicky?"

Nick nodded while German Annie filled up the empty glasses, bending over the cooler a little longer than necessary allowing the guys to look at her assets. The math was easy. More looks, more tips.

Frank continued, "We got our first assignment of a dead body over on Milverton Avenue at about three in the morning. Now, I figure we got a gunshot victim or a murder and with both of us being rookies and not knowing any better, we run lights and siren all the way to the assignment. So, we get there and had to knock on the door for a real long time before anybody answered. Now, I'm thinking, what is this shit about? A dead body and we got to wake people up! Finally some guy opens the door and he is yawning and acting all sleepy. I get pissed and start asking him where the murder victim is and he looks at me and Nicky like we're crazy and starts backing up stammering, 'I didn't kill anybody, he was dead when we found him!'

"Nick slaps cuffs on the guy and he starts crying and then some chick in her pajamas comes into the kitchen and starts yelling all crazy like, demanding to know what's going on. We tell her somebody at this address called in a dead body and this guy might be a suspect. She starts cussing us up one side and down the other and tells us that the dead body is her grandfather who lived on the third floor and was real sick for a long time and, 'you motherfuckers were called five hours ago and now you show up trying to arrest my man? He didn't kill nobody,' she screamed at us, pointing to the guy we got in cuffs who is still crying. Turns out, the old man died because he was old and sick. She called the cops 'cause Gramps had to go to the County Morgue because they didn't have a doctor sign the death certificate. 'You people told me that!' she was blabbering."

Willy-the-Couch was doubled over in laughter and several of the cops slapped the bar with their fists. "What happened next?" one of the Mounties asked.

"By this time me and Nicky are backtracking and apologizing all over the place. We call Radio to send the meat wagon because back then, the cops took dead bodies to the morgue before the coroner took over. Anyhow, after about another hour, Car 491 shows up with Olson and Williams and we tell them what we got and the dead guy is up on the third floor. Now, both of these guys were known to have a couple cocktails on occasion while on duty and they go off to the wagon to get the stretcher, bitchin' about 'damn rookies.' Meanwhile, me and Nick are sitting at the kitchen table with the granddaughter and her boyfriend getting the information for the report. It's morning now and the sun is coming up. All of a sudden we see a flash of something fly by the kitchen window. The boyfriend and the granddaughter are sitting with their backs to the window and me and Nick give each other a "what the fuck was that" look. I lean forward in the chair and look out the window and see Gramps splattered in the driveway!" Frank shook his head like he still couldn't believe it all these years later.

"I give Nick the high sign and he picks up on it real fast. I tell them I got to go to the car and get another report sheet. I meet the wagon guys coming down the stairs with an empty stretcher and I say to them, 'What the hell did you guys do that for?' Olson gets in my face and man, the sauce was really coming out of his pores now. He proceeds to tell me the old guy was too fat to bring all the way down three flights of stairs on the stretcher so they pushed him out the window!

"I didn't know what to say, almost pissed my pants!" Frank was laughing along with the crowd. "Then Williams pipes in and says, 'What the fuck do you care, he was already dead!' Then they go outside and put gramps on the stretcher like nothing happened, and off they go to St. Luke's Hospital to get the body pronounced dead by the emergency room doctor before they take it to the morgue for an autopsy. I go back into the house, scared shitless that some neighbor or a passerby saw what had happened," said Frank. "Nick had all the information for the report so we apologized again to the granddaughter for taking so long to get there and then scrammed outta there!"

Nick picked up the story. "I didn't believe what Frank was telling me. Who does something like that? But, when we get back to the Fourth District to go off duty we see Olson and Williams in the locker room. Those two assholes are grinning from ear to ear. Now, I get pissed and went right up to them and asked point blank, 'Did you guys really throw that guy out the window?' Olson looks at me and says, 'Welcome to the Fourth, kid,' and walked away laughing.

"Me and Frank are going crazy and don't know what to do. We go out into the parking lot so nobody hears us, just knowing we are goners. Then Frank spoke his words of wisdom," said Nick. "He says, 'Remember what that Shooting Range Officer, Lieutenant Roth, told our academy class, Nicky?' I tell him that Lt. Roth told us a lot of stuff, 'Pearls of Wisdom' he called it, and I didn't remember all of them."

Frank picked up the story. "The old timer told us, 'Admit nothing-deny everything-and when they got you by the balls-demand proof!' So we decide to say nothing and prayed no one would ever find out what those assholes did."

"After about a month," continued Nick, "we don't hear nothing so we get to feeling pretty safe that nobody found out. Then one night after Roll Call, we get called into Sergeant Welch's office and he starts asking us if we 'remember' getting a dead body run over on Milverton Avenue about a month ago. My balls are up in my throat now. I look at Frank and he looks at me and I say, 'Maybe, that was a long time ago.' Welch sits down in his chair and looks up at both of us and says, 'Might there be something you two want to tell me?' Both of us just stand there saying nothing, figuring our short-lived Police careers are over now.

"Then Welch stands up, shakes both of our hands and says, 'You two guys are all right! Olson and Williams told me what happened that morning and we all had bets on how long before one of you cracked and ratted them out, but you both kept your yappers shut. The whole platoon knew what happened. You guys passed the test. Welcome to the Fourth District, kiddies.'"

Frank continued, "So later I ask the Sarge how the morgue explained all the damage to the guy if he was supposed to die from natural causes. Turned out that some retired Fourth District cops worked at the morgue. They told the Assistant Coroner the stretcher was old and it broke bringing the guy down the stairs and he fell 'some' and it won't happen again!"

Frank laughed along with his audience. "After that we got assigned to cars with good training officers and saw a lot of action. We lasted another nine years in the Fourth before we got sent to the Narcotics Unit."

By this time the New York City cops were piling into the Roach and Willy had to help German Annie pour drinks to keep up with the crowd. Some of the guys were still in their softball uniforms and had just finished playing ball at the Gordon Park fields down off the Shore way next to Lake Erie.

As the bar talk grew louder and the night grew closer, Agent Reis and the Dickens Avenue killings faded to a nuisance buzz in Nick's head. *Sometimes, I wish tomorrow would never come.* He ordered another shot.

Chapter 9

JuJu awoke with the familiar gnawing in his gut; he wanted heroin. He had not used in a couple of weeks and was trying to stem the need he had through willpower alone. It wasn't enough.

Since the killings two weeks ago, he had been laying low in the Clevelander Hotel, waiting for the heat to die down. He purposely did not carry any heroin on him or keep any in his hotel room for fear of being either apprehended with it on his person or having some snoopy hotel housekeeper steal it or decide to call hotel security.

He used his disposable cell phone and called Darik and Tion to place his order but no one answered and voicemail did not activate. JuJu threw the phone onto the bed in a rare display of temper. While he prided himself on keeping his cool, the uncertainty of his current situation and drug craving only increased his agitation.

Then he remembered that he had Sydney's number. He dug her business card out of his wallet – a whore with a business card! He checked to make sure his caller ID was blocked and dialed the number.

She answered after the third ring with a husky, "Hello?"

"This is the big man from a couple weeks ago, you remember me?"

Sydney frowned when she heard JuJu's melodic voice but forced a smile to encourage a welcoming response.

"Sure Sugar, I remember you, what's up?"

"I need you to do something for me," JuJu responded. "Meet me in front of the Rock and Roll Hall of Fame. And leave your friend at home. Come alone." He didn't need a parade of people being able to identify him.

"Baby, I can't make it until after four this afternoon. Brandi has my car," she lied, "and she went with her baby's daddy to check out a new day care center." Sydney actually had a weekly appointment with a big-time downtown attorney she had been servicing for almost a year. It was an easy gig and she didn't have to worry about getting mauled. All she had to do was don a judge's black robe and deliver a "guilty" verdict and sexy punishment. Seems the man liked to relinquish control now and then, and she provided the outlet. For that, he paid her $500. Any other working girl might exploit this knowledge for her own benefit, but Sydney was smart. When it came to her clients, she kept her mouth shut. She actually received customer referrals from long-time clients who appreciated her discretion. Just like a real business woman.

The lawyer's office was in the Terminal Tower which was also on Cleveland's Public Square adjacent to the hotel where JuJu was staying. The historic Public Square occupied a ten-acre tract originally designed by Moses Cleveland in the 1790's as a common area to graze farm animals. Today, the Square was a bustling center ringed by the city's three tallest buildings. The fourth building was the Horseshoe Casino, formerly Higbee's department store, featured in the iconic movie *A Christmas Story*. It was also the first metropolitan area to be lit by modern electric lights in 1879 that were developed by Cleveland native Charles F. Brush.

"Just meet me at East 9th Street on the pier at four," he told her. JuJu showered, ordered room service for lunch, then left the Clevelander Hotel and started walking to the rendezvous site. The craving for heroin was still there, fluttering in his gut. He was Obeah Man and could control himself, unlike common junkies, he thought. A little dope and alcohol had always been enough to keep him wired, but lately he found he was spending too much time in the hotel bar and the jittery feeling that compelled him to ask Sydney to score some heroin for him was unsettling. It wasn't like him to allow a whore to know his business.

But now was not the time to get distracted; he could deal with this little problem after he left the United States. The immediate issue was to sell the coke stashed in his rented van and get back to Trinidad with the money.

He walked through downtown Cleveland and repelled the panhandlers working the Square with a glare. At the Justice Center, he turned and crossed Mall C toward the Rock Hall, as the locals referred to it. The closer he got to the Rock Hall's sprawling glass pyramid structure and the growing crowd of tourists, the less he wanted to be there. He changed course for the end of the East 9th Street pier and took a bench overlooking the water. From there, he could see out over Lake Erie to the boats crossing behind the large break wall built to keep the waves from slamming into the docks and shoreline of the Cleveland waterfront.

He stretched his long legs out and slouched down along the seat until he could rest his head against the back of the bench. The sun felt warm on his face and the lake breeze was comforting - but the urge to use was still there. *I'll just close my eyes for a minute.*

About fifteen minutes had passed when a large seagull looking for food scraps squawked, startling him awake. A glance at his cell phone told him it was almost four o'clock. Time to meet Sydney. JuJu rose off the bench in a graceful move that suggested a cat leaving its perch rather than a druggie looking for a fix, and looked over at the water one last time.

He had gone only a short distance when he spotted Sydney's brown Cadillac DeVille lumbering down East 9th. He stepped out into the street, waved her over, opened the car door, and slid in next to her. She didn't speak a word to him as she made a U-turn and headed up East 9th Street and then east on the Memorial Shoreway adjacent to the Lake.

JuJu spoke first. "I want you to get me a half ounce of good heroin. I want quality stuff." Without looking at her he pulled out a large roll of currency and put it on the seat between them. "Don't even think about gettin' any of that shit that's been cut to nothing," he warned. "There's more than enough cash here to make it happen," he said, tapping his fingers on the rubber-banded roll of cash.

Sydney glanced at the wad of cash on the seat. There had to be a couple thousand dollars in that roll and the dude didn't even seem to care what it might cost! "I'll have to travel some to get the good stuff. Are you up for the ride?"

JuJu did not want to be anywhere near the deal. "I want to wait somewhere for you," he told her. The Clevelander Hotel wasn't an option as he didn't want her to know where he was staying.

Sydney thought fast. She had just passed the downtown Cleveland Lakefront Burke Airport. The East 55th Street Marina was nearby and had a public bar called The Captain's Quarters. That would be a good place for the big man to wait while she made the drive to Shaker Heights to buy the heroin. She and Brandi sometimes acted as confidential informants for Cleveland detectives and they often met up with Detective Nick Silvano at the marina when the cops needed their special services to act as drug buyers. The marina had a locked gate to keep out non-members but Sydney knew the bar was a public place and all a visitor had to do was ring the buzzer and the bartenders would open the gate from inside.

Sydney made the turn into the marina and rang the button outside the eight-foot gated fence topped with barbed wire. In just a few seconds the gate rolled open and the DeVille rolled into the parking lot. She looked through the windshield to see if she spotted anybody she knew. Specifically, she was looking for Detective Silvano. Right now, he was the last person she wanted to run into. Technically, she wasn't doing business. She was just dropping off her new acquaintance at the bar.

She pulled the DeVille next to the Captain's Quarters entrance and turned to face JuJu. "You want to wait here? I will be gone for less than an hour and this is as good a place as any. You can either wait by the park benches facing the boat docks over there," she pointed her finger by way of explanation, "or here by the bar. There are tables outside and you can get a drink while I'm gone."

JuJu looked over the marina area. There was a good mix of people milling around; both blacks and whites. Some were in shorts and T-shirts but there were also people dressed in suits. He could easily pass for a boater, or someone waiting for his boating friend to show up. He was skilled at changing his voice, posture, or gestures to fit into any environment. It's what kept him alive for so long.

"This will do fine" JuJu replied. "I'll wait by the tables outside the bar on the patio. But don't be too long," he warned. The thought that Sydney would take off with his cash and never return didn't even occur to him; he was confident in his power over other people.

He exited the DeVille and watched Sydney as she drove out the gate. Only then did he walk through the bar to the patio. He chose a table in a corner where his back was protected by a wall but provided a clear view of the patio, the door to the bar, and the parking lot beyond. The white plastic chair's legs wobbled slightly as he lowered himself into it. A large yellow and white umbrella advertising Corona beer in large blue letters provided shade.

A blonde barmaid came out of the door and walked past JuJu to an adjacent table with a full bucket of Coronas. She appeared to be a seasoned waitress – somewhere between 25 or 30, he guessed. Even if he erred on the high side, she was still quite a prize with long, tan legs set off by trim red shorts. A white halter top barely seemed up to the task of containing the twin mounds of her breasts. JuJu looked for tan lines, but didn't see any. He took that to mean this girl spent a lot of time out on the water sunbathing in the nude, just like the girls back in Trinidad. She made change for the group of twenty-something professional males dressed in business suits.

Time's up boys, he thought as she approached JuJu's table.

"My name is Kat, and I'll be your server. What is your pleasure, sir?"

Even though he knew she probably said this to everyone, JuJu felt aroused but evenly responded, "Spiced rum and Coke."

"Coming right up," she said, then walked quickly through the swinging door connecting the patio to the white, one-story building that was barely large enough to contain the bar, bait shop, and restaurant. She returned a few minutes later and deftly set his drink order onto the table in front of him. "Do you want to run a tab?" she asked.

"No need," JuJu told her, still avoiding looking directly into her eyes. He gave her a hundred dollar bill. "This should handle my bill for now."

Smiling, Kat leaned over, picked up the bill, and slid it provocatively into the left swell of her halter top. She paused then, waiting for JuJu to look at her. When he finally turned his head and met her gaze, her practiced smile froze and it seemed as if she was being held in place by the blackness of his eyes.

Then his lips parted revealing even white teeth; a slight smile released her. She made herself turn away from him and practically fled into the safety of the bar. *That dude is one scary motherfucker...but he's got friendly cash.*

Chapter 10

JuJu sat quietly, sipping his drink for the next hour, watching the antics of the white dudes in business suits. They had removed their coats and were standing around with their shirt sleeves rolled up, acting like a bunch of juvenile school kids whenever the barmaid brought them another round of drinks.

Over an hour had passed. *Where was Sydney?* He reached for his phone, about to dial her number, then put it back on the table. He had to maintain the impression of aloofness and superiority over everyone he encountered. Calling her would only show the weakness of impatience. He knew she was afraid of him. That was part of his power. So far, it was working.

While JuJu waited for Sydney at the Captain's Quarters, Detective Nick Silvano was at the station. He completed the daily duty report, officially known as Police Report Form One, which would be dropped into his Supervisor's mail basket. Duty reports were a mundane but necessary part of the job. Officers recorded their daily activities and turned them in to the Narcotics Unit supervisors.

"C'mon Nick, it's been a long day. Let's get a beer at the Roach," Frank said.

"Yeah, Nick," Lenny echoed, cracking a big grin. "Just

one beer."

"Naw," Nick replied. "I'm tired. I'm just going to the marina and grab a burger and a beer and rest on my boat tonight. And besides," he added, "it's never just one beer with you guys!"

Nick left the Justice Center and drove his Honda Civic the short distance to the marina. The Captain's Quarters was jumping. Most of the cheap plastic tables at the outside cabana bar were fully occupied.

He parked in a spot by the D dock walkway, stowed his gun and badge in the center console, then locked the vehicle and walked across the lot to the bar. While nightfall was approaching, the late August evening was still hot and humid and felt like the tropical weather he endured as a jet fighter mechanic stationed at Moody Air Force Base in Valdosta, Georgia. It was twenty-five years ago; another lifetime. He was only eighteen years old then, but on evenings like this, when the air was swampy, it seemed like only yesterday.

The air base was next to the Okefenokee swamp, a vast, murky wasteland covering portions of both Georgia and North Florida. At night, alligators would leave the cool waters of the swamp to claim a spot on the concrete runways, still warm from being baked all day by the sun. Each morning, before the jets could take off, the crew chiefs grabbed ropes and headed out to the runways for an alligator roundup. If they didn't remove the ancient reptiles, an incoming jet could crash. Those alligators made for one hell of a speed bump.

Entering the bar, he was glad to see Kat was working. She was a welcome sight after the day he'd had. Even though the food was good there, Kat was the main reason the young men clustered around the establishment whenever she was on the schedule.

Tina, the owner, greeted Nick with a hug and placed a shot of Jack Daniels and a Bud Light beer in front of him. "You look hungry, Nick. What are you having tonight?" she asked, pencil poised above a notepad to take his order.

"Well, since you have the best burgers in town, I'll have the Bacon Swiss burger platter, no onions."

She read the order back to him, "Bacon Swiss burger with Portobello mushrooms, Swiss cheese, bacon, Dijon sauce, no onions."

"Don't forget the fries."

"It'll be up in a few minutes."

"I'm in no hurry," Nick said, drawing the beer closer. He took a deep swallow then set the bottle down on the bar and followed it with a mouthful of Jack. The bar was covered with colorful decals of shells and tropical fish submerged under an ocean of varnish to protect them from the wear and tear of glasses and bottles being pushed and pulled over the displays.

Kat gazed warmly at Nick and gave him a refill without charging his tab. During the past two years she had been working at the CQ, as it was called by the regulars, the pair had gotten close to the point that Kat knew where everything was to make the morning coffee in the Rinker's little cabin area. She also knew he liked his coffee strong with a little Bailys Irish Cream added, but only if he didn't have to work.

He knew he never got tired of looking at her. Short blonde hair and deep green eyes, slender waist, and smooth skin tanned a perfect golden hue. With her provocative look and amazing body, she could easily be featured in a men's magazine. And she was smart. Kat was working on a Master's degree in Clinical Psychology at Case Western University. Bartending was both her fun job as well as an extracurricular classroom; you met all types of people in the bar. All that, right here at the CQ. *How did I get so lucky?*

The bar was far too busy for Nick to converse with her so he eased himself back in the barstool and settled in. Tina set his burger platter in front of him and when he finished eating, he ordered another shot and beer, then got up to use the men's room.

The bathrooms were located outside and remained unlocked during the boating season so the fishermen and dock holders could have twenty-four hour access. Nick exited through the side door to the outside patio and walked through the group of people dancing to the reggae band that was the night's entertainment. The young, black musicians were dressed in colorful costumes singing a musical chant. Coming back, he looked over the crowd to see if any of his dock mates were present when a brown DeVille pulling into a parking spot next to the patio caught his attention. *I know that car!* He watched as the car's owner and his sometime snitch, Sydney, approached a large black man sitting alone at one of the tables. *What the hell was she doing here?*

Sydney sat down and passed a small package to the man. After a few minutes, the man got up and went into the bathroom. Nick knew what he just saw. No matter how discreet they had been, the whole exchange screamed "score" and the guy was going to take his treat right there in the bathroom – on Nick's own turf.

He casually retraced his route to the bathrooms and caught sight of the big man just as he entered a stall and shut the door behind him. Should he kick the stall door open and make a bust right here? He was off duty, alone, and his gun and badge were locked in the car. Might as well let the dickhead enjoy himself, tonight anyway. He went to the sinks and washed his hands to explain his presence, then left and made his way over to Sydney and tapped her on the shoulder. She turned around, and became agitated when she saw who it was. "Nick! You startled me."

"I guess I did," he answered. "What are you doing here, Sydney? You know better than to come down here with your customers. I know what that dude is doing in the men's room and I don't appreciate you coming into my sandbox with your shit."

Just then, Sydney's companion exited the bathroom and returned to the table, fixing Nick with a hazy stare. After hitting a couple long lines of heroin up his nose, JuJu was feeling pretty mellow. He resumed his seat and picked up his drink, his eyes never leaving Nick, who was still standing next to Sydney. Nick returned the scrutiny with a gaze of his own.

He did not recognize this man and decided to mentally file his description into the back of his mind for another day. His curiosity could wait until he could get Sydney alone and quiz her as to who this dude was.

Sydney twisted nervously in the plastic chair as she watched the two men stare at each other. Both were dangerous in their own way. Nick could put her in jail and JuJu, he could probably inflict a lot of physical pain. She wanted to avoid both scenarios and was relieved when Nick said, "Good to see you again baby, I'll call you later," and walked back into the bar.

Even though JuJu was high on heroin and warm from the rum, the man talking to Sydney made him uneasy. "Who was that man?" he asked her.

"He's one of my customers. Thought I was free and wanted a date tonight but I told him I was already booked, Sugar. I am booked up for the night, right?" Sydney wanted to keep the leftover cash from the dope score. He'd given her three thousand dollars and the drugs cost fourteen hundred. Her Shaker Heights supplier reduced the price for a blow job while he measured out the heroin.

JuJu thought for a minute before replying. "Go get us a room. I might as well get my money's worth out of you."

Nick watched them leave from the bar window.

Both men were instinctively suspicious of each other. Each was a hunter. One of them would be prey.

Sydney prayed the two men would never meet again.

Chapter 11

Silvano answered his cell phone on the third ring. "Hey Lenny," he said to his partner after seeing his name on caller ID. "What's up?"

"Where are you?"

"Where do you think I am?" Nick asked. "This is my day off and I'm sleeping in," he replied as he removed Kat's soft, tan arm from his chest. She stirred slightly and Nick could have sworn that she actually purred. It was a seductive sound and momentarily distracted him from what Lenny was saying.

"You're scheduled for a grand jury hearing at ten o'clock this morning."

"What?" Nick exclaimed, now wide awake. "I don't have any subpoena for a grand jury today!"

"You told Charley Goetz you would testify for Frank today, remember?"

"Is that today?" asked Nick.

"Yep," Lenny confirmed. "Charley doesn't want Frank anywhere near the grand jury and he called for you specifically."

"Okay," Nick answered. "Tell Charley he owes me." He looked over at Kat, now snoring lightly into her pillow. "A big one."

Nick slid out of the small sleeping berth, threw some

clothes in a small duffel bag, then headed to the shower house. Last night's encounter with Sydney and her dope-using friend still pissed him off. Should have busted that junkie right then, he thought. He had a feeling this one would come back to bite him.

After showering, Nick returned to the boat, scribbled a note for the still-slumbering Kat then drove to the Justice Center, mentally reviewing his testimony for the drug case along the way. Nick and Goetz had worked many drug cases together. He liked Goetz. Hell, he trusted Goetz and that was more important. There were lots of guys he worked with that he liked, but he wouldn't trust them to borrow his car. The last drug bust they had worked together had culminated in the seizure of twenty-two pounds of methamphetamine and the arrest of seven members of a biker gang. While Frank had been involved in the raid too, Charley didn't want him anywhere near a grand jury.

The raid had been conducted with a Federal DEA search warrant. When the Cleveland Police SWAT team hit the door of the double house in Cleveland's Tremont area, a middle-aged, white female came flying out of the second story window, landing face-down in the driveway, within feet of where they stood.

Thinking she was trying to escape, Detective Frank Hartness yelled at the woman to "stay put" and placed handcuffs on her. What he didn't realize, in the heat of the moment, was that she was unconscious and had two broken arms. It wasn't until later he learned the bikers thought she was a snitch, so they threw her out the window.

"The girl is nothing but a snaggle-toothed speed freak," Goetz explained to Nick, "but she hired herself a dirtbag lawyer to file a million dollar lawsuit against the DEA and you cops for breaking her arms when she 'resisted' arrest. The bikers got to the chick's boyfriend and told him that if she testifies against them for selling her the dope and throwing her out the window, then she and her whole family were as good as dead. Her only way out was to blame Frank, so you can understand how it would look to have Frank there and have some grand jury member ask him how this girl got so injured."

Nick wanted to protest but Charley had intervened. "For Christ's sake Nick, your partner handcuffed an unconscious woman with two broken arms! Don't give me any grief! Civilians on a grand jury can't understand what happens in a dope house raid, how fast things happen, how quickly things can go south. I know Frank didn't break her arms, I was there, remember?" said Goetz. "I just don't want to open a can of worms over this, alright?"

Nick grumbled over the request but knew if he was in Goetz's shoes, he'd probably think the same way. The grand jury testimony went off without a hitch and Detective Frank Hartness' name wasn't even mentioned. Nick picked up his overtime court card at the Court Sergeant's Office, stopped in at the Justice Center's cafeteria for a quick coffee, then went up to the Narcotics Unit office. He sat down at his desk and looked at all the case files piled on top of each other, wondering how he was ever going to get to them.

"Bunch of shit, huh," Lenny said, nodding his head at the stack of files as he sat down at his desk across from Nick's.

"Where's Frank?" asked Nick.

"Don't know," Lenny responded. "This morning he told me that Sydney called him late last night crying about how she might have screwed something up and wanted to see him right away. He went to meet her down by the Rock Hall. I was going to go with him but I had to go testify in Muni Court over a Fifth District case and he said he couldn't wait for me."

"I know what she screwed up,'" Nick said. "She took one of her johns down to my marina last night and passed off some dope to the asshole. And I saw her do it! I was going to pop the dirt bag but it was late and I didn't have my gun. The guy was freakin' big and scary looking so I decided to wait for another day." He shook his head, wondering at Sydney's choice in clients. "Someday," he predicted, "We will get the call to ID Sydney's body at the morgue."

"Well," replied Lenny, "Sydney and Brandi have scored a lot of buys for us. We do owe them a little slack."

"Yeah, I guess you're right about that," Nick said.

"But she sure has brass balls to operate in your territory!" Lenny added. "You wanna stay for a while and help me out here? You can use the overtime."

Nick and Lenny spent the next three hours working

on their case files. "She is scared to death of you, Nick," Frank explained when he finally returned from meeting Sydney, "But she is more afraid of this guy she has been seeing for the past month or so. Said she met him at the Interstate Inn with Brandi for a paid date that was set up by two little queers. She says you," he pointed a finger at Nick, "can put her in jail but this dude can kill her!"

"Did she say what his name was?" Nick inquired.

"All she knows is she heard one of the little guys referred to him as 'JuJu' and they seemed really scared of him," Frank related. "He won't give her a name and when he calls her, his number comes up as Restricted on her caller ID."

Nick looked like he was about to say something but Frankie beat him to it. "Before you get all righteous on me, hear me out. Sydney will help us get this guy but she says it has to be on her terms. She doesn't have a real name on him or the little queers he runs around with yet, but promised me that she will help us."

"Go on, I'm listening," Nick prodded.

"She also told me that the big guy has a heroin jones and carries a knife. She saw it last night when they went out to the Euclid Motel. She decided to do a little snooping while he was in the bathroom and happened to peek in his man bag. She saw a wad of hundred dollar bills and the knife but before she could look any further, she heard the toilet flush and had to stop. But you know how bitch crazy Sydney is, she'll nail it for us."

Nick answered, "No doubt. She knows we are the only reason she and Brandi are not in jail. But I'm still ticked off that she took that scumbag where I live!"

Lenny interrupted his two partners. "Let's not fight," he said in his best teacher's voice. "What about that Dickens Avenue murder case?" he asked changing the subject, looking from Nick to Frank. "We hear anything else about it from Homicide?"

"Fratello hasn't said much to me lately," Nick responded, "but since there are no suspects or arrests, I got a feeling we'll hear something soon. The streets are quiet on this one. Nothing from any of our usual informants or the Feds' CI's. Maybe we should take it up a notch, what do you guys think?"

"We can start looking into it more after we catch up on our cases here," Lenny answered.

"Yeah," Frank agreed, "but keep that asshole Reis away from us Nicky."

Nick relayed what had transpired in Chief Marinik's office, leaving nothing out. "The Chief wants the Cleveland Police to solve these murders."

"That's for you and Fratello to delve into," Frank said. "Our plates are full! We can back you up but the case is for Homicide, not us Narcs."

"Fair enough," Nick replied then thought of something else. "Hey, Frank?"

"Yeah?"

"When you met up with Sydney today, she said that she met that big dude through a couple of homosexual guys?"

"Yeah, that's right," Frank confirmed, meeting Nick's gaze. "She told me she met the big guy after her and Brandi were trolling for johns and two little Jamaican guys hooked them up at the Interstate Hotel. She said the dudes had copped some heroin for him and acted like they worked for him."

"Maybe we should follow this up since Sydney is passing it on," Lenny interjected. "If she doesn't know this guy or the two little Jamaican guys, they must be new in the play here 'cause those girls have a direct pipeline to all that goes on in this town. What with Sydney banging the top lawyers and probably a few judges too, you can bet this new guy and his little friends need a look."

"I agree," Frank said. He turned to Nick. "You still friends with that gay bar owner on the west side? If I remember correctly, he is the go-to guy for all things gay in Cleveland."

"You mean Michael's Body Shop?"

"That's the one," Frankie confirmed.

"Yeah, I know Michael. You want to pay his bar a visit?"

"Sure do," replied Lenny.

"I'm in," Frank said. "What we do for the people of Cleveland. If they only knew!"

Chapter 12

N ick pulled the red, dented, wooden door open and stepped over the worn threshold into Michael's Body Shop bar. It was exactly like he remembered years ago when he was a rookie walking the beat on second platoon. It was his first day out of training and he'd checked on the bar at the start of his afternoon shift; it was full of male patrons. He made a final pass at quitting time and found the same crowd, only now they were in drag, dressed as women.

Even as a rookie, Nick adopted a "to each his own" attitude that allowed him to cultivate informants from all walks of life. Michael, the owner, was always friendly to Nick, especially after Nick arrested two men who'd come into the bar one night for the sole purpose of making trouble.

Nick had walked into the bar and caught one of the men pistol whipping Michael, screaming "You and all of your faggot friends better find someplace else to drink!" An accomplice held the customers at gunpoint. The two men were arrested and Nick followed up on the case to make sure they were convicted. He stayed in touch with Michael in the years that followed and assisted him in other situations.

"Hey Nicky," the bar's owner greeted him. Michael

was a slim, elegant man in the vicinity of sixty years old. His long fingers, more suitable to playing piano than washing glasses, held the stems of two wine glasses in each hand. His graying hair was pulled back into a nub of a ponytail held in place by a rubber band. "You ready to change sides, sweetie?"

"Michael," Nick said, smiling. "You know I'm still straight, but if I decide to switch teams, you'll be the first to know!" Nick and his partners walked to the far end of the bar where it was quieter and motioned for Michael to join them.

"What can I do for you boys?" Michael asked.

"You got any information on a big black dude, about two fifty with a bald head and gold hoop earrings?" Nick asked in a low tone.

"Can't say that I do," Michael replied. "You know, most of my customers are white guys and now they are quite a bit older than when you first met them, Nick. The ones that were here that night you saved my ass still come in and ask about you. Matter of fact, James down there," Michael paused, pointing to a fiftyish man dressed in a pale blue tank top and extremely short shorts, "was here that night. Hey James," Michael called out, "remember Nicky?"

"Oh God, yes!" James exclaimed, raising his glass to Nick as if to toast him. "Our white knight in shining armor!" James stood up and pointed to the rest of the customers at the bar, who by this time, were now staring at the three officers. "Can we buy you and your friends a drink, officer?"

"Sure," answered Nick. "We're officially off duty."

While Michael was busy fixing drinks, Frank turned to Nick. "You got a little piece of heaven here don't you Nick?" he said, grinning.

"These guys are okay," Nick said, "And believe me, they are a good source of information."

Michael brought their drinks out and led them to a table.

"Frank, tell Michael what Sydney told you," Nick instructed his partner.

After Frank relayed Sydney's story, Michael said, "I do remember two Jamaican guys coming in a few times. The weird thing was, well, weirder than most of my customers," he allowed with a little laugh, "was the way they giggled. Like a pair of little school girls. They had some sort of Caribbean Island accent, sing-song like. I knew they were riff-raff. Definitely not classy enough for my place. The last time they came in was about two weeks ago. I had my security guy put them out when they put a line of cocaine on the bar. I mean really," he huffed. "Who does that anymore?"

Michael turned and motioned to a very large man sitting on a stool just off to the inside of the front door. "Hey Hoss, come over here."

Hoss lumbered over to the table. The bouncer was only a little over five-foot-five inches tall but was almost as wide and had tree trunks for arms. "Christ," Nick exclaimed, "How did we miss you sitting over there when we came in?"

Hoss shrugged in an I-don't-know gesture, causing

the cotton fabric of his T-shirt to stretch against the muscle movement. "Hey, I've seen you around the lifting circuit – how much can you bench?" Nick asked. Nick himself had taken a silver medal in the Police Olympics for power lifting and had competed in regional lifting competitions.

Hoss's wide face broke out in a grin at this acknowledgment. "I've benched six-fifty but my dead lift is over a grand. Most I've totaled is twenty-two fifty at the Arnold Schwarzenegger Invitational in Columbus last year."

"Yeah, I remember you," Nick said. "They call you Boss Hoss, right?"

"Yeah, that's right. You know, like from the Dukes of Hazard." He looked at Michael as if asking permission before saying anything else to the detectives. He had them pegged as cops the minute they walked in.

Most people didn't realize it but bouncers are great students of human nature. They could tell the measure of a person just by the way they walked through a door. Kind of like bartenders, Nick thought, his mind immediately fixing on his favorite bartender. Only Nick didn't think Hoss was pursuing a Clinical Psychology degree.

"These guys are all right, Hoss," Michael told him. "They want to know about those two Jamaican guys you kicked out of here a couple of weeks ago."

"Yeah, those guys," Hoss said, in a voice that sounded like he was gargling gravel. "I put them out and those two little weasels had the nerve to threaten me at the door. I followed them to their car to make sure they left and they were yelling how they were coming back and kill me!" He looked around the table. "I mean, I'm a big guy and can take care of myself. But dudes like that scare even me because they looked crazy enough to do it."

"What did they look like?" asked Frankie.

Hoss described them just as Sydney had told Frank earlier, only he was able to describe their car too. "They had a black Ford Focus rental. I saw the rental sticker on the window. I like to keep a lookout for troublemakers like that in case they come back."

"Thanks a lot, Hoss," Nick told the bouncer. "Stay strong, man!" Hoss returned to his post by the door.

Nick and his partners stayed for a couple more rounds. As they were leaving, James stopped Frank to thank him for his service as a Cleveland Police officer, held his hand out to shake, and then pressed a note into Frank's palm.

"What does the note say?" Lenny badgered his partner once they were back in the car.

Frank fished the note out from his pocket and, after reading it, crumpled the paper in his hand and threw it out the car window.

"Yeah, Frank, tell us," Nick echoed.

"James wrote that he would just 'love it' if I would stop by and show him my 'big gun'. You believe that shit?" Frankie exclaimed, shaking his head.

"Well, you gonna do it?" Lenny asked with a straight face. "Protect and serve and all that..."

Chapter 13

JuJu sat at the hotel bar, his usual spiced rum and Coke drink resting before him on a cardboard coaster imprinted with the hotel's name, and watched the early afternoon news cast on the big screen television positioned high on the wall. The same Greek bartender, who never seemed to leave the building, was working again. *Did he ever go home?*

With each passing day, the Dickens Avenue Killings received less and less attention. All the better for him. Or so he thought.

It had been over a month since JuJu and his two Jamaican accomplices had robbed and killed the two Mexican drug couriers and the two buyers from Cleveland. JuJu was biding time in the city, waiting for the heat to subside. That was the easy part; all the cops would do was toss him in jail. It was the Mexicans he was worried about. He knew he was dead if they ever found him.

He'd seen firsthand what the Cartel did to those who crossed them. The unfortunate son-of-a-bitch ended up wearing a Columbian Necktie on his way to the great beyond. No casket, just a 55-gallon gasoline-filled drum, a tire for a necktie, and a match to light the way. He had tied the necktie on a few people who thought they were smarter than the Cartel. But they didn't have my power, he assured himself.

He paid his hotel bill weekly using his dead brother's American Express card but wondered how long he could use that card before any red flags came up. He made a point to ask the front desk if there was an American Express office nearby so he could pay the bill in cash to avoid them cutting it off for non-payment. Just that morning one of the desk clerks had made a small inquiry into what his business was when he paid his bill. JuJu inferred that he was a consultant for a Toronto engineering firm and traveled the world extensively for the business. The clerk seemed satisfied with his explanation, gave him a receipt, and thanked him for his business. JuJu was confident the clerk's inquiries were nothing more than polite conversation. That was another benefit of staying in a large hotel in the middle of downtown Cleveland. They were used to guests who stayed for extended time periods.

After paying his bill, JuJu moved the rental van to another spot in the hotel's expansive parking garage. He moved it every other day to avoid the appearance that it was abandoned and therefore subject to being towed. The cache of drugs and money was still intact. While he was comfortable staying in Cleveland, he knew he had to get back to his native Trinidad-Tobago. The Mexicans could never touch him there and he'd have more than enough money to secure his future. No more worries then 'mon. *Just have to get there.* But first he had to unload the stolen cocaine.

Just have to get there.

His vicious reputation would precede and protect him in the east Port of Spain streets he called home. If he got another two million for the rest of the drugs, he could even buy his own small army to protect over him.

He had thought about using the Jamaicans to deal the stolen cocaine but decided it was too risky to trust them with such a large undertaking. They were good for the small tasks he assigned to them but he knew if they had access to that much money and cocaine, their greed would far outweigh their fear of him.

There was no way he could offer the drugs for sale himself. Even though he could change his demeanor and appearance to fit in with most any element, he was not known in Cleveland's drug world and as a newcomer, he would automatically stick out. He also realized that the scare he thought would result from the voodoo signs marked on the bodies had no effect on anyone but the two Jamaicans and the Coroner's assistant; but since he wasn't at the scene, he didn't see her terrified reaction.

The Cleveland dope gangs could give a shit about voodoo, the Jamaicans had told him. Those young punks were just as vicious as he was, JuJu mused, but probably not as wise. Maybe he should just dump the cocaine in the Cuyahoga River and get back to Trinidad with the two million he already had. But the lure of doubling his money was too great.

JuJu's brother Moon had Canadian connections. They could possibly sell the remaining cocaine, but how would he get it there? Driving a car across the border was far too dangerous and the two Jamaicans were way too noticeable. Customs would surely stop and interrogate them just to see what they were about.

He ordered up another drink and turned his attention back to the TV. A weatherman paced back and forth in front of a weather screen, pointing out the high temperatures for every city in the state of Ohio. Abruptly, the news went to a breaking story about a major drug arrest and video footage from the scene rolled across the screen. His gaze focused on one person in the background. It was the man Sydney had been talking to at the Captain's Quarters, the john she said was looking for a date. He was a cop!

"That whore bitch!" The words burst from his lips before he could stop them. Luckily, the only person close enough to hear him was the Greek bartender and he acted as if JuJu hadn't spoken.

JuJu watched intently as the newscaster described the drug scene. A police Sergeant identified as the department's spokesperson responded to reporters' questions. "Does this have any connections to the drug killings on Dickens Avenue last month?" one of the reporters yelled in a voice loud enough to drown out the others.

"This case is not related in any way to that investigation," the Sergeant responded. "We have an on-going investigation into those crimes and we hope to have a conclusion for all of you very soon. We are assigning a task force consisting of the local police,

DEA, and the FBI to work full-time to solve these murders."

JuJu fought to control his emotions and place a logical spin on the situation. *If that whore knew who I really was and intended to turn me into the police, I would already be in jail.* All she knew was he liked her sexual services and needed her to get heroin for him. She knew nothing about his past and even less about him. *She doesn't even know my real name.* Now that he knew what her cop friend looked like and where he hung out, he could keep an eye on him. Maybe he'd even start spending more time at the marina bar.

He charged the bar bill to his account, went up to his room and changed clothes. Even though it was late afternoon, the outside temperature was still in the nineties. He planned on staking out the Captain's Quarters until he could locate and identify the police detective that his prostitute friend had so nimbly managed to avoid telling him about. Information was king and he made it a priority to gather intel on his enemies; it had saved his life more than once.

It had been a week since he had last used heroin but he still felt good. The emotional excitement of playing cat-and-mouse with Cleveland's Finest was all the high he needed right now. He was no junkie. That's what being an Obeah Man was about; controlling yourself and the world around you.

Time to hunt the hunters!

Chapter 14

JuJu briefly considered calling Sydney for a ride then changed his mind. He hailed a Yellow Cab and instructed the driver to take him to the East 55th Street Marina bar. The less she knows about me the better, he thought as the city streets slid by the cab's window. JuJu grudgingly admired Sydney for her discretion. In that way, they had something in common; she didn't talk about her "business" dealings or mention her clients by name. Since he told her to leave the little white whore out of it, things were good between them. She was a good lay and had a reliable heroin connection. But he also knew if she got a whiff that he was involved in the Dickens Avenue killings, she would be all over those Crime Stoppers reward commercials playing on TV.

The cabbie rang the buzzer and the marina gate opened. JuJu paid the fare and gave the cabbie a $20 tip. While it was only a nine dollar charge for the short ride, he felt a kind of camaraderie with the cabbie, who trying to make a living in a strange country. Just as he was doing. Only his payday was several million times more rewarding. After receiving JuJu's generous tip, the cabbie gave JuJu a card with his personal cell number. "You need a ride sir, you call me."

The Captain's Quarters was decorated in a predictable nautical theme with fish nets and colored sea glass floats suspended from the ceiling. Small groups of men clustered around tables and the bar drinking and talking about that day's fishing. He immediately spied Kat, the tall, blonde barmaid that had waited on him when he was here with Sydney. JuJu had paid attention to what everyone was wearing and tonight, he dressed to fit in: worn jeans and a black 'Cleveland Rocks' T-shirt. He purchased the shirt in the hotel's gift shop and topped off his attire with a Cleveland Indians baseball cap. Tan boat shoes without socks completed the outfit and he'd removed his gold hoop earrings; he needed to blend in with the mixed crowd, not stand out. He took a table by the window where he could view the parking lot through the fish netting that served as a curtain.

"Oh, great," Kat muttered as she saw the big man from the other night coming into the bar. "Just what I need." She grabbed a menu and walked over to JuJu's table.

"Good evening," she said, setting the menu on the table in front of him. "Can I get you something from the bar?"

He knew she remembered him and decided to soften his approach. She could be his best source of information about the big cop. "How are you today?" he asked with a big smile; his attempt at friendliness.

"I'm good," Kat responded evenly. "What can I get you?" she repeated.

"A spiced rum and Coke," he said.

"Coming right up," she responded and headed toward the bar.

When she returned with his drink, he said. "Just start a tab for me."

"Will do," she said. "Do you need some time to look over the menu?"

His eyes left her face and moved quickly down the length of her body, returning to meet her gaze. "No, I'm not that hungry – for food." As if to soften the obvious come-on, he treated Kat to a dazzling aw-shucks-you-can't-blame-a-guy-for-trying smile.

Is this guy for real?

"It's been a long day. I just need to unwind," he said, his tone friendly and an expression on his face that wasn't unlike any of the other guys that came into the bar looking for a little diversion from life.

Kat retrieved the menu and gave him a professional smile. *Maybe I'm being paranoid.* After all, she was used to getting the once-over from customers – just part of the job. But this one felt different. The typical bar sharks in boater's shorts and Sperry Topsiders who frequented the CQ swam off at a respectful distance once their "bite" was rebuffed. She had the feeling that if she allowed this one within bite range, there'd be no letting go. Better to stay out of his depth.

True to his word, all JuJu did over the next couple hours was sit quietly over a succession of drinks while keeping an eye on the parking lot and wait for the cop to show up. He did his best not to scare Kat any more than he already had. After two hours he was about to leave when his quarry arrived. Nick came through the door, his arrival eliciting greetings from the CQ regulars. JuJu watched with interest as Kat planted a brief kiss on the detective's lips before hurrying back to the kitchen to pick up an order.

Nick took a barstool by the door. JuJu sat back and took measure of this new adversary. It was obvious he was a regular here, and it seemed that Kat had a special interest in the detective as well, if that kiss was any indication.

"Hey, Nick! We saw your ass on television today at the firehouse," the guy sitting next to him said. "That true about you being on some sort of task force hunting for the Dickens Avenue killers?" the man's voice boomed.

Nick started to answer but was cut short by another man two barstools away. "Shit Nick, the only people killed was four dope guys. What the hell is the City of Cleveland doing wasting my tax money looking for their killers? They ought to give them a reward!" Several bar patrons voiced their agreement with this sentiment. "Yeah, he's right, give the killers the reward money!"

Nick turned his bar stool around to face the small group gathered around him and shook his head before responding, "You people just don't get it do you? Drug dealers have feelings too!" he said sarcastically.

"Maybe if you cops shot more of the bad guys, this city would be a much better place to live in," said the off-duty Cleveland firefighter who started the whole exchange.

"God dammit, Hawker! You got away with shooting those guys you caught on your boat just because the prosecutor was your cousin," Nick replied jokingly. "And besides, you know a fireman can shoot anybody they want to and nobody would give a shit! The minute my gun goes off, I got Internal Affairs and FBI up my ass. It's like a circus parade!"

Nick was referring to two thieves Hawker Chambers had blown off the back of his boat when they had pointed their guns at him after he caught them stealing his gear. "You even got elected Commodore of this whole marina with that caper and it never even cost you a beer!"

"Go on, Nick," Tina the owner encouraged. "Tell the story – just in case there's someone in the State of Ohio who hasn't heard it yet!"

"Okay – about two years ago there were a lot of thefts from the boats. Nobody knew how the perps were getting in or out 'cause the gates are locked and the Park Rangers patrol all the time. Hawker here," Nick paused to gesture at the fireman, "was passed out on his boat but felt it moving when two bad guys crawled onto the back after floating over from the East 55th Street Park in one of those cheap rafts. You know, the kind they sell at K-Mart for little kids. These guys would float over in the middle of the night from the public park, steal stuff, and then float back to the park.

"When Hawker confronted them, they pulled guns and told him to get inside his cabin. They ripped off his radio, fish finder, and GPS unit and started to float away when Hawker came out of the cabin with a 9 mm pistol he had stashed in his tackle box, which luckily they didn't take, and told them to stop.

"One of the stupid bastards busted a cap at Hawker so he shot both of them and the raft too! After the Ports and Harbors Unit dragged the marina and found the bodies, they found both guys had guns that were ripped off from other boats. Hawker's first cousin is the County Prosecutor and the Homicide Detective assigned to investigate the case, Tim Costello, went to school with him, so no charges were brought against him.

"Now, I'm not saying there should have been any charges filed against my friend here but the Irish in this town have their own Mafia and they really take care of their kind! Back in the day, Cleveland looked like a fireworks display with bombs going off all the time what with the Irish and the Italians blowing each other up!"

The off-duty Cleveland firefighter chimed in. "Absolutely right, Nicky, I really didn't want to shoot those guys but they put me in a situation where I had to defend myself. Fighting fires is dangerous enough, but I was never shot at before and I didn't like it!"

The bar was crowded and dark and Nick never even looked in the direction where JuJu was quietly sitting, pretending to be engrossed in his own thoughts rather than listening to their boisterous exchange.

"So, Nick," Hawker said in a tone indicating he was

done joking. "What's the scoop on the Dickens Avenue murders?"

Nick took a long draw on his beer before answering. He had spotted JuJu as soon as he came into the bar and his cop "radar" had started beeping. But he didn't want to alert the man that he was aware of his presence. Little did Nick know that every word he said was being absorbed into the brain of the very person responsible for the murders they were now discussing.

"Hawker," Nick started, "we've got squat! No good leads or suspects. I really didn't want this case but the Chief and the DEA want me in on it, so there you go."

JuJu evaluated what he'd heard. Maybe the cop wouldn't be trying that hard. After all, enough time had gone by. They probably assumed the killer, or killers, would be long gone by now. Kat came by to ask if he wanted another drink.

"No, thank you," he replied. "I think I've had enough."

She presented his tab for $37 and he gave her a $100 bill. "No, you keep it," he said as she started counting out change.

"Thanks and have a good evening," she said, pocketing the $63 tip. Maybe he wasn't so bad after all. She watched as JuJu exited out the back door then disappeared into the patio crowd.

Nick waited for few minutes then walked out the front door and headed to the Short Bridge, a narrow, metal walkway with stairs leading to D dock and his summer boat home.

JuJu had been waiting for his cab when he noticed the

detective leave the bar. He looked toward the street and then at the detective's retreating back and decided the cab would probably wait for him. He followed Nick, hoping to find where his boat was docked in case he needed to take him out later. Cop or not, he had to protect himself. Back in Trinidad, he'd killed a few cops. He wasn't afraid to do it in Cleveland if it served his purpose.

What JuJu didn't know was that Nick was anything but another overworked city employee who wanted nothing more than to shed his uniform once five o'clock came. Nick had years of surveillance and observation skills he wore like a second skin; they were always with him. He'd had JuJu in his sights the entire night. Did this guy really think he could follow a veteran Detective without being seen? Nick wanted to turn right around and pound the piss out of his adversary, but he needed to know why this guy was on his tail. Better to let himself be followed.

Nick slowed and passed by the walkway to D Dock and his boat. His gun was locked in his car. He thought retrieving it but he didn't want his follower to know what kind of car he drove. He kept walking until he crossed over onto C Dock. Sailboat riggings squeaked and clanged with the rise and fall of the waves that nudged the boats against their moorings. He glanced behind him and saw the man stop at the ramp entrance to C Dock. Nick paused to talk to a couple lounging on their boat, positioning himself so he had a view of the dock entrance. "You folks have a good evening," he said loudly, then continued to the end of the dock.

He took a seat on a bench at the end of the dock and gazed out into the dark, waiting to see what his shadow planned to do next. Turning his head slightly as if watching a late boater returning to his slip, Nick could see the big man had retreated to the marina entrance and was standing by the gate. A few minutes later, a Yellow Cab entered the marina lot. The stranger got in and the cab left, heading west on the Memorial Shoreway toward downtown Cleveland.

Nick checked the time on his cell phone. Almost 10 p.m. He made a mental note to contact Yellow Cab tomorrow to see if he could identify the unknown stalker he had acquired. Now that his shadow was gone, he headed for his own slip in D Dock and checked the dock lines and electrical hookups before climbing aboard, as was his nightly ritual. That done, he stepped down into the cabin, stripped naked, and turned on the air conditioning. He would have left the hatch open but this time of year the mayflies were abundant.

Nick's bunk was in the aft cabin in the back of the boat. He was only in bed a few minutes when he felt the boat move slightly. Someone was on the deck. He reached into the cubbyhole by his right side and retrieved his off-duty Smith & Wesson 9 mm semi-automatic from its holster. He sat up in a low crouch, as far as the boat ceiling would allow, with the barrel of the gun pointed at the cabin door. If his stalker had returned, Nick was prepared to deal with him.

The door inched open and Nick caught a whiff of cigarette smoke, perfume, and whiskey. He lowered the gun and addressed his intruder by name. "Hello, Kat."

"Hello Nicky," Kat said. She peeled off her clothes, crawled into the bunk, and reached for him.

Nick forgot all about his dark shadow.

Chapter 15

*W*hump! *Whump!* Nick woke with a start as something hit the boat once, then again. The Rinker bounced in the water. "Asshole," Nick muttered. This wasn't the first time his idiot dock mate had bumped him with his thirty-foot Sea Ray. The guy had no clue how to handle that boat. Kat was still out cold. Nick pulled on some jeans and went up on deck.

"Sorry, Nick!" yelled the offending captain. "Every time the wind is from the west I end up running into your boat when I try to dock."

Nick looked over the port side of the Rinker. The oversized rubber fenders dangling alongside the cabin cruiser had done their job; the Rinker didn't appear to be damaged. "Dammit, Henry!" Nick yelled to the other boater. "When are you going to learn how to dock your boat?"

"Don't worry, Nick," he answered. "It won't happen again."

Nick knew that it would happen again as this bonehead said the same thing at least once a week. Nick threw his neighbor a look of disgust and then went below to check on Kat.

Still sleeping. *God, she was beautiful.* He grabbed his gym bag and headed to the public bathrooms for a hot shower. He thought about last night and knew that his first order of business was to identify the "big dude" who had followed him.

He returned to his slip, dressed for work, then grabbed Kat's foot and shook it. "Sleeping beauty – time to get up."

"Mmmmpf," she responded. "Are you aware," she continued in a still-sleepy voice, "that Sleeping Beauty is fraught with symbolism representing the shameful secrets of a dysfunctional family? Sigmund Freud and Carl Jung both have a lot to say about it."

"I'll take your word for it, Professor," he answered in mock solemnity. "But you know, sometimes a cigar is just a cigar."

"Meaning?"

"You're still a sleeping beauty."

Nick left Kat and drove directly to the Narcotics Unit office in the Justice Center. "Morning Captain," he said in passing to his Commanding Officer as he seated himself at his desk. He surveyed the mounds of paperwork and wondered if he could pass any of it off to Frank or Lenny. All of this DEA liaison work was beginning to cause his other cases to back up. Still thinking about his shadow last night, he found the number to his Yellow Cab contact and placed a call. Nick described what he was looking for and after a few minutes, his contact came back on the line.

"Our records show the fare was picked up at the East 55th Street Marina and taken to Public Square. Detective, that's all we have to tell you; he must have called the cabbie directly. A lot of our cabbies give their cell phone numbers out to get the repeat business. We don't condone it but as long as we get our fare money it's alright with us. That's the best I can do for now."

"Thanks, Patty," Nick said.

"Anytime, Nick," the cab company's office manager replied.

Shit! That didn't give him a lot to go on. He'd have to squeeze the information out of Sydney. He placed a call to her cell phone but she didn't pick up and her voicemail wasn't working. Since most of Sydney's business came through the phone, Nick surmised she was purposely avoiding talking to him. *She must know I'm looking for her.*

His departmental desk phone rang and he saw the number came up on Caller ID as Unknown Caller. *Maybe it was Sydney.* "Detective Silvano, Narcotics Unit," he answered crisply.

The person on the other end did not speak right away but when he did, the voice was a familiar one. "Nick, I got the heat turned up from my bosses about the Dickens Avenue killings," Charley Goetz said. "The amount of crap the FBI and that asshole Reis is feeding to my superiors is beginning to have an effect on them. The FBI wants the case - for whatever reasons - and I don't have any information to give my bosses. It's been over a month now and they want me to give them something concrete or a lead of some sort." Goetz paused, knowing that what he was going to say next would not be entirely welcome. "I had to call your Chief

Marinik and get you assigned to us full-time until we get this behind us, so pack your shit and march on over here."

"Damn it Charley!" Nick exclaimed. "I'm looking at a month's worth of work on my desk now. How do you expect me to do both jobs?"

"Well amigo," Charley said. "As of right now, you only have one job and that is over here with me, so get your white ass moving. I have two of my guys holding down the fort for now, but this case is going to be you and me until the bitter end. I'm going back to field work and you are my partner as of today." Before Nick could offer another excuse, Charley added, "Chief Marinik gave it the okay so saddle up my friend and let's go for a ride."

Nick went to his Commanding Officer in the Police Narcotics Unit and started to speaking even as he walked through the door. "Captain....."

The Captain held up his hand as if to ward off the anticipated outburst. "I already know Nick," he said. "I'll have your cases reassigned. Go get 'em."

Nick spent the remainder of the morning clearing off his desk and leaving notes on files for Lenny and Frank. It was late afternoon before he left the Justice Center for his "new" home over at the Drug Enforcement Administration office a few blocks away. He parked his car in the secured and guarded level reserved for DEA vehicles and entered the office from the same floor. After exchanging greetings with Agents Max Magruder and Lee Silverstein, he made his way to Charley's office.

As the Agent-in-Charge, Charley had the best office, which was probably the only job perk. It had a window that faced the center of Cleveland and the Terminal Tower building. The Tower dominated the view. Originally built as part of the Terminal Union Station, the Tower was completed in 1927 and home to the Horseshoe Casino. Now, it was the second tallest building in Cleveland, overshadowed only by Key Tower, which boasted fifty-seven floors.

"Hey Charley," Nick said, taking a seat in one of the two leather chairs facing the Agent in Charge's desk. "What's the game plan?"

Ever the cowboy, Charley wore pressed jeans, western boots, and a western shirt topped with a loose fitting sports coat to cover the Glock he kept anchored in his shoulder holster. Charley had been a California State Highway Trooper before joining the DEA. Between his time as a cop and twenty years in the DEA with assignments in Pakistan and South America, he'd pretty much seen it all. "Well buddy boy," Charley said, leaning forward in his office chair, "it's already approaching the end of the day so let's go get a beer at the Roach. Hey guys," he called out to Frank and Lee, "let's go grab some beers with our new ace investigator, Nicky!"

The Roach had the usual groupies and a couple of off duty cops. Charley ordered rounds for his group and the cops, leaving out the civilians. DEA Agents were welcomed in the bar by Willy and the cops and felt no threat from them unlike the FBI. A sign posted on the door said, "NO FBI ALLOWED" did not need explaining to the bar's patrons. Snoopy FBI Agents had no place mingling with cops. Even the civilians agreed.

The usual banter began with Agent Lee Silverstein doing most of the talking. Lee was especially critical of the drug culture in Cleveland and the Midwest in particular. He was from New York City and continually complained about the druggies. Charley told him, "Hey Lee, if it wasn't for the druggies you wouldn't have a job and you couldn't afford those stupid looking penny loafers you're wearing." Lee liked to wear brown penny loafers, socks optional. He called it the "fashion statement of true New Yorkers.

Nick tried to steer the conversation to his new assignment but Charley cut him off. "You'll find out soon enough what the game plan is Nicky, and I can't guarantee you will like it. Let's just have some beers and enjoy ourselves for the time being."

Nick had the feeling this was the calm before the storm.

Chapter 16

S ilvano was fuming.

The Chief had just ordered him to turn over his Dickens Avenue murder files to the FBI in the "spirit of cooperation"! He had already turned over all of his "good" files to Charley Goetz at the DEA. Five weeks of note taking and time invested that were now going to that prick Reis, but nobody told him that everything was to be surrendered and Nick knew his chief well enough that he would not object him to be "subjective" in his reporting.

He reviewed the case file and removed all the identifiable and personal information pertaining to his informants. He made sure there was no mention of "gays" or any references to his friends at Michael's Body Shop or to Sydney. The information she had told Frank about the "big guy" she was seeing had him thinking. Something about this guy was nagging at him. Nick knew it was common for informants to throw information out there that wasn't true or only half-true to curry favor from the narcs for future consideration. "Like an insurance payment," a junkie had once told him. A future "get out of jail free card". Information gained from the street, no matter how much crap was wrapped around it, always had some sort of merit, no matter how unusual or bizarre it sounded.

He placed the file into a brown envelope marked for delivery to the Cleveland FBI office then took the elevator to the first floor mailroom. "I don't care when they get this information," he told the Patrolman behind the desk. "Put it on the back burner and deliver it when you get time."

The Patrolman assigned to the mailroom was retiring in a couple months. He looked at the intended receiver's name and address and gave Nick a wink. "I get your drift, Detective."

Nick thought about getting in a quick workout in the Police Gym but decided to skip the exercise and punched the elevator button for the 6th floor housing the Homicide Unit instead. He found Fratello in his office, closed the door, and sat down across from him. His friend spoke first. "Alright, Nick. I know that look."

"Damn right, Jon," Nick replied. "I got blindsided and you never even gave me a warning. When were you going to tell me that I had to drop what I was doing and investigate this case?"

"I'm telling you now. I need you. You have connections with the DEA and at least they should be on equal ground with their federal counterparts in the FBI. The FBI runs with this and we get shut out, I may as well retire now because they will take all of the credit. This is also an election year and Mayor Somerville wants this feather in his cap. Chief Marinik wants you in particular to keep Reis in line because the Chief knows you won't take any shit from him. It has to be you, DEA and the FBI working together. Hear me Nick? I am putting emphasis on the word 'together'. You're the best cop I know for this job and we need the best."

"I appreciate your bullshit reasons, Jon," Nick countered, "but there's nothing new to tell. We've been looking when we have time, but have no definitive leads. You got any?"

The Lieutenant answered, "We have some calls to Crime Stoppers about a couple of little crazy guys with a kind of island accent, maybe Jamaican," the Lieutenant shared. "Detective Liptak in Crime Stoppers took the call and said he can get back to the caller. This person told him that these two hopped up crazies were talking out loud about voodoo shit and cutting people up." Nick raised his eyebrows. Those details hadn't been shared with the media. Either someone had leaked information or these guys had been at the murder scene. "The caller said he sold these guys some heroin a couple of times and is afraid – he wants to make a deal."

"We have information from our sources - possibly those same two guys," Nick said. "Can Liptak get a location or a plate number?"

"You think we might have something?" asked Fratello.

"It's worth a shot," answered Nick. "We have a good source that is passing similar information to us. We have nothing else right now so let's run with this."

"I really appreciate this Nick," the Lieutenant said.

"Anything you need, just let me know, okay?"

"Yeah, Jon," Nick replied. "And after this, leave me the hell alone!" he joked, giving his friend a fake punch on the arm before leaving.

Maybe they finally had something. Both Crime Stoppers' unknown caller and Sydney's intel put the same two crazies with that big guy who followed him. He mulled over the possible connections. I've had lots less to go on, he thought.

Nick left the Justice Center and drove east on St. Clair Avenue. It was rush hour and most of the main streets were clogged with commuters trying to get out of town after work. He jogged his Honda over to Payne Avenue to avoid traffic and drove by the old Third District Police Station at East 21st Street. Back when he was a rookie, the traffic court and jail were housed in the now historic building where Elliot Ness used to be the City's Safety Director. One time when he had to testify in traffic court, he had used the bathroom in what was then the Police Headquarters. Written on the wall above the dirty urinals were the words, "The Untouchables pissed here."

He turned down East 40th Street toward the East 55th Street Marina and felt a pang of mortality. He had no wife, no family, no property, and no money saved. He could retire in nine years when he reached fifty, but then what?

He drove past a three story brick building that was home to the David Gray Publishing Company. A couple of years ago he had met Les Roberts, the famous

Cleveland author who wrote crime stories based in and around Cleveland. Roberts had lived in Hollywood before landing in Cleveland – it didn't seem to hurt his career any. The man had written fifteen novels featuring the fictional detective Milan Jacovich and was one of Nick's favorite writers, that is, when he had the time to read.

The author told Nick he thought every retired cop should write a book. What was the old saying – write what you know? Nick often joked that his book would be about drug dealers and the title would be "Heroin Has No Holiday." Although he could probably fill ten books on his own, the trouble was that some of the best stories could never be told! He was probably better off to leave the writing to guys like Les.

Cops were a different breed, he mused. You could have two cops who absolutely hated each other, but neither would ever place the other in danger or in jeopardy of losing their job. They would call each other names and screw each other's wives but the Thin Blue Line held fast and they would go to their graves without divulging each other's secrets.

Nick's cell phone rang, bringing him back to reality. When he saw the caller ID pop up, he didn't even bother with hello. "Where've you been, Sydney? I haven't heard a peep from you since you took that big junkie to my marina, and I'm really pissed at you! He was there the next night and followed me. Who the hell is he Sydney, and don't give me any of your hooker bullshit! I want it straight and I want it right now. Why didn't you call me instead of Frank?"

"I was scared of what you might do to me, Nick," she stammered, her voice trembling. "I'm caught in the middle of something and I don't know what to do! This dude has me scoring heroin for him. I'm laying him too, and he's been calling me to meet him more and more," she paused. "I think he's big trouble, Nick."

"What's his name and where is he from?" Nick demanded.

"I don't know his name but the little dudes call him JuJu. I met him a while back, maybe a month and a half or so, when me and Brandi was trollin'. Didn't Frank tell you?"

"Yeah," replied Nick. "But I want to hear it from you."

"Me and Brandi were picked up by these two little Jamaican guys. The way they were constantly touching each other made it clear they didn't want our services – they were getting us for someone else. Crazy little dudes driving a black car, I don't know what type. They took us to the Interstate Inn downtown and gave me a room card and good cash, all in hundred dollar bills. This big black dude opened the door and we partied with him all night. He had some good heroin and we did it with him. Nothing really strange until he got really drunk and high and started chanting shit and talking in tongues, like what you see in zombie movies! He never will give up his name or a phone number. He just calls me and tells me when and where to meet him."

"That's all you got?" Nick asked incredulously.

"That's all," Sydney whined. "He calls and has me get heroin for him and sometimes we spend the night together, but I really don't know anything else about him. I pick him up when he calls and I always drive. He never talks about himself. You saw him, right?" Sydney asked. "He is as scary as he looks, believe me. But now he's calling more often and using a lot of heroin – more than the first couple times. I snooped in his man purse when he went to the bathroom and there was a big knife! He almost caught me - I don't care about the drugs or money or even if I go to jail, at least I'll be alive!"

"What about the Jamaicans?" Nick inquired. "Know anything about them?"

"Never saw them after the first night," she said. "I gave them my business card and I gave one to the big guy too. All it has on it is my first name and cell number. And why does everyone think it's so funny that I have a business card. A girl's got to network too you know!"

"Look," Nick said, "I need to learn more about him and his two friends. You stick with this JuJu dude, or whatever his name is, until I tell you to stop. Find out everything you can about all three of them. We've heard some street talk about two island boys bragging about hanging out with a new big player. Supposed to be some cutting and voodoo involved with them too."

"Oh my God, Nick!" Sydney exclaimed. "You think these guys are involved in that?"

"I don't know," he replied, "but it might be a good

start."

Nick didn't tell her about his talk with Michael. Sydney was spooked enough. He had to keep her on the chain and the information coming. "When was the last time you heard from him?" he probed.

"A couple of days ago, I was with him the night before at the Euclid Motel. That's when I saw the knife in his bag and he got all weird on me. He usually calls me once or twice a week."

"What about Brandi? Does she go with you?"

"No," Sydney answered. "Not since the first night. He just wants me."

"Well, aren't you the lucky one," Nick commented sarcastically. He had the feeling they were onto something big. Three sources, with basically the same information, and none of them related to each other.

"Alright," Nick said, sensing he'd gotten everything he could out of her. "You let me know the next time you hear from him. And Sydney?" he asked, waiting for a response.

"Yeah?" she answered warily.

"Do not take him back to my marina or there will be hell to pay, you hear me?" warned Nick.

"Yeah, I hear you Nick."

Chapter 17

Back at the hotel, JuJu was trying to figure out how to get the stolen cocaine into Canada. If he could just get it across the border, there was probably another two million in profit to be made. Less any expenses, of course. The sound of a vacuum cleaner in the hallway made him jump off the chair and rush to look out the door's peephole. Nothing but a maid, he confirmed. *I've got the jitters. Time to get a little something to settle that down.* But first, business. He used his cell phone to call Andre, his dead brother's Toronto, Canadian partner. It was risky, but it was a chance he'd have to take; he stood to lose a lot of money if he couldn't convert the coke into cash.

Andre answered on the fourth ring. "Hello, Andre," said JuJu. "This is Moon's brother. I have a business proposition for you."

"Yeah?" It was more of a challenge than a question. "If you're Moon's brother, what's your real name?"

"Lusa Tomari," JuJu said. "You satisfied now?"

"Yeah, man. What's up?"

JuJu described what he had for sale, leaving out the parts about the killings and the cocaine's real owners. If Andre knew where the cocaine came from, he'd bail. Andre gave a low whistle after JuJu described the amount and quality of the cocaine he had. "The problems I have are many," JuJu explained. "I don't know how to get it into Canada. Driving it in is too risky. Can you move the product out from here?"

"Man, I can't come to the states," Andre told JuJu. "But there may be a way for you get it to me with minimal risk."

"Tell me!" JuJu demanded.

"I know some guys who come back and forth across the border on the gambling buses from the States to the Windsor Casino. Usually the buses are almost full and the custom border guards from both countries just take a quick glance and pass them right through. They like to check car trunks and fender wells on the cars and trucks," Andre explained, "but for some reason, the bus traffic doesn't get looked at as much. Yeah," Andre concluded. "Check out the buses."

"Okay mon," JuJu said. "I'll get back to you." Could it be so easy? JuJu wondered, or was it a trap? He had never heard of such a thing. But then, sometimes the simplest plans were the best. He'd check it out. He picked up the complimentary room copy of the Cleveland Plain Dealer Sunday newspaper, opened it to the travel section, and found numerous bus companies offering trips to Windsor Casino. Most were for day trips but there were a couple overnight trips too.

JuJu picked one at random and placed a call. A passport and twenty-five dollars would get him a round trip ticket. All he had to do was meet the bus in a Cleveland suburb hotel parking lot. He wrote down the bus schedule and the locations along with the pickup times. Unbelievable! With Moon's passport, he just might be able to pull this off! JuJu entertained the idea of inviting Sydney to go with him to make it look like they were a couple on vacation, but decided against it. He'd go this alone. No need to complicate things.

Outside of JuJu's hotel window, the sun was beginning to set over Lake Erie and backlit the boats going back and forth out of the mouth of the Cuyahoga River like a scene from a movie. It reminded him of Trinidad.

He decided to make a dry run to the casino, without any drugs, just to see if it would be as easy as Andre made it sound. He'd catch the first bus trip in the morning.

He dialed the front desk to request an early wakeup call, then settled into bed and thought about what tomorrow would bring. He felt exhilarated again – he had a plan. He placed a line of his remaining heroin on the table next to the bed and took a snort. The powder gave him a warm feeling of power and control as he rolled the beads of his necklace between his fingers and chanted his own dark rosary of petition for protection against his enemies. *Ogun is with me, showing me the way.*

He fell asleep to the city's lullaby of horns and sirens.

Chapter 18

The ringing came from far away. JuJu stood over Detective Silvano's dead body and stared at the blood pulsing from the open wound in his neck. The ringing continued. A telephone! Who was calling now? He reached a bloody hand toward the phone...

"Yes," he said huskily into the phone, his Island dialect turning the word up on end as if it were a question.

"Mr. DeBoissiere," a soft, feminine voice spoke. "This is your five a.m. wakeup call."

"Yes, thank you," he replied, then replaced the handset of the phone back into the cradle. He stared at his hand. No blood. No dead body on the floor. Just a dream.

The bus schedule required him to be in the parking lot of the Quarry Inn Hotel in Independence at 6:30 a.m. According to Google Maps on his smart phone, it was a twenty minute cab ride. JuJu got out of bed and walked to the window, stretching his arms above his head. He could see the dawn breaking over a large ore boat being pushed up the Cuyahoga River by a much smaller tugboat. Ahead of the large ore carrier, the mammoth steel railroad drawbridge rose slowly to accommodate the carrier's passage as it made its way up the river to the steel plant where its cargo would be unloaded. Automobile headlights on the Shoreway adjacent to the lakefront were focused on the downtown area. And so began another day for the hundreds of thousands of workers commuting into the city and for the island man looking for a way out of the city.

Room service knocked with his morning order of coffee, toast, and juice. He would be glad when this was done and he could go home and retire. Just a few more weeks. He checked his messenger bag for items that might arouse any suspicions in the event a Customs Agent stopped him at the Canadian border, and removed the knife concealed in the outside zipper pocket. It was the same one Sydney had seen when she was searching his backpack – a Tac-Force Speedster Spider knife. He turned the knife over in his hands, admiring the sleek, blue aluminum handle adorned with a black spider and web design. He flicked it open and the black, stainless steel blade sprung from its case, revealing a deeply serrated edge. Firefighters and paramedics liked these knives because the handle could break windshields and the blades could easily slice through seat belts. Criminals like them too, for other reasons.

He flipped the blade closed and paused to stare at the handle. For a moment, it looked as if the spider had moved. He heard a story once, about a voodoo curse that had been placed on a man who had stolen from the wrong person. The man developed a bump on his neck, like a mosquito bite. Only the bump never went away;

it grew larger and started to itch. When the man started scratching, it burst open, releasing a hoard of spiders that swarmed over his body, biting him. His family found him the next day on the floor where he had fallen; his eyes gone and his flesh disappearing as the spiders feasted on his body. JuJu said a brief prayer to Ogun then put the knife underneath the mattress.

The hotel maids he had known in Trinidad had aided him tourist robberies and he had no reason to think that the housekeepers in this Cleveland hotel were any different. He always made sure he left a tip each day on the table by the bed in the hope it would dissuade them from snooping through his things or worse, robbing him.

He showered and dressed in casual clothing: tan slacks, brown loafers, and a black polo shirt. A glance in the bathroom mirror reminded him to remove his gold loop earrings. He placed a Cleveland Browns football cap on his head. He knew his size and muscular build attracted attention to himself but he had learned to adopt a smaller, less intimidating posture when needed.

JuJu took the elevator to the lobby where he picked up a Cleveland Plain Dealer from the front desk. He walked out into Public Square and hailed a cab. The hotel was a hot spot for cabbies whose fares usually consisted of business people going to Cleveland Hopkins Airport and a new batch of suits waiting to go from the airport to downtown Cleveland.

He breathed in the heavy morning air. Yesterday's

heat was already being transferred from the buildings into the morning dampness. The stench of garbage from the city's back alleys and the constant "beep beep" of delivery trucks going in reverse were the same in every large city in the world. JuJu got into the back seat of the taxi and told the driver his destination. The cabbie deftly moved his fare through the streets and then southbound on Interstate 77. This trip would either lead him into the last portion of his quest or make him question everything he had done.

"We're here," the cabbie said, driving the cab up the steep incline leading into the rear parking lot of the Quarry Inn Hotel. A large bus idled in the corner of the half empty lot. A group of people stood by the open door the bus driver had just exited.

JuJu peeled off a pair of twenty dollar bills from the roll of cash he pulled from his backpack and paid the cab driver. "Keep the change," he said, surprising the cabbie with a seventeen dollar tip. He only brought five hundred dollars for this first trip. Five hundred would be about right for a person taking a bus to a casino, he rationalized. Too much money would be suspicious. He needed to remain as unassuming as possible in every aspect of this foray into a different country.

JuJu stood apart from the others in the parking lot so he could watch what they did and follow their lead. There was one white couple and three elderly black women waiting to board. The three older ladies each carried large handbags with travel pillows sticking out of the tops of the bags. *Perfect.* He walked toward them slowly, with his head down. "Is this the bus to the Windsor Casino in Canada?" he asked timidly.

"Why yes, it is young man, is that where you are going?" one of the ladies replied.

"Yes, Ma'am" JuJu replied respectfully, looking down on her. "I am in town on a business trip and had this day to myself. I was told the Windsor was a good place to try gambling while I am here."

"Where are you from, son?" one of the other ladies inquired.

JuJu saw the opening he was waiting for and told her his name was Moon. "I work with the Red Cross in my native Haiti," he explained. "They sent me to Cleveland to obtain training to help the many homeless people who lost everything in the earthquakes." That piqued the interest of those waiting to board the bus and an immediate kinship was formed as they projected their sympathies from seeing the devastation played out on the television news onto this man who, they incorrectly assumed, was trying to help his people. The least they could do was take him under their wings, so to speak, and show him they were all kindred spirits.

While his appearance would scare the hell out of these old ladies if they knew his true nature, his soft, respectful demeanor and convincing story won them over. After all, he couldn't be a bad person if he was dedicating his life to help the less fortunate.

JuJu made small talk with the ladies while they waited to board and then asked permission to sit next to the woman he had first approached. The woman, who introduced herself as Ms. Sarah Burton, "but you can call me Miss Sarah," now felt it was her duty to watch over JuJu and kept calling him "son". She instructed him to give the bus driver his name and twenty-five dollars in cash before they left the parking lot for the next pick-up location where more gamblers were waiting to board the bus north to Canada. He learned that the three ladies took the trip twice a week. "It's practically free," his new friend explained, "because when you get to the casino they gave you twenty dollars back to play with."

The driver made four more stops before getting on the Interstate highway toward Toledo. They arrived in Detroit after only a couple of hours and the driver angled the bus containing the two dozen gamblers into the designated lanes approaching the bridge leading into Canada and the casino located in the town of Windsor.

"How long do we wait here?" JuJu inquired to his seat companion. He looked nervously out of the window toward the group of uniformed agents waiting to greet the bus passengers eager to try their luck at the foreign casino.

"If we're lucky we won't get a new customs agent," she answered as she reached into her large handbag and came out with her passport that identified her as a U.S. citizen. "You better get yours out too, young man," she instructed.

JuJu reached into his pocket and took out his dead

brother's passport. He willed his pounding heart to slow down and forced himself to continue the small talk with his companion while the Canadian Customs Agent boarded the bus and shouted instructions into the driver's microphone.

The agent began his walk down the aisle, reaching out for each passenger's photo identification. He examined each document, then held it up next to the passenger to compare the photo ID with the passenger. After assuring himself the photo and face matched, he handed the passport back to the owner and gave a quick nod acknowledging that he agreed they were indeed the man or woman they purported themselves to be.

He took JuJu's passport and looked at him for what JuJu thought was an alarming amount of time before handing it back to him, nodding his approval, then asked to see his companion's identification. "Hello again, ma'am," the agent said to the woman. "You ladies have a good time," he said to all three before handing the passports back to them without even looking at them. He gave JuJu another glance before he moved on to the rear of the bus and the remaining passengers.

The Canadian Customs Agent then left the bus and the driver roared the engine before placing it into gear. The hissing of the air brakes sounded loudly in JuJu's ear like a victorious trumpet call, and the bus lurched onto the bridge toward the Windsor Casino.

When the bus reached its destination, a casino hostess boarded and read the rules. The passengers ignored her instructions; they'd all heard it before, and instead squirmed in their seats and stowed their pillows and carry-on-coolers into the overhead bins to await their return six hours later.

JuJu's companions had already attached their casino players cards to their wrists with the long, yellow bungee cords preventing them from leaving their machine with the card still inserted. JuJu heard the instructions on how to receive his points card but had already decided to forego obtaining anything that would place him in this location. Even though he was using his dead brother's name, he didn't want to take any unnecessary chances.

After all the passengers departed the bus JuJu said "good luck" to the ladies and walked into the casino. He located a bank of payphones and called Andre. The phone was answered quickly and after JuJu identified himself, they agreed to meet in a couple of hours to plan how to transfer the drugs into Canada for distribution to the Canadian cocaine users.

JuJu ate lunch at one of the casino restaurants and then hit the blackjack tables. In a casino, you were more noticeable if you weren't gambling. The casino was full of people. Some walked with purpose, perhaps returning to the machine that had been lucky for them the last time they were there. Others wandered aimlessly through the rows of machines with their colorful displays and loud noises carefully placed to lure in the gamblers like fish to a worm. His cell phone rang while he was cashing in his winning chips. "Where you at?" inquired Andre.

"The cashier cage next to the smoking area on the first floor," JuJu replied.

"Wait there," Andre told JuJu. "I need a smoke anyway."

JuJu walked outside the casino to the designated smoking area, which consisted of a small fenced-in area adjacent to the street. He sat at one of the small tables reserved for smokers. A few minutes later, Andre came through the door and, without any greeting, sat down at the table with JuJu. He lit up a cigarette, took a long draw, and watched the smoke curl into the air as he exhaled.

"Been a while man," Andre said, giving JuJu the once over. "You looking fit like you could tear somethin' up."

"You look good too, brother," JuJu replied.

After some small talk, JuJu got to the business at hand. "Mon, I got a shitload of cocaine I fell into down in Cleveland but I got no 'in' with anybody there. I've been sitting on it for almost two months. And with Moon dead, I'm out my Canadian connection. I need to move it, but I can't do it by myself." Andre didn't visibly react but JuJu saw the cigarette twitch in his fingers.

"Cleveland is a rough town and the gangs run all the dope," JuJu continued. "I can handle myself, as you know, but the numbers don't match up in my favor. Since you and Moon did business together, I thought you could take the delivery off my hands – for a substantial reduction in the total price – if you can take all of it."

"How much you looking to unload?" Andre asked.

"Forty bricks at a pound apiece. That should get two million American," JuJu answered.

Andre stood up then, almost hitting his head on the cheap umbrella covering the table. He turned away from JuJu and stubbed out his cigarette in the cement ashtray before turning to face him. "I don't doubt that you got good stuff, but I have to reach out to get that kind of cash. Me and your brother Moon was doing good for a while, until he got careless and got his ass shot off in Toronto. I could get rid of the stuff for you, but I got to see some samples first. And you got to get it to me. I ain't going into Cleveland to pick any of it up, JuJu." Andre paused. "I been hearing some stuff about a Cartel looking for someone who ripped them off. I ain't saying anything to you about it 'cause it ain't none of my business and I don't aim to make it my business. I'm in it for the money and if you got good stuff and can deliver it, I think we can make a deal."

"Alright," JuJu told him, neither confirming nor denying Andre's observation. "I'll use the casino buses; you were right about the customs agents. But it will take several trips."

"Okay," Andre responded. "Let's go and get a drink, partner. We'll celebrate my new beginning and your continued wealth and long life. Moon always said you were the one to make it big and I believe you may have done it for both of us."

At four p.m., JuJu dutifully returned to the bus for the

ride back to Cleveland. He saw his three new friends sitting on a bench, and they waved for him to join them. As JuJu approached the ladies, a plan began to form. They inquired if he had been "lucky" and he opened his hand to reveal several colorful casino chips he had purposely not cashed in.

"You only have a couple of minutes to run back in and cash in those chips before the bus leaves you stranded here," Miss Sarah warned.

"Well, Miss Sarah, I plan on coming back here on the next trip in two day's time. And I would very much like it if you and your friends could accompany me. Since I am walking away a winner, I would like to pay for all of your fares. You have been very kind to me and I return kindness with more kindness," JuJu continued. "I learned that lesson from my beloved Grandmother who has since left this earth some ten years ago."

The three women cooed in delight. His Grandmother must have been a special person to have raised such a polite and generous grandson. After a chorus of polite protestations, the ladies gave in and agreed they would meet again in two days and let this young man pay for their bus trip. After all, they didn't want to seem rude!

The gods have again blessed me with these three women. The number three had a special meaning in JuJu's voodoo upbringing. It was the number of Legba, the guardian and opener to the crossroads of the world who provided clear pathways and protection for those who called upon him. JuJu took this as a sign. Legba was providing the path for him to follow. The return trip was uneventful. At the border, the bus was again boarded, this time by United States Customs Agents asking if anybody had anything to declare. Back in Cleveland, JuJu exited the bus and said goodbye to the three women. He entered the lounge of the Quarry Inn Hotel and enjoyed a spiced rum and Coke before asking the bartender to call him a cab for the short trip back downtown to his hotel.

Entering his hotel room, he quickly checked his belongings to see if anything had been disturbed in his absence. His knife was where he had left it and his things were still arranged as he had left them. He placed a call to room service for dinner and ordered up a bottle of rum and a six pack of cola. Time to celebrate his good fortune. Trinidad was getting closer.

He fingered the beads of his necklace, murmuring, "Ogun, hear my plea. Return me safely to my homeland. Keep those who would spoil my plans apart from me."

Chapter 19

It was Saturday before the annual Labor Day Cleveland Air Show. This year, the Air Force Thunderbirds would take to the air over Lake Erie to celebrate the beginning of the end of summer. The Air Show was based at Burke Lakefront Airport in downtown Cleveland and the East 55th Marina was the perfect place to watch the acrobatic biplanes, military flybys, and the Army Golden Knights parachute team. Nick was partial to the Thunderbirds. As a veteran Air Force jet fighter crew chief, he had fueled them many years ago at Amarillo Air Force Base in Texas.

Since he was off duty today, he'd go to the Cockroach Inn for some beers before settling in on his boat to watch the jet planes in the late afternoon show. Willy-the-Couch was behind the bar talking with Paulie-the-Pig, another veteran cop and regular customer, and some uniformed motorcycle cops who were killing time until the end of the show when they would have to return to the streets and resume their respective traffic flow assignments.

Civilian cop groupies played pool in the back room. Like rock 'n roll groupies, these men and women felt that just being in the same place as the cops somehow made them part of that inner circle. They were wrong, of course. While some cops fed off the hero worship and cult-like status of having their own groupies, others were just plain annoyed and ignored them. An industrial fan hummed loudly from the rear of the bar as it tried vainly to push back the holiday heat from the September day. Nick squeezed in between two other cops, ordered up a Bud Light, and waved a hand over his friends' drinks indicating he was buying the next round.

Willy was pouring beers and retelling a story from a couple of years ago when the Navy Blue Angels were the featured act at the air show. Some of the pilots and crew came into the Roach late one night and consumed more alcohol than they should have. The traffic cops dared the Navy daredevil pilots to break the sound barrier during the next day's performance. In exchange, the cops would let the pilots drive their police motorcycles and ride the Mounted Unit's horses.

"Those Navy Pilots are really something!" Willy said. "One crazy pilot took off right up East 9th Street flying between the high buildings about a hundred feet off the ground. Nobody knows how fast he was going but he managed to bust a whole lot of office windows with his fly by. We heard he got grounded for a little bit, but he was their best pilot so he wasn't canned. They came back in that night and the cops had to make good on their bet and let them ride the cop bikes and the horses."

Nick enjoyed the banter right up until his cell phone started to ring. The caller ID was from the Second

District Jail. *What the hell!* He seriously contemplated not answering. But after a couple of rings he pushed Talk. "What's up?" he asked without even inquiring who it was.

"Nicky, I got big trouble, you gotta help me!" he heard Sydney's pleading voice.

Dammit! Nick cursed himself for answering the phone on his day off. His father always told him "the phone and the mailman are not your friends." So true. The phone calls he received now were an annoyance and the mailman only delivered bills and junk mail.

"What's wrong, Sydney?" Nick asked wearily, plugging his open ear with one finger so he could hear over the bar noise.

"She gone, Nicky, she's gone!

"Who are you talking about, Sydney?" asked Nick, "You're not making any sense."

"Brandi is dead, Nick. She finally overdosed herself on a bad batch of heroin laced with fentanyl. She called me last night from some shooting gallery over on the west side and asked me to come get her. When I got there she was dead. I called 911 and the cops came with the ambulance and they arrested me! I kept telling them I had nothing to do with the dope house but they locked me up anyway."

"Where are you now?" Nick demanded.

"The Second District jail. I been here twelve hours already and this is my first phone call. They wouldn't let me make a call until now and court ain't until next Tuesday and this is just Saturday. I just kept yelling and finally the jailer that just came on duty said he knew you and let me use the phone to call you. Nick, you gotta get me out of here, I can't take three days in here!"

"Who gave you the phone?" asked Nick.

"All he told me was 'tell Nick he owes Teen Angel a beer!' and kept eyeing up my tits but otherwise he's been okay," Sydney relayed. "There must be over fifty people in here. It's wall-to-wall assholes!"

"Well, you're one of the assholes," Nick told her. "Let me talk to Teen Angel." Teen Angel's real name was Ricky Dolan, and he was far from being a teenager. The moniker had been bestowed on him years ago when someone said his pompadour hair looked like a 1950's heartthrob crooner. Now in his late forties, the nickname had stuck, along with the hair style.

Teen Angel picked up the phone and said, "Hey Nick, big tits here says she knows you, that be true?"

"That be true," Nick acknowledged. "What's she in for?"

"She was in a dope house with a dead junkie. Probably had nothing to do with the dead chick but First District Vice Cop Danny Colegrove put a hold on her until he can figure out where the bad dope came from. He said they have had five dead junkies in the past twenty-four hours!"

"Shit!" exclaimed Nick. "I work the Narcotics Unit and we haven't heard anything about that yet - but I'm sure we will now. I know Colegrove," Nick said to the jailer. "He been in yet to charge her?"

"Naw," answered Teen Angel. "It's Saturday and the Prosecutor won't be in until Tuesday morning. Because of Monday being Labor Day and all, the courts are closed, so it looks like she's stuck here."

"Put her on the phone, will ya?" Nick asked. "Maybe we can work something out with Colegrove so she can work it off or at least get her outta there. She does come up with some good intel from time to time."

"You got it, Nick," Teen Angel replied. "Give me a minute to get her out of the bullpen and into the interrogation room and transfer the call so she can talk without these other assholes listening in."

Nick drank his beer while he waited. After a few minutes Sydney returned to the phone and again pleaded with Nick in the fashion that only a street hooker can do, alternately sobbing and then yelling demands. "Me and Brandi have done a lot for you, Nick, and now she's dead. You owe me! Get me the hell outta here!"

"Goddamn it Sydney, why'd you have to pick a holiday to get arrested? No – don't answer that. Let me try to find the vice cop that picked you up and see if we can work a deal."

Sydney spoke in a much more subdued tone now that she realized that Nick was going to help her, and she played the only get-out-of-jail-free card she could think of. "You know that big dude I been telling you about? I can give him to you next time he's holding."

"Shit, Sydney, you're the one giving him the heroin. He'll know it was you who gave him up."

"Bust me with him, Nicky, I need to get rid of him anyway. I'm scared of him. He hasn't called me for a couple of days and he's about due. I still don't know what his game is yet 'cause he don't say much but he's gotta be into something. Maybe if you bust him he can turn snitch and help you get something big. He always had a big wad of money on him. Where's he getting it, I ask you? He don't buy his own dope, he don't give up a phone number or where he's staying. It's like he's hiding out from something or somebody. I have to do all the driving – he doesn't even have a car. What do you think Nicky? Will that square us?"

"Tell you what Sydney," said Nick. "I owe that son of a bitch one for following me at the marina. Sit tight and I'll be there in a few."

Sydney sighed into the phone. "Nicky, I think I love you more than I should. Too bad we didn't meet in different circumstances. Who knows what might have happened?"

Nick responded, "Hell, the day's still young babe, don't write me off just yet." Then in a more serious tone, "What about Brandi - she got any family?"

"Yeah, she's got a brother in Minnesota. Kept a picture of him in her crib. You're gonna call him – right?"

"We'll take care of it. Now – you're sure you want to do this?"

"Yes! I get outta jail and I get that scary bastard out of my life." At least she hoped that's how it would go.

Nick contemplated his next move. First, he had to talk

to Vice Detective Colegrove. It was his pinch and he wanted to do the right thing by him. He called Willy over to settle up his bar tab. *There goes my day off.*

Nick left the Roach, got into his Civic, and drove to the near west side of Cleveland to Fulton and Daisy Avenue where the Second District Police Station was located. The Second was a melting pot for Hispanics and Appalachians with some eastern Europeans thrown in. The area close to Lake Erie was turning metrosexual and the Ohio City area was where the people with money bought and restored century homes only to barricade themselves in with tall fences, big dogs, and expensive security systems to keep the "have nots" from stealing all their stuff.

Nick headed west over the Lorain Avenue bridge spanning the Cuyahoga River that separated the West and East sides of the city and saw the planes flying overhead entertaining the half million Air Show fans enjoying the late summer day. Continuing south on West 25th Street, he passed people sitting out on the sidewalks craning their faces skyward to get a glimpse of the F-22 Raptor Air Force jets streaking overhead.

Crap! He was missing all of it because of a whore and his stinking dedication to a job that kept threatening to put him in jail, he thought disgustedly, recalling cops that impersonated him and his partners. Nick wheeled his car into the Second District parking lot and saw the wagon loading up several female prisoners, all handcuffed together like a Georgia chain gang. He looked for Sydney among the tethered assortment of prostitutes and vagrants. Maybe somebody bailed her out. *I should be so lucky.*

He entered the jail; it stank of piss, puke, and body odor. Nick found Teen Angel at the booking desk, smacking some Puerto Rican over the head with a Yellow Pages phone book. "Do you piss on the floor at your house you piece of shit?" he yelled. The prisoner held his hands over his head trying to avoid the harmless blows. His pants were down around his ankles. The man was so intoxicated he had no idea what was going on but knew that he didn't like it and was screaming in Spanish for the jailer to stop.

Nick locked up his service weapon in the gun locker and waited by the big garage doors of the Sally Port for the commotion to stop. The Sally Port was a big garage where prisoners could be safely transferred from police cars to the jail. When the cops drove in with a prisoner, or prisoners, the door closed behind them, effectively cutting off any chance of escape. It also prevented other people from getting in and interfering with the transfer, like a pissed off wife or girlfriend. If you were out on the street trying to walk a guy into jail, it would be easy for a carload of the guy's family or friends to follow the cop, pile out of the car, and then overpower the cop as he tried to transfer the prisoner. Nick often wondered why it was named after a woman – who was Sally anyway?

Nick waited until the man had been put in a holding pen then walked around the booking desk window and approached Teen Angel and the other jailers. "What's up?" Nick asked, his gaze acknowledging all three officers.

"Just tuning up Hector there," answered a burly veteran cop Nick knew as Roy.

Elroy Knuckles and Tommy Seitz were famous for keeping discipline in the jail and would not tolerate any bullshit, especially from prisoners who used their jail floor for a bathroom. "It stinks bad enough in here without assholes like that pulling out his junk and whizzing all over the floor," Elroy said disgustedly. The other two officers nodded their agreement and Nick saw that Hector was now sitting on his cell floor in his own piss.

"Jesus! I sure don't miss this shit," Nick said. "Hey, Teen Angel man, where's my girl? I didn't see her being put into the wagon."

"I got her in the interview room waiting for you. Detective Colegrove is coming in with another hooker arrest for soliciting from the airport, so I figured I'd just keep her here and you and Colegrove can discuss her problem."

"Thanks," answered Nick. He walked into the Police Station's main office and spoke briefly to the Desk Sergeant, filling him in on why he was there. He then located the interview room where Sydney was waiting for him. Nick hadn't even sat down before Sydney jumped up and began apologizing, trying to explain away her actions that led to her arrest.

"Don't even go there," said Nick. "Let's wait for the Vice cop to get here and see what he has to say 'cause he does not mess up, Sydney. If he popped you, you had it coming."

Sydney plopped herself back into the wooden armchair and leaned forward so her head rested on the metal interview table. Nick sat across from her, contemplating what to say to the Vice cop when he showed up.

Vice Detective Danny Colegrove entered the room, grinning. After shaking Nick's hand, he looked at Sydney and then back to Nick again. "Okay, Nick, let's have it. This girl one of your CI's?"

Information was gold on the streets and detectives all had confidential informants, or CI's, who provided valuable information regarding crimes; those already committed and, more importantly, crimes that were about to be committed.

"Not officially," Nick answered. Detective Colegrove, in his mid-forties, was six-foot-one with blonde hair that just touched his shoulders and clear blue eyes. His looks were helpful as a vice cop, especially with women. The two men had patrolled together years ago.

Once, while on a vice mission to arrest an extremely beautiful, high-priced escort, Colegrove left his partner outside of a bar high and dry. As his partner told the story, he waited over an hour for Colegrove to come out with the hooker. When he went inside to check if something was wrong, he found a message written in lipstick on the mirror in the men's room. "Sorry partner, this one is too good to pass up!"

Colegrove's partner said he was in the wind for two

days, and to this day, still won't admit what happened, invoking an "I-don't-kiss-and-tell" excuse.

"Sydney here helps us out in the Narcotics Unit from time to time," Nick explained. "You know how it goes. The minute I register her with the department as an official Confidential Informant, everybody will want to use her for her street knowledge. We just let her and her partner, the dead girl you found with Sydney, take a dip from the bag when they make a buy for us and try to keep them out of jail. Sort of why I'm here now. How big a case you got on her?"

"It's okay, Nick. I could give a shit if she goes to court or not. I'll tear up the arrest report right now if you want, but," Colegrove paused, looking straight at Sydney while still talking to Nick, "I don't want any grief over this. I can make it like it never happened if you want me to."

"That would be great," Nick said. "Sydney has agreed to give us a big dude who's into heroin. Calls himself JuJu. She cops it for him and can let us know when he is holding." He paused. "There's just something about this guy that just doesn't add up," Nick continued." He's been in Cleveland for about two months now, has Sydney buying half ounces about every week, and is banging her at the downtown Interstate Inn. I'd like to know where he's getting the cash. And besides, he pissed me off down by my boat one night."

"Yeah," chimed in Sydney, wanting to be part of the conversation since the situation now turned in her favor. "He fancies himself as some sort of voodoo dude but won't let on anything about his personal life. Most dudes can't wait to tell you all about themselves. When he gets high he chants some sort of mumbo jumbo and says he's a Spiritual Baptist and sacrifices blood to the Gods. And he has a big-ass knife in that man purse he always has with him." Sydney looked from the vice cop to Nick. "He saw me with Nick and knows Nick is a cop. He asked me about Nick but I just told him that I throw him a freebie once in a while to leave me and Brandi alone to do our business. He seemed satisfied with that but I still don't trust him. He's got these two gay Jamaican guys doing his leg work for him like booking the rooms and stuff. It's like he's a spy or something. This dude gives me the creeps. I need him gone out of my life. I'll do whatever you want to get rid of him!"

"Cool," Colegrove said. "I'll talk to my boss and this will all disappear," he said, pointing at Sydney's arrest paperwork.

"Great," Nick said. "Come on, Sydney. Let's get out of here before he changes his mind."

Colegrove stood up and shook Nick's hand. "I'll call you soon as I get the okay. And you," he said, pointing a finger at Sydney. "Why don't you go straight and sell yourself out of Craigslist like all the other girls nowadays? You could get at least four hundred a throw if you got a pimp to go between yourself and your customers."

Sydney tossed her head contemptuously, her red curls flying. "I'm already online," she informed the Vice cop. "I do just fine by myself."

"Yeah, I can see that," the detective replied.

On the way out of the station Nick stopped and thanked the Teen Angel and retrieved his gun from the locker. "Where you want me to drop you off?" Nick asked Sydney.

"Why don't you take me to your boat, Sweetie," she suggested. "I got the weekend free now."

"For Christ's sake, Sydney," Nick muttered.

Chapter 20

JuJu spent the next three weeks moving the van around the parking ramp and piecing out the remaining cocaine from the robbery into double sealed plastic bags. He taped the bags to his waist before each bus trip to Canada. He and Andre met in men's room of the casino where they exchanged the cocaine for cash from the previous delivery's sale. In the event a customs agent wanted to look inside his carry on, all they would find was a change of clothes and some newspapers. Nothing suspicious. He made even more points with his new lady friends when he explained his stay was extended and since he was so lucky at the blackjack table, he would continue going to the casino and donate his winnings back to the Haiti relief effort. "It's the least I can do for my country when I have been so richly blessed," he humbly explained.

After numerous trips to the casino, he was able to unload the entire shipment, convert it into cash, and "deposit" the money into the duffel bag in the van, still parked in the hotel parking ramp.

Another two million in cash! JuJu triumphantly exclaimed to himself as he placed the final payment into the duffel. Time to celebrate! He had avoided using heroin while making the drug runs and had done nothing illegal to bring any attention to himself. He'd leave Cleveland on a high note, and he knew just who to call to make that happen. All that was left was the return trip to Trinidad.

JuJu used the internet in the hotel's business suite to check on Greyhound Bus fares to Florida. The bus service had less security than the airport, but he could dump the car at the airport. That way, if anyone found the car and made a connection, he'd still be long gone; the cops would never think of looking for him on a bus. If he could get to Key West, he could get a plane back to Trinidad. Between Cleveland and Key West, there were three bus changes: Nashville, Atlanta, and Miami. The whole trip would take almost two days and although inconvenient, the extra stops gave him the chance to get off the bus if he thought he was being trailed.

He booked the ticket online using his dead brother's American Express Card and printed out the confirmation that served as his bus ticket. What's another $178? This would be his last night in Cleveland.

JuJu walked out into the parking garage and, after making sure no one was around, went to the van, opened the back door and climbed in. To anyone passing by, it would look like he was re-arranging his cargo. The cash was tightly bundled and weighed almost eighty pounds. He emptied the duffle bag and divided the cash bundles throughout the three compartments of the Gregory Contour backpack he had purchased at a L.L. Bean store in Cleveland just for this purpose, and placed the bus ticket confirmation in the outer zippered-pocket. He wedged the backpack underneath the van's rear seat, covered it with newspapers, then exited the back and closed the doors. Casually, he knelt beside the right rear wheel and reached his hand inside the wheel well, feeling for the magnetic case that held the spare key. To anyone watching, it would appear he was inspecting his tire. Being a thief himself, he knew most cars were stolen using the spare keys the owners thought they had cleverly hidden. But since the hotel parking lot had security, he thought it was a calculated risk. He wanted to make sure he had the key handy in case of an emergency. Assured that his private Fort Knox was secure as it could be, it was time to relax. He dialed Sydney's cell phone from memory.

She answered with a husky, "Hello," not knowing who was on the other end of the call as JuJu always had his caller ID restricted.

"You ready to go tonight?" he spoke into the phone.

Sydney's knees wobbled when she heard the deep and strangely melodic voice through her Bluetooth headset. *Damn!* She hadn't heard from him in three weeks and had hoped he had left Cleveland so she wouldn't have to make good on her promise to Nick. "Think Sydney! Think!" she coached herself. "Sure, Sugar," she responded calmly, as if expecting his call. "I can make some time for you. What kinda night you want it to be?"

"Meet me at the marina in an hour and I'll give you

the funds to pick up some stuff. I'll wait for you there and then we can start our evening together."

Damn and double damn! The marina! Right where Nick had told her NOT to go. Now what....now what?! "Okay," Sydney said and hung up the phone. When he had called, she was just getting in her car to leave from her weekly appointment with a lawyer. She loved lawyers. They always paid. Remembering her deal with Nick, Sydney called him. It was her only chance to get this guy out of her life. And besides, she had promised. If she reneged now, she knew Nick would never help her again, CI or no CI.

Nick was at his desk in the Narcotics Unit office when his cell phone rang. He glanced at the caller ID – Sydney.

"Hi, Sydney," Nick said.

"Nick, he just called me. What should I do?"

Nick knew immediately who she was talking about. "What does he want?"

"He wants me to meet him at the marina in an hour. He said he's going to give me some money to buy heroin and then we'll go to a motel for the night. I don't want to go with him Nicky, you gotta help me!"

"Let's just stick to our plan," he instructed. "Go and meet with him. I'll be there waiting when you get back and we'll bust both of you so he doesn't get suspicious. Just make sure you have him in your car and the heroin is on him and not you - got it?"

"Yeah, I guess so," she answered in a quiet voice.

"Don't screw this up, Sydney," Nick told her. "This is

your 'get out of jail free' card you owe me. If you mess it up I'll talk to Detective Colegrove and have the drug house charges re-filed and you'll get six months at Warrensville Detention Center. You got that?"

"I got it," she told him. "You gotta make it look real, Nick!"

"Don't worry about it," he told her. "Just do your part and the score will be even between us."

Nick called his partners and explained the plan to arrest JuJu. The three detectives took an undercover vehicle from the lot, drove to the marina and parked in the back corner. The lot was full and the detectives were easily absorbed into the approaching dusk.

JuJu walked to the Taxi stand in front of his hotel and hailed the lead cab in line. While passing through the gate to the Marina he saw Sydney's car parked next to the Captain's Quarters Bar. He had the driver circle the lot slowly before stopping by the Cadillac. "Wow," Lenny said from the back seat of the surveillance van. "Look at that – he was looking for surveillance. That son of a bitch sure is being careful."

JuJu paid the cabbie and, after looking around the parking lot again, got into Sydney's car. "Here's enough for a half ounce," he said, pressing money into her hand. "How fast can you be back here?"

"Just take me a minute, baby," she answered. "Wait in the bar and give me your cell number and I'll call you when I'm on the way back."

"No need for you to have my number," he told her, frowning. "Just be quick and I'll be here."

Sydney nodded and JuJu got out of the car, watched her drive away, and then went to the patio bar to wait for her. It was a pleasant evening. The September sun still had some heat to it. JuJu ordered his usual rum and Coke and looked for Kat, but she wasn't around. However Tina, the owner, was just as easy on the eyes.

Although Sydney had said it would take 'just a minute' for her to get the drugs, forty-five minutes passed before JuJu spotted her Cadillac come through the gate. She pulled up next to the outside patio bar and waited while JuJu paid his bill. He walked out the patio gate and got into her car. Sydney handed him the bag of heroin he had ordered. JuJu shoved the packet of drugs into his pants pocket and was buckling his seat belt when he felt the barrel of Nick's 9 mm service weapon pressing on his right temple.

"Don't move," the detective spoke sternly. "You – driver!" he yelled at Sydney. "Turn off the car and put your hands on the dash! I told you the last time not come back here with your johns. You didn't listen, now you're going to jail."

He ordered JuJu out of the car and had him place his hands on the roof while Detective Frank Hartness patted him down. "What do we have here?" Hartness said, holding a baggie of heroin up in the air before placing it on the hood of the car. He handcuffed JuJu and placed him into the back seat of the black and white Zone Car that had just pulled alongside Sydney's Cadillac. Nick had another Zone Car called to the scene with a female officer to search Sydney and made it a point to have JuJu observe the arrest.

"You got warrants for prostitution and grand theft," he said loudly. "Who belongs to the dope?"

Sydney wailed and cried, basically putting on a good show. "I don't know nothin' about no dope!" The female officer cuffed Sydney and helped her into a Police car.

JuJu was stunned. He'd been so careful and now he was being arrested for some dope? It was almost laughable. This had to be a setup. But Sydney's tear-streaked face looked convincing. He closed his eyes and whispered, "Protect me, Ogun. Let not my enemies defeat me."

Chapter 21

"Take him to the Narcotics Unit and hold him there," Nick instructed the uniformed officers, "but don't put him into a holding cell until we get there."

"No problem, Nick," one of the officers replied.

The booking officers handcuffed their prisoner to a chair until Nick and his partners arrived. Hoping to move things along, one officer asked, "What's your name?"

No answer.

"Where are you from?" an officer prodded.

Silence. They emptied the prisoner's pockets and found some cash and the keys to the rented Dodge van that pulled double duty as a bank on wheels. "Where's the vehicle that belongs to these keys?" another officer asked. The prisoner remained silent. JuJu had stashed his dead brother's ID along with his cell phone and hotel key card in the Dodge just in case something like this occurred.

Nick had Sydney "released" at the scene of her fake arrest after JuJu had been taken away by police car.

"You did real good, Sydney," Detective Hartness told her.

"You sure that bastard is in jail and he can't get out?"

she asked him. "He's gotta know it's me who set him up. He'll kill me for sure!"

"He's gonna stay locked up," Detective Moore assured her. "Don't worry."

Nick and his partners returned to the Narcotics Unit office and found JuJu handcuffed to a chair.

"You pissed at me because I'm fucking your girlfriend, Detective Silvano?" JuJu broke his silence to taunt the detective, adopting the grittier demeanor of the streets.

"How do you know my name?" Nick asked.

"You're famous," he continued without answering the question. "All over the television and in the papers."

"Okay, you got me," Nick answered. "Now, tell me who you are smart ass!"

"All you need to know is your girlfriend calls me JuJu. I am being framed by you and your whore friend but I will be out of here before long, and you know it, Nick." JuJu deliberately used the detective's name to rattle him.

"You never saw me buy or use dope except for that first night you saw me with Sidney at the marina. You lost your chance to arrest me then. Now it's too late. You know that bitch will never testify against me." JuJu glared smugly at Nick.

"You know what JuJu?" Detective Silvano said to his prisoner. "I don't give a shit if you get charged or not, I just want you out of my city. But I can guarantee you one thing."

"What's that?"

"You will leave my city and you will not look back. I don't know why you're here and I really don't give a fuck, but you will leave."

JuJu went silent. He didn't want to push the detective's buttons any further. Since they didn't have a full name, he was booked as "John Doe" for heroin possession and held for investigation until fingerprint results could help establish his identity.

Now what? They had him dead to rights on drug charges. He knew they wouldn't find anything out from fingerprints, since he'd never been arrested in the United States. But the longer he stayed in custody, the better the chances were that he would be identified. His best option was to stay quiet and refuse to cooperate until he came up with a plan to either get released on bond or make a deal. He should never have trusted that whore. How could he have been so stupid? *I'm gonna kill that bitch!*

Nick and his partners finished the arrest reports. One last check with the CSI to see if any identification came back on their prisoner yielded a big fat negative; they called it a day.

The next morning Nick tapped CSI again. Still nothing on JuJu's real identity. Nick had JuJu brought to a interrogation room. If the night in jail had rattled the big man, he didn't let on.

"Alright, let's get things straight between us," Nick said. "It's just you and me in here. You followed me a couple of weeks ago at the marina. What was that all about?"

"I don't know what you're talking about," JuJu replied. "I never saw you before last night."

"Well, that's obviously a lie since you already accused me of being jealous over my 'girlfriend'. Look," Nick said, "I'm not a rookie and neither are you. You know how this works. You give up information to us and we make a deal for you, but, you've got to start cooperating. Now, what is your name?"

JuJu's eyes had never strayed from Nick's gaze. "You're right, Nick, I do know how to play this game and I don't have to say shit to you," he countered. "If you're so smart, figure it out. You're just pissed at me for banging your girlfriend, Sydney, so you set me up. I saw that hot, blonde barmaid pat you on the ass in the bar. You banging that too?"

"I don't have to continue talking to you," Nick said, caught off guard at the mention of Kat's name. "Let's see how bad your heroin jones is. You're the one in jail, not me, and since you're a John Doe, you might be here a while."

Nick left the small interrogation room, instructed the jailers to take JuJu back to his cell, and returned to the Narcotics Unit office.

"That guy is being too careful," Nick said to his partners. "Let's let him sit a couple of days in jail before taking the case to the Prosecutor. Maybe he'll realize that he has no recourse but to confess and start talking."

JuJu had no intention of talking to him or anyone in the Cleveland Police Department. Back in his cell, he closed his eyes and sought to connect with his spirit protectors. JuJu spent a restless night in the Cleveland City Jail. The yelling and screaming all night long by other inmates didn't allow him any rest and he was irritated. The last thing Detective Silvano had mentioned was that he was "going to sit in jail for a couple of days" until he volunteered information as to his identity. Well, that was just not going to happen. But he knew he couldn't make bail without a name. After some deliberation, he came up with an idea that just might work.

"Jailer," he called out. "Can I get a phone call?"

The weary looking Corrections Officer unlocked JuJu's cell door with a giant key attached to a very large, circular metal ring deliberately fashioned so that it couldn't fit into a pocket and get lost. He escorted JuJu to another locked cell with a pay phone attached to a wall. The wall was covered with numbers inked by other prisoners. Some numbers were for lawyers, others for bail bondsmen. It was a criminal directory of sorts.

JuJu dialed 411 and when a voice requested, "city and state please."

"Cleveland, Ohio – the Federal Bureau of Investigation."

Chapter 22

Agent Reis had just left the morning briefing when he overheard another agent asking if anybody was interested in information concerning four drug-related homicides that happened on Dickens Avenue three months ago?

"Who has the information?" Reis barked out.

"Some guy in the Cleveland Jail just called and said he wants to trade the information for a drug charge he got. Says he's being railroaded by a Detective Silvano because he was with some whore he says this Silvano is banging!"

"What's this guy's name?" asked Reis.

"He says his name is Moon DeBoissiere but Silvano booked him as a John Doe so he couldn't get bonded out. Sounds like he's got an island accent; don't think he's from around here. Says Silvano and his partners are really screwing him over and wouldn't listen to him when he tried to tell them who he was. But he did say he overheard a couple of druggies talking about some dope house robbery and killing people. I don't know Reis, there may be something to it but I got my plate full of cases. You want to take it?"

"Yeah, I'll check it out," Reis said. Moments later, he informed his supervisor that he was going to the

Cleveland City Jail to interrogate a prisoner. Reis and his partner drove the four blocks from the Federal Building to the Justice Center and parked in the lower level reserved for visiting police agencies. The police officer assigned to the parking garage was indifferent and waved them through without asking for identification.

"Incompetent assholes," Reis said to his partner as they entered the elevator reserved for the jail. The two FBI Agents deposited their service weapons in the gun lockers outside the jail unit before being allowed to enter the secure area containing the prisoner population.

A corrections officer brought JuJu from his jail cell into the prisoner interview room and seated him across the table from the two FBI agents. "Okay, let's have it," Agent Reis spoke to JuJu after he was seated. "Let's start with the information you said you have for us."

"As I told your office on the phone," JuJu said in a calm, precise voice, "I was arrested on a trumped up charge by this Detective Silvano. He planted heroin on me and he had threatened me before because I was seeing his girlfriend. She's a prostitute I call when I am in town on business. I didn't have my identification on me because I didn't want to be robbed but he wouldn't listen to me when I told him my name and where I was staying. None of the other policemen would listen to me either. That's why I called the FBI." He paused, trying to gauge whether the agents were buying his story. Seeing the expectant look on their faces, he continued spinning his tale.

"I admit that I do some drugs, for my own recreation, but that bag was not mine! I was just trying to get some time with the lady, not robbed, and certainly not arrested on these false charges. I know the police stick together but I really did overhear some talk when I was in town a couple of months ago."

"What did you hear?" Agent Reis asked him, trying to maintain a look of bored indifference.

"I was in a bar looking for some, uh, recreation and two Jamaicans hooked me up. That Detective's girlfriend had introduced me to them. They were two little, how you say, men who like men?" he paused while looking from one agent to the other.

"Homosexuals," supplied Reis' partner.

"Yes, homosexuals," JuJu repeated as if trying a new word for the first time. "Those two – they were high and talking loudly. I heard one say, 'Did you see the blood when that guy's throat was cut?' I asked him what he was talking about and he said that he and his partner had done a dope robbery that had a lot of blood involved!"

"You know who these guys are?" Reis asked.

"No names, just a phone number so I can contact them when I am in town. I could probably call them and arrange a meeting if you want, but I need to know - what's in it for me?"

JuJu was careful not to mention anything that might implicate himself in the killings. He wanted the FBI

Agents to think he was a man being railroaded by the Cleveland Police and didn't know that the information he was providing them was needed to solve four murders.

Agent Reis hid his excitement beneath a stoic expression. How lucky could he be to have this thrown into his lap? Here this big, dumb guy was giving him the chance to nail Silvano and solve one of the biggest homicide cases of the year at the same time. *Could it be this easy?*

Reis got up and paced the floor of the small interrogation room. He stopped behind JuJu and placed a hand on the large man's shoulder in what he intended to be a supportive gesture. "You do what I tell you and maybe we can get you out of this mess you got yourself in with the Cleveland Police. But you can't lie to us, you understand?"

JuJu looked the Agent in the eye and responded, "Sir, what I am telling you is the God's honest truth. I don't know why that police officer would do that to me. My name is Moon DeBoissiere and I live in Toronto, Canada, but I'm originally from Trinidad-Tobago. I come to Cleveland for business on occasion. I didn't have my ID on me when I was arrested because I didn't want to take the chance of being robbed. My passport and other identification is in my vehicle in the hotel parking garage. I didn't think it was safe to leave it in the hotel room. If you'll just let me get those, then you'll have proof of my identity. The detective never would allow me to show it to him, but I guess he was mad at his girlfriend for dating me."

Agent Reis instructed his partner to contact the Officer-in-Charge of the jail and tell him that the FBI was removing this prisoner from their jail. His partner came back with a uniformed Captain and a plainclothes officer from Internal Affairs. When they asked Agent Reis what grounds he was using to remove the prisoner, he responded, "This man has accused one of your narcotics detectives of falsely placing heroin on his person and violating his Constitutional Rights by false imprisonment! We are placing him in our custody until further notice and any attempts to impede this action will result in charges being filed on you also."

The Captain wasn't in any position to question the FBI's actions and the Internal Affairs Detective was relieved that it would be handled by the FBI and not his office.

"Do what you gotta do," the Captain told the agents. JuJu was handcuffed and escorted out of the Cleveland Police Justice Center. When JuJu was secured in the rear of the FBI car, he knew he had a real chance to escape with his money intact if he acted quickly. JuJu read these guys like a book. The agents were obviously seeking the glory that would come with solving murders and corrupt cop cases.

"We don't have much time," JuJu implored the agents. "The woman, she told me the Jamaicans who sold the drugs are leaving town soon. They're scared because they stole the drugs from a Mexican Cartel." He paused, letting that little nugget sink in. "Put a wire on me. I will locate them for you and then you will let me go, yes?" he pleaded.

"Hold your horses," Reis told him. "First we have to prove you are who you say you are. Where is your vehicle parked? We need to see your identification."

JuJu's heart began to pound but he decided to bluff it through all the way. He didn't really have any other choice. "Go to the Clevelander Hotel," he directed. "My vehicle is on the fifth floor. I'll prove to you that I am telling the truth."

The agents followed JuJu's directions and when they pulled next to the parked van, JuJu asked them to remove his handcuffs. Reis's partner was reluctant to do so but Agent Reis rebuked him saying, "For Christ's sake man, this guy is going to break a multiple homicide case wide open and take down a crooked cop in exchange to drop a bogus drug charge. Take the freaking cuffs off the man!"

After the steel bracelets were removed, JuJu rubbed his wrists, then asked Reis if he could get his ID from the van. Reis told him, "Go ahead but keep your hands in sight at all time, got it?"

"Yes, sir," JuJu answered, smiling to himself. He pretended to drop something and quickly reached into the wheel well of the rented van and removed the extra key hidden in the magnetic case. He opened the driver's door, removed his dead brother's wallet containing the driver's license and credit card from over the sun visor, then retrieved the passport from the glove box. *Calm, remain calm, Ogun is with me,* he assured himself even as he could feel the sweat sealing his shirt to his skin.

"Here you go, Sir," he said, handing the items to Agent Reis.

"All right," Reis said. "Get back into the car. We're going to my office to plan our next move. I must remind you, Mr. DeBoissiere, that any attempt to escape or lie to me will be met with severe consequences. Do we understand each other?"

"Yes Sir, absolutely Sir," JuJu responded. "I just want this over with so I can get back to my wife and children in Toronto. I am very ashamed of myself just hope that you will forgive me." JuJu thought the added touch of a family back home would soften the agent's attitude toward him, but all he got was a silent nod.

The FBI agents drove directly to the Federal Building where they recorded JuJu's false information into their computers. No criminal information was returned from a search of the name and birth date JuJu had provided and he breathed a sigh of relief that his brother had been thoughtful enough not to get himself arrested in the United States.

After a short meeting with his supervisor, Reis took JuJu into a side room and started asking him questions about the two suspects and Sydney. Did he think Detective Silvano knew more than he was saying in the murders and the drug thefts?

"All I know is that detective is crazy. I was with the woman at the bar in that marina a couple months ago and he threatened me with a gun and said he would kill me if he saw me with his prostitute girlfriend again. When I came back to town, I called her and she picked me up and drove me there again and the next thing I know, I'm in jail and he said I was going to get twenty years in prison. You must stop this lying police officer," JuJu sounded righteously indignant now. "I might have done something wrong for calling a whore, but I don't deserve to be threatened to be killed or put in jail for twenty years for something that I didn't do! I admit that sometimes I do a little bit of drugs - but not this time. The drugs belonged to her! I didn't know anything about that." JuJu kept talking. Anything to keep the FBI Agent from realizing that he was being duped by the Dickens Avenue killer.

Agent Reis was giddy. DeBoissiere's words were like a lover's murmur – he couldn't get enough! That asshole Silvano really fucked up this time. "Alright, here's what you are going to do. Call the two Jamaicans. Can you order up some drugs from them?"

"Yes," answered JuJu, "I will do whatever you say – anything to make this nightmare go away."

"Call and tell them you want to meet by the Horseshoe Casino Valet parking garage. I am going to place a wire on you and when you meet them and buy the drugs, we'll arrest them and get you out of there."

"And then I am free to go?" asked JuJu, still playing the innocent victim with the agent.

"Not right away, but soon - if your information checks out. You may have to wait a day or two but I believe you have a good chance. You understand you have to sign charges against Detective Silvano, right, and will have to come back to testify against him in court?"

"Sir, I have no problem with that. I just pray that he is stopped before he harms someone else with his actions," answered JuJu with feigned concern.

The next hour was spent readying JuJu for the drug buy. The agents fitted him with a body wire and supplied him with marked FBI money. Each bill was photocopied and the serial numbers registered in the buy book that tracked drug buys.

"Alright, let's give them a call," Reis said.

JuJu pretended to have trouble remembering Tion and Darik's cell phone number before using a special line in the FBI office used to make unknown calls such as this one. He must continue to act like the scared informant they thought he was.

JuJu reached his accomplices and spoke into the phone. "This is the man from Toronto," he said, playing the role of an occasional recreational buyer. "Can I get some heroin soon – in an hour?" he requested, trying to keep the conversation to a minimum. "Yes, the same amount as before." He did not know which of the two he was speaking to so he just kept on and said, "Meet me by the Horseshoe Casino over by the rear door by Prospect Avenue." He ended the conversation before they could respond further. He didn't need one of them volunteering any information that could damage his story.

"That was quick," Reis said to the person he thought was Moon DeBoissiere.

"I'm sorry," replied JuJu. "I'm pretty scared and I got confused. Did I do it right?" he asked the FBI agent.

"You did fine," Reis told him. "Let's hope they do as you said but I wanted them to meet you at the front entrance by Public Square, but this will have to do. Be sure you speak clearly when you pay them and receive the drugs. We want you to say these words when the sale is completed, 'Can I call you next week to get some more?' That will be our cue to move in and arrest them. Do you understand?"

"Yes," replied JuJu. *I understand that you will never see me again!*

The agents obtained backup to assist in the buy-and-bust operation and drove JuJu to Cleveland's Public Square adjacent to the rear casino entrance and let him out of the car with instructions to stand on the sidewalk until the two supposed drug dealers came to meet him. He was not to get into the car with them. "Just do the deal through the open car window," Agent Reis coached. "That way we can see it go down and you just back off."

JuJu managed to appear nervous and went to the spot where he had instructed the men to meet him. After a few short minutes he saw the rented Focus approach. He quickly walked to the driver's side and got into the rear seat.

"What is he doing?" Reis remarked into the radio. "He's supposed to stay outside the car to do the deal."

JuJu put his finger to his mouth communicating they should be quiet. Darik and Tion watched as JuJu pulled off the body wire taped to his chest. He silently mouthed, "wait here" holding up one finger and slithered out the other rear door into the crowd of people facing away from the agents, and walked into the casino. The agents were still watching the car they thought contained JuJu and the drug sellers, waiting for a conversation that wasn't going to happen.

"What's taking them so long?" Reis spoke aloud to no one in particular.

"Maybe the wire is bad," responded one of the backup agents into the radio.

While the FBI agents continued to watch a car containing the two Jamaicans and no informant, JuJu had already crossed the casino floor and exited from the north end of the building, close to the Clevelander Hotel parking garage. He entered the garage unobserved and retrieved the van containing his four million dollars. In less than five minutes, JuJu was southbound on Interstate 71 intent on reaching the Cleveland Hopkins Airport where he could abandon the Dodge Caravan. Thank the Gods he already made escape plans. Everything he needed was in this vehicle: money, bus ticket, and a change of clothing.

Meanwhile, Agent Reis nervously watched the drug dealers' car, waiting for the signal to move in. *Why couldn't he hear anything? Was there something wrong with the wire?*

"Holy Christ!" he blurted into the radio. "Move in! Move in!" Reis and the other agents jumped out of their cars and ran to surround the black Ford.

"Oh my God!" Reis exclaimed when he got to the car. His informant was gone! The accomplices in the front seat were unmoving, almost transfixed, by some object only they could see through the windshield. Reis reached into the empty back seat and pulled out the listening device wire he taped to JuJu's chest just one hour ago.

"Holy shit, Reis!" exclaimed one of the other agents. Night had fallen on the city and Reis stood under the glare of the Casino lights not believing what had just happened. He'd be lucky if he even had a career after this!

The group of agents stood there waiting for some response from Reis. Another agent yelled at Darik and Tion, demanding to know what happened to JuJu, but the pair were unresponsive; almost as if in a trance. Finally Reis barked orders and the backup agents fanned out and began searching for the man who had successfully duped all of them – right under their noses!

While Reis and the other agents were trying to salvage the situation, JuJu dumped the rental van in the long-term parking lot at Cleveland Hopkins Airport and was now riding the Rapid Transit back toward downtown Cleveland. The FBI and the Police would think he had taken a flight out of town and while they were trying to determine where he was headed, he would be traveling south on a Greyhound bus to the Florida Keys. He changed his clothes inside the caravan from a stash previously assembled in the rental car and the four million dollars in cash was safely packed away in the grey backpack now strapped to him. He thought about bringing his knife but decided it was too risky and put it under the seat of the van after making sure he had wiped it and the interior clean of fingerprints. The money was bulky but the backpack was designed to easily distribute the weight of its contents. The manufacturer probably didn't imagine a cargo of over eighty pounds of cash! He didn't care if it weighed eight hundred pounds. He wasn't letting it out of his sight.

The Rapid, as it was called, brought him beneath the Terminal Tower and the Horse Shoe Casino - right back where he started from. He knew that Agent Reis would immediately check the hotel parking garage for the Dodge but chances were slim he'd ever think of looking back downtown for him. The police would set up roadblocks and check traffic cameras which should waste enough time to allow him to evade their search.

JuJu was right. The FBI put out a BOLO alert and were looking for the van instead of him. And he wasn't in the van anymore. As he exited the Terminal Tower out onto Public Square, JuJu felt bold and hailed a cab, even as the FBI frantically searched the area for clues. Amazingly, he saw that the cabbie was the same driver that drove him to the East 55th Marina two months ago when he had followed Detective Silvano. *The Gods are watching over me.*

The Cleveland station would surely be watched, he figured, but Greyhound made so many stops between Cleveland and Florida, he could board anywhere along the way. JuJu pulled out the bus schedule he had previously printed out and decided to board in Akron, which was forty miles south of the scene of his crimes. He instructed the cabbie to drive to Akron. From there, he would catch the Greyhound Bus to Key West, Florida.

JuJu settled back in the seat and glanced out the cab's right rear window at the fire coming out of the tall stacks from the enormous steel mills just south of Cleveland. Two hours had passed since he lost the FBI tail. If he could make it to the bus without any mistakes his bid for freedom was assured. He just had to remain calm and focused. He watched as the lights of Cleveland faded behind the speeding cab.

May the Gods of my ancestors watch over my journey. May Ogun deal with those who would choose to stand in my way!

Chapter 23

Finishing his workout in the Police gym, Silvano was in the process of deciding whether he should go to the CPPA Bar or to the Cockroach Inn for a couple of beers when he heard the overhead page.

"Nick, come to the phone immediately," the voice called through the gym's ceiling speakers. The voice sounded urgent and Nick suspected he would have to put his thirst on hold. He set his weights down, picked up his sweaty towel off the vinyl-covered weight bench and walked over to the wall phone hanging next to a fire extinguisher.

"Who is this?" The caller better have a good reason to interrupt his post-workout plans.

"Nick! Get cleaned up and come up to my office right away," Lieutenant Fratello spoke urgently.

"What's up?" Nick asked.

"Your friend at the FBI lost JuJu!" Fratello answered.

"C'mon Jon," replied Nick. "I don't have time for jokes!"

"This is not a joke, Nick," Fratello answered. "Reis lost your prisoner!"

Nick was stunned. *How the hell could this have happened?* He skipped the shower, quickly changed into his street clothes, and ran up the single flight of stairs to the sixth floor Homicide Office. Frank and Lenny were already there. Fratello was red-faced. "What happened, Jon?" Nick demanded.

"It seems that FBI Agent Reis took it upon himself to interfere with your arrest. He signed that JuJu character out of our jail this morning. He made a lot of noise about you violating the prisoner's constitutional rights and was going to use him as a Confidential Informant to catch the Dickens Avenue killers."

"Who authorized him to do that?" Nick asked incredulously.

"The Captain of the jail and the Internal Affairs Detective who came to the jail to take the complaint against you for 'violating' the asshole's rights allowed it to happen. I don't know, maybe they're afraid of the FBI or something, but their asses are on the line now and I hope they get burned for this screw-up!"

The three detectives just stared at Fratello as he continued. "I am lodging a complaint against both of them for the absence of notification of the prisoner's release to the arresting officers, which is you and your partners, and for failure to notify this office, and more specifically myself, of withholding knowledge of murder suspects. Needless to say, I don't think the complaint made against you is going to be investigated now!"

"Jesus Christ!" Nick exclaimed.

Frank jumped into the conversation. "Remember when we went to Michael's Body Shop and that bouncer Hoss told us about those two Jamaican guys?"

"Yeah, I remember," said Nick. "Sydney told us about them too."

"Well, the Detectives on the scene described the two guys that JuJu met up with in company of the FBI and they fit with what Sydney and Hoss told us. Of course, they are in jail so we will have to follow up on them later. We've got to find this JuJu or whoever the hell he is! The two guys said all they know is that they call the guy 'JuJu' and he is supposed to be some sort of voodoo priest. They're more scared of him than they are of us!"

The Lieutenant turned to Nick. "These guys told me that this JuJu character was the person who killed Pookie and the three other dudes on Dickens a couple months ago and of course they deny being there. The voodoo part fits with the marks on the dead bodies and the pile of sand and bones left in the house."

"So what now, Jon?" Nick asked.

"Manhunt," the Homicide Commander replied. "You and your partners go to the hotel and see what you can dig up about this JuJu. What we have learned from the FBI is that his name is supposedly Moon DeBoissiere and he is from Toronto, Canada. But, after calling the cops in Toronto we find that the real Moon DeBoissiere was killed a few months back in a drug dispute in their city. So, we are back to square one as to this guy's real identity."

The Commander continued, "My guys will start the investigation and maintain the crime scene. There will be no interference from Reis or the FBI as the Chief has already made his calls to Reis's boss and to the U.S.

Attorney. As far as we're concerned, the FBI is complicit and they will be treated as witnesses just as any civilians would be.

"Our information so far is this JuJu person had a vehicle parked on the fifth floor of the Clevelander Hotel and I've got the Vice Squad staking it out as we speak. My guess is that he is long gone but just to make sure, I want it watched until you and your partners get there," he said, nodding toward Nick.

"If his vehicle is still there, it stands to reason that he was staying there also," Nick offered.

"Here – take these copies of his mug shot for distribution," Fratello said, passing out eight-by-ten glossies of their fugitive to the cops in the room. "Canvas the airport, Amtrak, and the bus station just to be sure."

"This guy is clever," Nick reminded them. "We need to turn over every last stone."

"This office will be the Command Center," Fratello continued. "Unfortunately the FBI will have their personnel here also. And it is my understanding from the Chief that the FBI misfits who allowed this whole fiasco to happen, including Agent Reis, will also be assigned here." This statement was met with groans from Lenny and Frank.

"I didn't want that either," Fratello commiserated, "but the Chief feels they are better off here so we can watch them, but –"

"Yeah – I knew there'd be a big but," Lenny interjected.

Fratello shot a warning glance at the detective, then continued, "But, as I was saying…. they are to think they are bringing valuable information to this situation."

The assembled group of law enforcement officers prepared for the fugitive search. Some grabbed shotguns from the gun locker and tossed extra shells into their pockets. One of the Homicide Detectives remarked to no one in particular, "Better dead than alive for this asshole!"

Nick hung back. He wanted to speak to Fratello alone. "Jon," Nick began. "Can we have Frank or Lenny stay back to keep an eye on the FBI? I don't trust them one bit and I'd feel a lot better."

"Sure," replied the Lieutenant. "Tell you what - let's leave your partner Hartness and my guy Richie Allen here with him. Maybe they'll learn to like each other or maybe they'll kill each other, but either way, both will remain in the Command Center until I relieve them."

Nick pulled Frank aside and told him of the Lieutenant's decision to have him and Detective Allen stay in the Command Center. "Aw Nick, come on," Frank began to object.

"Listen Frank, I need someone I can trust back here keeping an eye on that prick Reis."

"All right," Frank conceded. "But you owe me!"

"Thanks," said Nick as he and Lenny prepared to leave the Justice Center. "And Frank, Any important information is to be texted. The Feds probably have our office phones tapped 'cause they seem to know a lot of our business."

Nick and Lenny went to the hotel parking garage where they met with Vice Detective Colegrove and his partner. "Hey, Nick," Colegrove said. "We've been here for over two hours and we didn't see anybody that looked like your guy anywhere near this garage. His car is gone and so is he."

"This guy is not dumb, that's for sure. Thanks for holding down the fort," Nick told the vice cops.

"Sure, no problem," Colegrove replied. "Oh, by the way, your big-titted girlfriend is off the hook. I got the Prosecutor to drop all the charges. Did she do all right by you guys?"

"She's the reason we're all going crazy looking for this guy," Nick replied, then radioed the Command Center telling the team that the suspect's car was gone.

Fratello issued another BOLO on the van using the description reluctantly obtained from the FBI and within twenty minutes, a Zone Car reported they had the tan Dodge Caravan under surveillance at Cleveland Hopkins Airport. Nick and Lenny immediately went to the long-term parking garage at the airport and met with the uniform car watching the suspect vehicle.

Nick borrowed a Slim Jim from one of the cops at the scene. He worked the long, thin bar through the window's rubber seal and down to the door lock, catching it in just the right way to release the lock and open the van's door. "Good job, Detective," said the black-uniformed patrolman as Nick returned the Slim Jim to him. Both cops and tow truck drivers used the tool to unlock vehicles. Criminals did, too!

Nick and Lenny searched the van. "Look what I found," Lenny said, holding up a blue aluminum knife housing with a black spider design on the shaft. Using his thumb and index finger, he carefully held it for everyone to see. The light reflected off the blue handle, making it appear like the spider was actually moving. "Right under the driver's seat."

"That might be our Dickens Avenue murder weapon," Nick said. "Treat it carefully."

The knife was bagged and tagged for CSI to check for blood residue. While the detectives searched the van, Command Center ran the license plate and determined it was an Enterprise rental from Independence, Ohio. A call to the rental agency confirmed it was rented by a Moon DeBoissiere from Toronto, Canada almost three months ago and had been being paid for with an American Express card issued to the same name.

"We know that's bullshit," said Nick.

He directed the uniformed cops to have the van towed to the police impound lot for processing. "Sure," one of the uniforms said. "Let's hope you find this prick. Let us know if you need anything else."

Lieutenant Fratello was holding a debriefing session as Nick and Lenny entered the Homicide Office. "We had a team check all of the downtown hotels. They showed the guy's photo everywhere but nobody could ID him as of yet. It's getting late and we'll have to check again in the morning. If his car was parked in that garage, he had to have been staying close by. It's possible that another shift of hotel employees might know who he is."

The night turned into the next day as the team worked around the clock, tracking down leads that went nowhere. At 10 a.m., the Lieutenant told everyone to go home, get some sleep, and report back at the Command Center at four o'clock.

When the teams reassembled as ordered, Lieutenant Fratello said, "We are going to start again. Let's show this picture to all of the downtown hotel workers. Someone had to see him." Lenny agreed to take his turn replacing Frank, remaining behind to 'watch over' Reis and the FBI who were angrily protesting their restrictions. A quick phone call by Fratello to the U.S. Attorney quelled their objections.

Nick and Frank took the Clevelander Hotel where the FBI last saw JuJu's vehicle. Upon entering the expansive lobby Nick spotted the bar. "Bartenders see everything," Nick noted. "Let's try there first."

Nick approached the bartender, showed his badge, and asked the man's name. "Niko," he responded in a thick Greek accent while continuing to wipe down the spotless bar top. "How may I help you?"

"You ever see this guy around here?" Nick asked while holding up JuJu's arrest photo.

"Yeah, he come here every day and drink spice rum and Coke," Niko said. "Maybe two, maybe three month. You go see that man," Niko said pointing across the lobby to the clerk behind the hotel's front desk.

Nick and Frank approached the hotel clerk and

placed the photo on the counter. "You ever see him here?" Frank asked.

"Sure, I know him," replied the young man. "He's been here for weeks. Said he was from Toronto and worked for an engineering firm. Let me look him up on the computer," he said, pounding the buttons on the keyboard in front of him. "Ah yes, here he is," the clerk said.

"Let me guess," Nick remarked before the young man could say anything further. "His name is Moon DeBoissiere, right?"

"If you already knew that, why did you ask me to look him up?" the young man responded with a bit of sarcasm.

"We need to look at his room," Nick stated, ignoring the clerk's tone.

"Show me some ID first," the clerk said, "and I'll have to contact the manager also to get her permission. What did this person do, anyway?"

"He murdered four people, that's what he did," said Frank.

"Whoa," responded the young man, "that's all I need to hear."

Nick and Frank flashed their badges to the desk clerk and waited impatiently while he made his calls.

"Okay," he said. "Here is a key card, bring it back when you're done. He never checked out so the room has not been changed out yet. Maybe his stuff is still there."

The two detectives entered JuJu's hotel room. "Nothing out of the ordinary yet," Frank said as he tossed the mattress off the bed. A check of the trashcan revealed some hotel stationary scribbled with web site addresses and phone numbers to airlines and car rental agencies.

"Let's call the CSI - do this up right and treat it as a crime scene," said Frank.

"You are right, my friend," Nick agreed. "Let's not screw this up 'cause I've got a feeling that these pieces of paper are going to be mighty important before this is all over!"

They made the calls and stopped searching the room until the Crime Scene Investigation could get there. While they waited, Nick called the front desk and asked if the resident in that room had used the internet. The same clerk confirmed that Mr. DeBoissiere might have used the internet in the business center.

Nick told Frank to wait for the CSI while he went and checked JuJu's computer history. Nick met the clerk in the business center, a room that was no bigger than a closet. "Sure is small, isn't it," the clerk said as he led Nick into the room off of the main lobby.

"I've seen bigger ones in a Motel 6," answered Detective Silvano. "You know we're going to have to confiscate this computer," Nick told the clerk. "It might be evidence."

"Dude, you can't do that to me," said the young man. "Can't you check it while it's here?" he implored.

"Maybe," Nick said.

He contacted his partner Frank using his portable

police radio and asked him to place a call to the White Collar Crimes Unit and see if Detective Jim Rodes could come to the Clevelander Hotel to run a search of the computer.

"You sure you want Rodes to do this?" his partner asked Nick. "After all, he is married to your ex-wife and I remember the last time you two were together it ended up in a battle royal."

"Aw, we were both drunk," Nick explained. "We smoked the peace pipe since then and after all, he's the best computer geek around."

"All right," Detective Hartness acknowledged. "I'll make the call."

Detective Jimmy Rodes came right away and met with Nick in the hotel's business center. "Hey Nick, what do we need?" he asked.

"I think this computer might hold information as to what the subject of our manhunt was planning. Can you get inside it and see if there's anything there?"

"No problem," Rodes said. After obtaining the suspect's name and room number, it took him only fifteen minutes to produce a printout of a Greyhound bus ticket. "This is what he used this computer for," Rodes told Nick. "Looks like he got a ticket from Cleveland to Key West, Florida and he probably left out of here yesterday. According to the time schedule he should be in Florida by now unless he got off when they changed buses in Atlanta or maybe someplace in between. The next change is supposed to be in Miami but it has made a lot of stops between here and there.

He could be anywhere by now."

"Well, that narrows it down," Nick said wryly. He copied the information and placed a call to the Command Center to update Commander Fratello. "Jon, I think we might have a possible on JuJu. He bought a Greyhound Bus ticket online from Cleveland to Key West the other day. The bus number is 1444 and it makes three transfers before hitting Key West. The first is in Nashville, the second in Atlanta, and then Miami, but it makes a lot of stops in between to drop off and pick up passengers."

"Okay, Nick," said Lieutenant Fratello, "Good work."

"And Jon? Let's set up a meeting with Detective Unit Commander Gary Payne and Chief Marinik so we can avoid any 'mis-communication' that may result in case the FBI tries to throw their mistakes on us, okay?"

"Sounds good," Fratello agreed. "Now go get some sleep. We will keep working on this. I'll see you in the morning."

Nick turned to Rodes. "Thanks, Jimmy," he said as the White Collar Crime Detective was packing up his gear. "Tell Cheryl I said hello, will you?" he asked.

"Sure thing, Nick," Rodes said. "If you need anything else, you know where I am!"

Yeah – with my ex-wife!

Chapter 24

Nick was wired from the days' events and chose to go with his original plan rather than follow Jon's instructions to go home and get some sleep. *Choices....*

The Roach won. All this JuJu crap and the extra work and the backstabbing from the FBI was wearing him out. He needed a drink. Maybe five. He claimed a barstool at the very end of the dimly lit bar. The large moose head mounted on the wall behind the bar was in tatters. Over half of the antlers were missing and the left ear was gone.

"What's up with your moose, Willy?" Nick asked.

"You know the drill, Nick," Willy said. "Out-of-town cops get a shot at Mr. Moose here and those New York City cops did a number on him! Shit, he must have a hundred pounds of lead in him! I'm surprised he's still hanging around. One of these nights he's going to fall off the wall and hurt me or one of my barmaids. I guess I better start thinking about moving him."

"Well, he looks particularly distressed right now," joked Nick. "How long you been letting the troops shoot at him?"

"Probably about two or three years now," Willy answered. "It started off as a joke when one of the guys brought him in here. He had gotten it from some cops ex-wife who wanted to stick it to her former husband. Seems the guy had bagged the animal while on a hunt up in Canada somewhere. Problem was that the guy took his girlfriend with him hunting. The wife found out and gave all his shit away while he was at work."

Nick nodded. *Cowboy Cop phase.*

"She called the cops and tried to turn in his guns as she was moving out of the house," Willy continued. "She took everything, including the light bulbs and the toilet paper. Bet that guy was surprised when he got home and saw what the little lady did! Anyway, one night after that, the guys got drunk and started plugging away at Mr. Moose here. I should have put a stop to it then but I was right there with them, shooting away! I had to move the mirrors away from it because some of the cops are terrible shots. Look at all the holes around Mr. Moose's head!" he exclaimed, pointing to the dozens of holes in the back wall of the bar.

Nick sat alone at the bar drinking his beer with a few shots of Gentleman Jack. Usually, this would relax him but his thoughts returned to this current puzzle. JuJu, the two Jamaicans, the Dickens Avenue murders, Sydney – somehow it all fit but he couldn't put the pieces together. He forced himself to focus on the television where the Cleveland Indians were getting the shit kicked out of them by the Toronto Blue Jays.

"Every year the Indians start out not so bad but fall apart after the All-Star Game, don't they?" Willy said.

"Yeah. Maybe the Browns will finally do something,"

Nick commented, "but we both know we will probably be dead and gone before Cleveland gets any kind of championship trophy."

A young man entered the bar and approached an off-duty cop everybody called Paulie-the-Pig. It was now almost eight o'clock. "Hi Dad," he said.

Paulie didn't even turn around to greet the kid but continued staring straight ahead at the televised baseball game. He held out one arm in the kid's direction, a check in hand. "Happy Birthday, kid," Paulie said, still without looking at the boy. "Tell your mother she can stop robbing me of child support money. You're eighteen now - I'm off the hook." The boy took the check, turned and walked out the front door of the bar without making any kind of response.

"Finally - the Bitch from Bucharest can stop taking my fucking money!" Paulie said. "Hey Willy, give the bar a round of drinks, I'm celebrating! For eighteen years she has hauled my ass into court over my kid and told him what a bad person I am. Couldn't even get visitation rights due to all the different shifts I had to work. I finally just gave up and let her blackmail me, but now it's over."

"Congratulations," said Willy while the scattered patrons raised their drinks to Paulie's new found freedom from child support.

A few minutes later, the young man returned and stood just inside the door looking like he was going to pass out.

"What's wrong, kid?" Paulie asked his now adult son.

In a wavering voice, barely audible, the kid said, "Mom told me to tell you that I ain't your kid anyway!" and he turned and ran out, leaving the stunned cops staring at the front door as it slammed shut.

"Unbelievable," said Willy. "You named your ex-wife right Paulie."

Another cop yelled down the bar, "Hey Paulie, who the baby daddy?"

"Shut the hell up!" Paulie yelled back. "I gotta go find my lawyer, maybe there is some way I can get my money back off the bitch." Paulie slammed his beer, pushed himself off the stool and stomped out of the bar.

"Wow," said Nick as he picked up his change from the bar. *Helpless and Hopeless phase.*

"Where you going?" asked Willy, "thought you were gonna get drunk?"

"That was my game plan," said Nick, "but I have a big day tomorrow."

"Doing what?" asked Willy.

"Gonna go JuJu hunting!"

Chapter 25

JuJu instructed the cabbie to drop him off two blocks from the Akron Greyhound bus station. He didn't know if the FBI or police knew his whereabouts yet but if they found his rental van at the Cleveland Hopkins Airport, he was probably safe for now and hoped they were only checking for flights and not the train or bus stations. He had no idea Nick was close to identifying his mode of escape.

Just to be sure, he walked the last few blocks to the station, looking for any signs of surveillance. Nothing. He checked the schedule again and saw that the bus left Akron at 10:05 p.m. He wanted to board just before it left.

He knew Detective Silvano was not as clueless as the FBI has been. The Detective had put the drop on him and he never saw it coming. He had to be extra careful. JuJu prepared for the thirty-six hour trip from Cleveland to Key West, a distance of 1,630 miles. He dressed in shabby clothing, frayed Nike baseball cap, dirty tennis shoes, and carried a backpack. From his appearance, no one would ever guess the backpack was full of one hundred dollar bills worth four million dollars. To place that much cash into a bus luggage compartment was too great of a risk. He wasn't letting the money out of his sight.

JuJu walked slowly and circled the entire bus station before going inside. He shuffled along like he had mental problems and for extra effect, had taken a Bible so thoughtfully left by the Gideons from his hotel room, and now held it up over his head as he walked slowly and mumbled to himself. Like the hotel industry, the bus station also employed off-duty cops in addition to their own security personnel. JuJu's appearance earned him a quick once-over as he was assessed and dismissed as a potential threat. To them, he was just another homeless drifter carrying all that he owned in a backpack. The sight was commonplace and not worth the hours of paperwork for them to even question him and perhaps find out he was wanted on some obscure outstanding warrant - no one would bother with him.

He made his way to the boarding lines and stood ready to board the beat up Greyhound bus, his own personal Freedom Ride. JuJu followed an overweight woman dragging a wheeled suitcase. One of the wheels was missing and it scraped the concrete floor, like fingernails on a chalkboard. While everybody in the bus station was looking at the fat woman with the noisy suitcase, nobody paid any attention to him, he correctly assumed.

He took an aisle seat behind the driver and placed his backpack in the window seat. From the numerous bus trips to the Canadian casino, he knew that customs and border agents always gazed immediately toward the rear of the bus and stood next to the bus driver. From that position they could see everything and everyone at once. Next came the slow walk down the narrow bus aisle. They'd turn their heads from side-to-side looking for any squirrelly individuals. All JuJu had to do was just meet their gaze, like any innocent person would do, and remain calm. The female law enforcement agent employed by the bus company did exactly as JuJu predicted. She stood up front and rested her hand on the back of the driver's seat. She glanced briefly at JuJu and then began her walk to the rear of the bus. JuJu could hear her asking questions, but not the exact words. Whatever was being discussed was of no importance to him and he knew that the agent would pass right by him on her hasty exit from the bus.

It was going to be a long ride. He wrapped his left hand through the backpack straps and vowed to stay awake and alert. The bus made scheduled stops every couple of hours to drop off and pick up passengers. JuJu stayed the course and only left his seat twice to use the bathroom, located at the rear of the bus. Each time, he took his backpack with him. The miles rolled by and night turned to morning. After Detective Rodes discovered the bus ticket JuJu purchased online using the Clevelander Hotel's public computer he turned the information over to Nick, who was still fuming at how the FBI could have allowed JuJu to dupe them so badly. How could those dickheads not know what their informant was doing? While they were asleep at the switch, JuJu had made fools of all law enforcement agencies in the process. The news media was having a field day. The apparent escape of the suspect while he was in custody was the lead story and even made the national news.

Maybe now, Reis will get what he deserves, Nick hoped. While JuJu had been filling Reis and his agents' heads full of useless information, Nick and his counterpart DEA Agent Charley Goetz, were left to clean up the mess.

It had been over twenty-four hours since JuJu had boarded the bus in Akron and Nick knew that every minute wasted would increase JuJu's chances of getting away. *Shit!* JuJu had taken so many twists and turns in the past twenty-four hours he could be almost anywhere! Maybe the bus ticket was a ruse and he was still in Cleveland. Wouldn't that be something.

While still unsure what his next move should be, Nick was sure about one thing; he was not going to tell the FBI what he had learned. Nick called Commander Fratello and agreed to come to the Justice Center to discuss their next moves.

Nick contacted Greyhound Security and filled them in on the situation. In response, they supplied the bus's current location and the driver's contact information. The TSA agent assigned to the Greyhound bus station also heard the Detective's request and, in the spirit of inter-agency cooperation, placed a call to their supervisors in the Federal Government at the TSA office. The TSA called their counterparts in the FBI. But in this case, cooperation was the last thing Detective Nick Silvano needed.

JuJu was in a dreamlike state as the bus continued south through the State of Florida. An uncomfortable premonition took hold of his thoughts. *Something is wrong!* He willed himself not to panic. It must be the drugs. He hadn't used for five days. He always had drugs available to settle his unease and he wished he had some heroin to help calm his nerves now! But the possibility of a dope dog sniffing him out was too great a risk to take when he was so close to his goal.

He forced himself to take deep breaths and imagined his future steeped in opulent surroundings; wanting nothing and having everything. It was a beautiful picture. When he returned to Trinidad-Tobago, he'd be so powerful no one could touch him. He'd have a mansion with a pool, maybe a helicopter. And women! Perhaps he'd lure Sidney to Trinidad and show her what happened to people who betrayed him. He had almost gained full control of his emotions and was settling back into his seat when he heard the musical chirp of a cell phone. He noticed the bus driver fumble in his jacket pocket and retrieve a ringing cell phone with one hand, his other hand still driving the bus.

Bus drivers aren't supposed to talk on the phone. Whoever was on the other end was doing all of the talking. JuJu kept his gaze fixed out of the window on the left side of the bus. From his seat he could see the aging driver's reflection in the window. The man's face looked concerned, but his mouth didn't move as he continued listening to the caller while simultaneously scanning the passengers' faces through the large rearview mirror. When the driver's gaze met JuJu's eyes, the man's expression tightened and he looked back to the road and said something to his caller. That was all it took for JuJu to know that he was indeed the subject of the phone call. *They had found him!*

There was no way that a Greyhound bus driver was going to have a conversation on a cell phone while barreling down the Florida Turnpike at seventy-five miles an hour! One complaint from a passenger and his job would be yanked out from under him in a New York minute. Panic began to set in and with it, the hunger for some smack to reel him back from losing control and bolting from the bus. He had to stay with it now. It was just another obstacle to overcome. If he could get off this bus before it was stopped by the Florida Highway Patrol, he might stand a chance. The bus began to lose speed and swerved into the far left lane of the turnpike toward the marked exit lane for an upcoming turnpike plaza. The bus driver lurched the bus into a spot by a walkway leading into the main entrance marked for Burger King, the machine's air brakes hissing like a giant snake.

"Folks," the driver announced. "I'm sorry for the inconvenience but I have a personal emergency to attend to and then I'll be right back." There was a murmur among the passengers. "Please stay on the bus – this should only take a few minutes. Thank you for your patience."

JuJu saw panic in the old driver's eyes even as he was trying to project calm. After the driver exited, some of the passengers were looking at each other as if to ask, "Why does he get to get off and not us?" They thought his "personal emergency" was an untimely call of nature. JuJu saw this as his opportunity to make a move and stood up as if to get off the bus.

A young father across the aisle grabbed his daughter by the hand and told her, "C'mon honey, let's go get something to drink," and walked off the bus toward the main plaza building. Other passengers followed.

JuJu picked up his backpack and exited with the stream of passengers, now disobeying the driver's instructions en masse. He listened for sounds of approaching sirens and looked around for evidence of any law enforcement, but didn't see anything. Maybe the driver really did have a personal emergency. *Maybe I'm just being paranoid.*

Seeing no visible signs of danger, he walked to the rear of the parked bus, still spewing diesel fumes into the humid Florida night air, and casually wove his way between the rows of gas pumps and idling giant trucks. He had to get out of this area fast and get as far away as possible.

He spotted a group of Hispanic men just finishing pumping gas into their beat up brown Ford van. They appeared to be migrant workers and JuJu saw their vehicle was pointed North, the direction he had just come. He approached them with as pleasant a look as he could muster and called out to them. "Hola dudes, I need a favor, por favor."

The four men looked him over with suspicion. Although JuJu was a big man, there were four of them. JuJu saw the suspicious looks he was getting and surmised the men were probably in the U.S. illegally. Well, that was one thing they had in common.

"I ain't the law or nuthin' like that," JuJu said quickly, lapsing into the language of the street. "I got cash to pay for the favor I am about to ask you," he continued, pulling out three one hundred dollar bills he had stashed in his pocket and holding it up so they could see the money.

JuJu weaved a story about his "bitch" who took off and left him there after a fight. He held out the three bills to the tallest man, who happened to be the one holding the keys to the van.

"Can you guys give me a lift?" JuJu asked them. "I gotta get back to Atlanta before that bitch gets to my pad and cleans me out. Por favor," he ended his plea.

Fortunately for JuJu, his new friends saw an opportunity to score some much needed cash as their work had been slowed by the numerous storms that recently pounded the state of Florida. The apparent leader of the group replied in a heavy accent. "I dun' know man, we was going to Jacksonville to look for some pickin' work. We might be talked into goin' that way but this old van eats a lot of gas, you know man?"

JuJu reached into his pocket, removed two more hundred dollar bills, and held out five hundred dollars out to the driver.

"You got a deal man, jump in," said the driver who introduced himself as Juan. Everyone relaxed then, and it was all smiles as JuJu, Juan, and the others got into the van. JuJu slid the door shut and took a seat in the third row of the beat up van, vowing to keep his mission intact even if he had to off all four of these guys! Ogun will keep me alive, he assured himself.

Juan and his crew exited the Travel Plaza and drove northbound on the turnpike then veered off to continue northbound on Interstate 75. JuJu surveyed the van for any possible weapons just in case his new traveling companions decided to rob him - or worse. It appeared that his hosts were living out of the van; it was stuffed with smelly clothing and empty fast food bags.

JuJu's fears were unfounded as Juan and his crew seemed happy with the money. Eight hours later they approached the outskirts of Atlanta, Georgia. "Where you want dropped off, man?" Juan asked.

It was early Wednesday morning and the Atlanta traffic was beginning to fill Interstate 75. It seemed every car in Georgia was funneling onto the freeway from various exchanges. Through the windshield, JuJu saw a collage of billboards ahead offering gas, lodging, and food. "Next exit will be fine, my friend," JuJu answered the driver. "My bitch ex-girlfriend is probably already at my place now, and it's not far from here. I'll call my people to pick me up from here."

The van pulled into a McDonald's parking lot. JuJu exited the van and walked toward the fast food restaurant. He glanced back and saw the van headed down the exit ramp to the freeway. The aroma of a fast-food breakfast assaulted his senses when the door opened and his stomach started growling. He hadn't planned on stopping, but he was hungry so he approached the counter and ordered coffee and two Egg McMuffins.

Those guys were really dumb. I would have robbed me if I was them! JuJu's natural mistrust of other members of the human race was founded on his own life experiences. As far back as he could remember, it was "take everything you can from everybody you can by whatever means necessary."

The coffee helped but he desperately needed sleep; it had been almost forty-eight hours since he left Cleveland. He finished his food and walked across the street to a Mom-and-Pop motel. There were some nicer places to stay; a Holiday Inn Express and a Comfort Inn were also next to the exit, but he had no intention of using a credit card or his emergency identification. He glanced around. There were only a few cars in the lot. Probably the maids. The motel units were open to the sidewalk and two housekeeping carts were parked in front of open doors. The exterior was painted a couple shades of grey to blend with the dirt. Cigarette butts littered the parking lot. There didn't appear to be any cameras installed. Another good sign.

He entered the run-down lobby and approached a pimply-faced young man, no more than nineteen or twenty years old, sitting behind the cloudy, smeared Plexiglas window separating him from whatever dangers he might encounter.

JuJu stood at the window, waiting to be acknowledged, while the motel clerk pretended to be busy shuffling pieces of paper. He could see the boy's real reading material was stacked on the floor beside his chair, a telltale rabbit emblem giving the true content away. JuJu knew immediately he was in the right place. This kid had no interest in anything except for the smut books on the floor. When the boy couldn't ignore the silent presence one minute longer, he looked up and asked, "Can I help you?" in a squeaky voice.

"You got a room?" JuJu asked. "My rig broke down on the interstate a couple of miles from here and it's going to take all day to fix. Tow truck driver brought me here," JuJu continued, answering a question that hadn't been asked but was implied as the clerk peered around him to see if what kind of car the big man pulled up in.

The young clerk pointed at the registration book, asked JuJu for his identification and credit card information, then retrieved a key attached to a green, plastic fob hanging on a greasy wall covered with motel occupancy permits.

"Oh man, I left my shit in my truck. All I got on me is some cash." He held out two one hundred dollar bills. "Do I need to call the garage to bring it to me?" JuJu asked.

"Naw," responded the clerk, taking the bills as JuJu fed them through the slot in the bottom of the window.

"Will that cover it?" JuJu asked

"I ain't got no change."

"Don't need none," answered JuJu. With the key to #9

in his hand, he walked out the motel office, passing a motorcycle parked under the portico. He assumed it belonged to the pimply-faced desk clerk. He found his room at the far end of the building, stowed his backpack under the bed, then flopped down and fell asleep atop the thin bedspread.

Chapter 26

U naware that the FBI was already actively involved in his case, Silvano headed to his meeting with Detective Bureau Commander Gary Payne and Chief Marinik.

After the TSA called and "shared" information with the FBI, Agent Reis made the call to the bus driver. Detective Frank Hartness, who had been left behind in the Command Center, heard Reis tell his cohorts, "We got him! I just talked to a Greyhound bus driver. That bastard is definitely on his bus! He just pulled over on the Florida Turnpike and we have agents on the way. He should be in custody shortly."

Hartness texted Nick with "problem-problem," their emergency code, then relayed what he had overheard Reis telling the law enforcement personnel assembled in the Command Center.

Nick was driving at the time but still read the emergency text. *Damn that Reis!* Everything he did only served to benefit him! Perhaps the FBI would get lucky and capture JuJu. Nick was hopeful but seriously doubted it. The wanted man was a ghost; materializing for a moment and then fading beyond human reach.

In Atlanta, JuJu awoke refreshed after ten hours of uninterrupted sleep. He stood in the motel's narrow shower, letting the hot water remove the remaining stress from his tormented brain, and reviewed his current situation. Stranded in a nameless Atlanta suburb with only the clothes on his back and four million in cash. It took a few minutes for him to redirect himself. Breakfast would be a good place to start.

The motorcycle was still parked next to the motel office and it gave him an idea that temporarily stamped out his hunger. He entered the motel office and saw the same clerk. JuJu approached and spoke through the quarter-sized speaker holes drilled into the Plexiglas.

"That your bike out there?" he asked the kid.

"Yeah, it's an 88 Kawasaki Vulcan 1500. Not a Harley but it will run the balls off any Harley made!"

"I used to ride," JuJu told him. "But too much time on the road doesn't allow me the pleasure anymore."

"Uh, yeah, I suppose," said the kid, looking back down at his magazines.

"I think I want to make some time for it now," JuJu stated in a more direct tone. "How much would you take for your motorcycle?"

"It's not for sale," the clerk said firmly.

"I think it is," JuJu countered.

Suddenly the Plexiglass shield seemed as secure as a piece of plastic wrap. The young man sensed danger, and the magazine wavered in his hand. "Ten thousand dollars is what I want," he blurted out, knowing that was more than twice the value of the Kawasaki. That ought to make him leave. No way someone would pay that!

JuJu glared at the kid. Now was not the time to lose his temper. He removed an envelope from the front pocket of his backpack, counted out ten thousand dollars, then pushed the money through the open slot at the bottom of the window. "Here is more than it is worth. Give me the title, registration, and keys." He fixed a dark gaze into the boy's watery blue eyes. "Also, you will not say anything about this sale to anyone. I can come back here at any time and discuss our 'arrangement' and I don't think you want me to do that, right?"

"Right," the clerk said as he took out his wallet and produced the requested paperwork and keys. "I won't say a word. I was thinking about getting a different bike anyway." His hand trembled as he pushed the keys through the slot and he thought he might wet his pants right there. *I ain't saying a freakin' word.* The clerk took a deep breath and counted his money.

JuJu fired up the motorcycle and took off northbound on Interstate 75 intending to double back south at the next exit. If the kid decided to call the cops, they'd be looking in the wrong direction. The next exit was twelve miles down the road. JuJu turned the bike off the exit ramp and headed to a Wal-Mart Store a few hundred yards away.

The new mode of transportation required a change of clothes. He bought a full-faced helmet, black boots and a waterproof riding suit with riding gloves to disguise his appearance. He put the newly purchased items on in the parking lot. Nobody would be able to tell what he looked like now.   JuJu gassed up, then turned the motorcycle southbound.

A couple more days before I am home free.

Chapter 27

"No way is that JuJu prick going to put a black mark on my cop career," Nick told Commander Fratello as they waited in the hallway outside of Chief Marinik's office.

"What do you want me to do about it?" Jon asked. "He's in Florida now. We don't have jurisdiction there. The FBI made sure of that!"

Chief Robert Marinik called the two officers into his office. DEA Chief Charley Goetz and Commander Gary Payne were there, all smiles.

"What are you two so happy about?" Nick grumbled.

"Well," replied the DEA Chief, "we have to make a trip, you and me. Turns out JuJu got away from the FBI....again!"

"No kidding," Nick dryly responded. "Where to?"

Chief Marinik answered his question. "You and Goetz are going to Florida to find that son-of-a-bitch! The U.S. Attorney's office has had enough and pulled Reis' ticket to operate. He's been suspended from duty until further notice," he paused, letting the news sink in. "And the FBI is off the case entirely. The Mayor wants this murdering bastard behind bars for what he did here. Goetz and the DEA have the authority to operate in Florida and he requested your assistance."

"Chief," Nick started, "I know the Mayor is up for reelection and all that but–"

Marinik cut him off. "I need you to do this, Nick. You know what he looks like and how he operates. Not only do I need you to do this, I am ordering you to do this! Pack your bags. You're leaving now!"

Goetz told Nick to pack a bag and meet him at Cleveland Hopkins Airport in an hour to catch a flight to Miami. From there, the Miami DEA office would supply the manpower needed to continue their search for the elusive killer.

While Charley and Nick prepared to catch a flight to Miami, their quarry was entering the Florida Keys.

JuJu rode the Kawasaki non-stop eight hours from Atlanta to Homestead, Florida using Interstate 95, avoiding the Turnpike and the array of cameras installed to photo capture vehicles skipping out on paying the numerous tolls. It was morning when he arrived at the end of the road before turning toward the Florida Keys. Tired from the drive, he found a small motel. He paid cash for a room and again was able to convince the weary night-shift clerk that he had "lost his wallet and all his ID" and all he had was cash. An extra fifty dollars to the clerk and JuJu had the key. These types of transactions happened all the time.

He slept until late afternoon, then showered, dressed, and added the extra layer of the rain suit. With the full helmet and gloves, he was once again covered from head to toe. No one would ever recognize him. He fired up the motorcycle and pointed it toward the Key Largo sign. One mile later he pulled into a RaceTrac gas station for gas and something to eat.

The road to Key Largo was a narrow stretch that went on for twenty some miles with no place to exit until you reached the Florida Keys. From prior experience running drugs in the Keys, he knew the Florida Highway Patrol and Monroe County Sheriff's office had a tight control over the road. Even if he thought someone was tailing him, he couldn't double-back like he did before.

Monroe County, Florida encompassed the entire Florida Keys. From Key Largo to Key West, it was 106 miles of mostly two-lane highway with the Atlantic Ocean and the Gulf of Mexico shouldering each side. Since there weren't any off ramps or other avenues of escape, any crimes occurring in the county received quick action by local law enforcement. It was not uncommon for the police to place roadblocks at Jewfish Bridge, the only way in and out of the Keys, and stop and check every car until the criminals were caught or the locals' cried bloody murder about the inconvenience.

JuJu sat on the motorcycle between the gas station and a fish bait store, eating one of his two sandwiches and contemplating his next move. Even though he felt sufficiently camouflaged in his motorcycle gear, he didn't want to be a lone rider as he approached the bridge, just in case there was a roadblock. He appealed to Ogun for protection and guidance. As if in answer to his prayers, a large group of motorcyclists pulled into the gas station. This was the last gas stop before continuing on the road to Key Largo and the Jewfish Bridge.

There were about thirty riders, mostly younger men. They didn't wear any "colors" that identified them as belonging to an organized gang and most were wearing rain suits and full helmets just as JuJu wore. *Ogun has provided for me again. I cannot be defeated!*

He waited until they finished gassing up, then fired up his Kawasaki, along with the other riders. As the group pulled off towards Key Largo, he eased into the back of the line as they headed out, two-by-two, southbound on the Overseas Highway with the early afternoon sun reflecting off their full-face helmets.

The ride was uneventful until the rising slope of the Jewfish Bridge appeared on the horizon. The cyclists slowed as they approached the bridge and JuJu noticed three Florida Highway Patrol cars parked in the grass to the right of the road.

If they had to stop for an inspection, he'd have to make a run for it. He fought the urge to gun the bike and pull away, falling back on the good fortune Ogun had provided for him so far. The line of bikers slowed to a crawl, but at least they were still moving.

JuJu felt like the troopers' eyes were solely focused on him as the motorcycles slowly rode through the gauntlet of law enforcement. Some of the bikers waved or gave the "thumbs up" sign but there was no response from the stoic troopers.

The September Florida sun beat down on the riders

and the temperature approached ninety degrees. JuJu could feel the sweat flowing down his neck and back, underneath the black helmet and dark rain suit. The motorcycle's engine radiated heat from underneath his overheated body and JuJu hoped he wouldn't pass out from the heat and the stress. The line of bikers continued on without any interference from the Florida Troopers and JuJu was soon coming down the southern end of the bridge that entered into Key Largo.

The Obeah is with me. The line of bikes stretched from the base of the bridge to the first red light; JuJu was in the group bringing up the rear. Time to break off from his fellow travelers before one of them realized they had an extra rider. After the light turned green, the line of bikes continued south. JuJu gradually fell back from the pack until he had completely separated from the group.

He proceeded carefully through the afternoon Key Largo traffic, then turned left at mile marker 101. He guided the motorcycle down the shady, tree-lined approach road into a shopping mall containing a Publix Super Market, Kmart, and numerous smaller stores and businesses. He parked the Kawasaki in the furthest corner from the main drive and removed his helmet, riding gloves, and rain suit. Immediately, he felt cooler. He wiped down the motorcycle with a rag from the saddlebags to get rid of any fingerprints. "No point in making it too easy for the cops," he remarked. He stuffed the rain suit under his arm and carried the bundle, along with the helmet and backpack, into the

Kmart store and headed to the customer service desk.

"My motorcycle broke down in your parking lot," he told the teenage girl behind the customer service counter. "I need to call for a tow, but first, can I purchase some more appropriate clothing in your store and wear it out? My riding clothing is far too warm for your wonderful weather."

"Sure," the girl replied. "Just bring the tags back to me and I'll ring up your purchase."

JuJu picked out several items of clothing and changed in the fitting room. He discarded his motorcycle duds, including the helmet, into the large trash can in the men's room at the rear of the store. He removed several hundred dollar bills from the backpack and stuffed them into the side pocket of the khaki cargo pants. He pulled a navy blue knit golf shirt over his massive upper body and folded the additional items of clothing under his arm. A pair of brown boat shoes completed his vacationer outfit and he made his way to the front of the store to pay for his items.

That done, he exited the store and carefully surveilled the parking lot. The Kawasaki was still parked in the corner of the lot by a RadioShack store. By the time the cops found and traced the cycle back to that little punk in Georgia, he would be long gone.

He walked into RadioShack and purchased three prepaid cell phones. The sun cast long shadows in the tree-lined parking lot as he left the store with his purchases. The Monroe County Public Library was just across the commercial square and it gave him an idea.

Most libraries had free internet access. Maybe it was time to see what was in the news.

The library was a cool contrast to the outside heat. He approached the front desk, adopting an apologetic smile for the two older ladies behind the counter. "Might there be a computer here that I could use to check my e-mail?" he softly inquired. "My mother has been ill and while I am on the road I need to check up on her."

"Yes," one of the ladies answered. "We have six computers at that table over there," she pointed to the center of the library. "Just sign your name in this registration book and there will be no charge, unless you want to make copies."

"Thank you very much," JuJu replied, adding "I won't need any copies." After writing a name into the book, he pulled out a heavy, wooden chair and sat down in front of a computer at the furthest end of the table, away from the front doors. He googled the Cleveland Plain Dealer newspaper and the Channel 19 Cleveland news station to see if he was mentioned. Nothing. Good! Next he checked back to the date three days prior to leaving Cleveland. Not so great. He was in many reports.

One of them quoted a "law enforcement official" who stated that DEA Chief Charles Goetz and an un-named Cleveland detective were enroute to Florida on a manhunt for the Dickens Avenue killer. It further revealed that voodoo markings were found on the four dead bodies and other occult items were found at the scene.

Damn! That meant Silvano was on his trail. He had to get back to Trinidad-Tobago now! The only way to out of the Florida Keys was by boat or airplane. There was a pilot he had met a couple years ago when he was guarding the Cartel's shipments from South America. What was his name......Mark.....Max.....Marshall! That was it. Marshall was an ex-heroin user who traded one addiction for another – alcohol. Most of the time he was drunk but he knew how to fly a plane and remain undetected by law enforcement. He had to find Marshall. Hopefully, before Silvano arrived in Florida.

JuJu created a new Google Gmail account, e-mailed his friend Gerard in Trinidad, and asked for an immediate response. JuJu and Gerard had grown up together in the slums of Trinidad-Tobago; they were partners in crime. JuJu knew Gerard's BlackBerry seldom left his palm as it was the lifeline to his drug business.

JuJu only used cell phones when absolutely necessary – he had a healthy respect that the technology was available to track him if the authorities knew he had a phone. He wasn't worried about e-mail; there was no way the police could connect the two men. Even if they somehow tracked his childhood friend down and traced the IP address back to the computer in the Key Largo library he was using, he would be long gone before they figured it out.

Gerard responded almost immediately with an email. "Dude, where you at?"

JuJu typed in one of the phone numbers of the newly purchased cell phones and instructed Gerard to call it, then exited the email account and answered the ringing cell phone despite the "No Cell Phones" sign posted on a nearby wall.

"Dude, where are you?" his friend repeated.

"Ah you know 'mon – here and there," JuJu replied, being deliberately cagey. He kept his voice low. "Do you know how to contact that pilot, Marshall?"

"Sure," Gerard replied. "He be in the Florida Keys somewhere, probably drunk. Why, you got some business man? You know you can count on me!"

JuJu had used Gerard to help him rob an unsuspecting buyer last year of his six kilos of cocaine he had just bought from the Mexicans. Then, just to be sure the man couldn't complain to the Mexican sellers, JuJu killed him. "Naw, man," replied JuJu. "I got some people asking about using him to fly some pot in from Texas. Get me a number for him, yes?"

"How do I get the info to you dude, call this number?"

JuJu told Gerard to call the same number. "And mon," he said, "do not mention this call to anyone!"

"It's cool," answered Gerard. He understood exactly what JuJu was saying to him and also knew that it wouldn't be healthy for him to ignore his instructions. Childhood friend or not – JuJu was a dangerous man.

"Later," said JuJu. He punched End Call, then the off button.

JuJu thanked the two women at the front desk as he left the Monroe County Library. "We're glad we could be of help Mr....." she paused to look at the register, "Mr. Silvano. We do hope your mother will be alright."

JuJu went to the pay phone on the corner and called the local taxi company. He had to limit his cell phone use as much as possible to lower the possibility of the Feds tracing his calls. Within a few minutes of the call, a cab arrived. Knowing that the cabbie probably accepted kickbacks from local establishments wanting more business, JuJu asked him if he could recommend any quiet motels. For incentive, he placed a fifty dollar bill into the cabbie's hand and watched as it disappeared into the man's rumpled shirt pocket.

"Sure," answered the driver. He had the typical dark, leathery skin that came from spending a lifetime in the South Florida sun. His black baseball Bass Pro Shops cap was incapable of covering a straggly mass of overgrown gray hair and the cap looked like it was in danger of sliding off his head. The driver spoke briefly into the mike and hit the meter.

"What kind of place you looking for? We got thousand dollar a night places and twenty buck a night dives, what's your pleasure?" said the driver, eager to demonstrate his knowledge.

"Just someplace clean with food nearby," replied JuJu.

"Got just the place down the road in Marathon, but it's almost fifty miles." He glanced in the rearview mirror at JuJu. "That gonna be okay with you?"

"Yes, that will be fine." JuJu settled into the back seat, still grasping his backpack. His future was packed inside.

Traffic was light and JuJu was dozing when he felt the cab slow and then stop at a small motel and restaurant just off the road by a bridge. A gas station was just across the road.

"This will do," said JuJu. He paid the one hundred and eighteen dollar fare by giving the driver a hundred and forty dollars. "Keep the change. Do you have a direct number in case I don't want to call your office?" JuJu suspected the grizzled driver could prove to be invaluable to him for transportation and information.

"Yep," the cabbie said. He reached into his shirt pocket and pulled out a card with nothing but a hand-printed phone number on it. "Name's Clyde. You call me direct."

JuJu entered the small lobby of the aging one-story building. The female clerk sitting in the office was watching a small television set and was startled by the man standing at the counter. She hadn't even heard the door chime. "Sorry Sir, I didn't hear you come in. What can I do for you?"

JuJu remarked that a cab driver had recommended the motel and before he could say anything else she interrupted, "Oh – you're the one Clyde called about. How long are you staying?"

"I don't know yet," JuJu answered her as he looked around suspiciously. He must have been asleep in the back seat of the cab when Clyde had called to inform her of his arrival. JuJu pulled out a wad of cash and told the clerk his identification had been stolen. "Can I give you a little extra for your trouble?" he asked placing two one-hundred dollar bills onto the counter.

"Clyde said you were a good customer," she said as she pushed a registration book toward him. "Just sign your name here," she pointed to a page with the current date. She glanced at the name and handed him a room key without any further questions. "Have a nice stay, Mr. Silvano."

Chapter 28

N ick Silvano and Charley Goetz had been in Miami for almost forty-eight hours before they accumulated enough information to begin their manhunt.

"The two Jamaicans thought JuJu might be from Trinidad-Tobago," Goetz said to the six men assembled in the Miami DEA office. "They were eager to talk and we heard it all - from their first encounter with JuJu in Miami a couple years ago to the Dickens Avenue killings. Homicide tried to put them at the scene on Dickens Avenue but the evidence wasn't there and they denied being there. There were no charges to hold them on and we had to let them go. Word is now they're in the wind. We still don't have full identification on JuJu," Goetz continued, "but we think that he's somewhere in the Keys trying to get to Trinidad. He bought a bus ticket for Key West and was headed there before the FBI screwed up. Make no mistake – this man is ruthless and intelligent!"

The briefing room was silent as the Miami agents absorbed the details. Goetz held up a photo and Silvano passed copies around to them. "This is a photo of him when he was booked in Cleveland. He's using an American Express card that belonged to a Moon

DeBoissiere. We think he stole it from his brother who was murdered in Canada during a drug deal. JuJu was last seen on the Florida Turnpike a couple days ago after he fled off a Greyhound bus. An alert is out on the credit card so if he uses it, we'll pick it up. But I'm not holding my breath. This guy is one sharp bastard. He won't use it unless he absolutely has to."

One of the agents raised his finger.

"Yeah," Goetz acknowledged. "You got something to add?"

"We have an informant here in Florida who told us the Mexicans are looking for somebody who ripped them off for almost two million in cocaine. Maybe this is the same guy. We can circle back with him – see if he has any more information."

"Okay," Goetz said. "Check it out. The rest of us are going to start at the top of the Keys in Key Largo and shop this photo everywhere we can. Maybe we'll get lucky. I don't want him spooked into doing something stupid. He might be feeling comfortable and safe enough now to hunker down somewhere. My plan is to get him in custody and off the streets before he hurts anybody else.

"Detective Silvano here knows him on sight. He arrested him in Cleveland for drug charges before we knew he was good for the murders. The FBI lost him twice. The less noise we make searching for him the better our chances of avoiding interference from other agencies, or worse, like having armed citizens looking for him. Those rednecks in the Keys could be more dangerous than JuJu!"

"You got that right," said one of the Miami DEA Agents.

"We'll start at first light," Goetz declared.

JuJu was indeed "hunkered down" as DEA Agent Goetz had suspected, but not because he felt safe. JuJu was suspicious and careful. The small, Marathon, Florida motel would be adequate for a couple days at the most. He had food nearby at the gas station and if he stayed in his room and came out only when necessary, he could make it until he heard back from Gerard about the pilot.

Now that he wasn't running, the early tremors of need returned. He knew the signs; his body was at an internal boil that only heroin could cool. If he didn't get a fix soon, the physical stress could drive him to do something that would ruin everything he had accomplished so far.

He vowed to Ogun, *If you get me through this and get me back home, I swear I will kick this drug and become even more faithful!* Since the only people he knew were the cabbie and the motel clerk, the cab driver seemed to be the most logical choice for what he needed; cabbies were plugged into their environment; they knew everything. He used the payphone at the street corner adjacent to the motel and dialed the number on the card. When Clyde answered, JuJu asked if he could meet him at the motel. "Sure I can," he replied. "You make it worth my while?"

In JuJu's current state of need, the man's reply made

him angry. Maybe he shouldn't have tipped him so well the first time. He paused before replying just to make sure he had his temper under control. "It will be well worth your while, just don't say anything to anybody and come alone."

"I'll be there in thirty," Clyde said. "I just dropped off a fare in Islamorada and it'll take me that long to head back your way."

JuJu sat in a plastic chair just outside his motel room and watched the sun disappear into the Gulf of Mexico sky while he waited for Clyde. The air was oppressively hot and humid but it felt like home. *I'm so close!*

Behind the motel's tight grove of Mangrove trees, the plunks and plops of swamp predators slipping into the dark waters to hunt prey among the twisted mangrove roots hovered just above human hearing levels. While most guests never even registered these sounds, other predators, including those on two legs, recognized them for what they were. JuJu had picked the motel, in part, for the natural barricade the mangrove swamp provided. It was unlikely he would be surprised by anyone circling the motel the back way as the only things that lived back there were alligators and snakes; no sane person would be foolish to enter them, in the night or the light of day.

Clyde arrived as promised and JuJu slipped into the back of the cab. He placed two hundred dollars into the cabbie's hand and said, "I need some heroin, can you get that for me?"

"Usually it's women and booze," the driver said. "I

know somebody who can get what you want, but you gotta come with me."

"Why do you need me?" JuJu demanded, his suspicions aroused. What if he had traveled all this way, with all this money, just to get busted in some small-town sting to catch vacationers trying to score a dime?

Clyde seemed oblivious to JuJu's concerns. "I ain't no dope man, mister. I wouldn't know heroin from sugar and I don't need you pissed at me if I get ripped off."

JuJu's instinct told him to remain at the sanctuary of the motel, but his gnawing need for the drug overrode common sense. He was beginning to break down physically. The tremors came in waves and he never knew when the next one would hit. "Okay," he said. "Let's do this."

The cab driver went south on Florida Highway One into the City of Marathon, passing the private Marathon Airport and a large hangar named The Jet Center. JuJu observed several rows of private planes tethered onto the tarmac. Maybe he could rent a plane and fly out of Florida. He started to ask Clyde if he knew anything about renting planes but then changed his mind. He could find out himself. No need to leave clues in case the cops started flashing his picture at the cab companies. The growing need for heroin was making him careless, but he was under Ogun's protection, which was more powerful than any drug. He would have never seen the private airport if he hadn't gone with Clyde.

Clyde turned left into a Kmart parking lot which was part of a small shopping center and stopped in front of a bar called the Copper Dog. Clyde told him to wait in the cab and he would be right back. In any other circumstance, that alone would have made JuJu incredibly nervous. But his heroin craving and faith in his voodoo beliefs all but erased those fears.

A few minutes later, Clyde exited the bar with another man. The pair talked briefly, then the man approached the cab, opened the front door, and leaned in. "You the guy who wants some smack? Clyde here don't want to touch the stuff," he said, nodding his head back at the cabbie, "but that makes no never mind to me. They call me Bobby G. I can hook you up. You got any money?"

JuJu was furious with the cabbie for fronting him off to the dealer, but again, his need was greater than his anger. "Give me what you got, mon," JuJu gave a clipped reply. Skinny white dude looked like he just crawled out of a ditch. Bobby G's shirt was dirty and torn and he had meth-head teeth, black and broken. The dealer pulled a zippered leather bag out from a side pocket of his ragged cargo pants and held it out to JuJu. It contained several wrapped packages of white powder.

"You don't want all of this, do you man? 'Cause it's gonna cost you eight thousand dollars if you do," remarked the dealer.

JuJu was impressed by the amount of heroin offered by what he had assumed was a homeless derelict.

"Not what you expected, right?" said the drug dealer. "This is good shit."

JuJu eyed him up and down and then said, "I will take half of what you got." He counted out four thousand dollars and handed it out the window to Bobby G. The cash disappeared into a different pocket. "You got any guns?"

"I don't leave home without one!" the dealer joked, pointing to his waistband while backing away suspiciously from the car window.

JuJu spoke quietly and carefully; he didn't want to spook the dealer into thinking he was about to be robbed. "I want to buy it from you. Will you take another thousand?"

"Hey man, you don't even know what kind of gun it is and you want to buy it? Are you a cop or somethin'? You know what – keep your money. Hell, keep the drugs too! I'm walkin'," he said, turning to leave.

"Wait!" JuJu exclaimed. "I am not law enforcement. As a matter of fact, I am wanted by the police and need a weapon to defend myself. Look – I'll give you another two thousand for your gun."

The drug dealer stopped and stared at the big man in the back of the cab. Dude didn't look like any cops he knew. The Marathon County Sheriff could have brought in a ringer from another county, but this man gave off a vibe Bobby G knew well; hunger tinged with barely contained desperation topped off with a dash of menace.

"All right," he said. "Clyde vouched for you so maybe

you ain't a cop. But just to be on the safe side, I will give Clyde the gun after you give him the two grand. I will be in the bar. I still don't trust you and I don't need you pulling my own gun on me and taking back the dope, money, and the gun. It's a nice Beretta 9 mm and I hate to see it go, but I'll get another one."

Bobby G instructed Clyde to get the money from JuJu and bring it to him in the bar, and then he would give Clyde the gun. "I ain't made for this kind of shit," Clyde balked, backing away and holding his hands up. "I'm just an old man trying to make ends meet and live to see another day."

He started to say more but JuJu cut him off. "Okay old man, there's another hundred in it for you."

"I'll throw in another hundred too," Bobby G said. He turned to JuJu and said, "Nothing personal man, just that I don't trust anybody!"

They both looked at Clyde. "Alright, I'll do it but I don't want any trouble," he said while simultaneously holding out a hand to each man to receive his money.

The old cabbie followed the drug dealer into the crowded bar and came out holding a paper bag. He climbed into the front seat of his cab and turned and handed the bag to JuJu. "Here ya go," he said and turned the ignition key. "Where to now?"

"Take me back to the motel," replied JuJu. He tore open a bag of heroin, anticipating the immediate release it would provide, his promise to Ogun forgotten.

Chapter 29

T he morning traffic on Florida Highway One outside the motel was loud and woke JuJu shortly after sunrise. He washed up and walked across the
four lane highway to the Speedway Gas station, purchased two breakfast biscuits and coffee, then sat
outside his motel room and devoured the breakfast. He
felt at ease for the first time in days. His mind was clear
and the boiling in his stomach was gone. Time to make
his final plans. He abandoned caution and called
Gerard on his cell phone. "You find Marshall yet?" JuJu
asked.

"Yes. And he needs money," replied Gerard. "Where
and when do you want to meet him?"

"Give me his number," JuJu said. "I'll contact him
myself."

Marshall's contact number was a bar in the Florida
Keys. According to Gerard, Marshall drank up all of his
money and didn't even have a cell phone. "He said to
tell the barmaid your phone number and he will call
right back."

"One additional thing," said JuJu.

"What's that."

"I plan to fly into Trinidad and will need you to pick
me up at the Camden Airfield outside of Couva," said

JuJu. The Couva airfield was just thirty miles from Port of Spain, Trinidad and was the primary point of transportation for workers bound for the oil fields of Venezuela. "You need to be there when I land."

"When?" Gerard asked.

"Maybe a couple of days, no longer than that I hope. Just keep your phone close and be ready to move quickly."

"You got it, old friend." Gerard frowned after the call was disconnected. "JuJu still has the power over me," he whispered. He'd always done what JuJu wanted – it'd been that way ever since they were kids.

Chapter 30

JuJu was in a dangerous mood. He dialed the phone number for the Jamaicans, daring anybody to listen in.

"Hello, who is this?" Tion asked, his soft voice tainted with suspicion.

"You know who this is! I understand you've been talking your way out of trouble by telling the police about me, is that true?" he asked, fishing for information.

"What do you mean?" replied Tion, panicked.

"You are not in jail and you still have the cell phone I gave you," JuJu stated. "The only possible reason you are not in jail is that you are cooperating with the authorities."

"No JuJu, we ain't said nuthin' man, that's the truth!" he stammered.

"You be lying man, I know things. An Obeah man see all, know all," JuJu said to the terrified Jamaican. "Where is Darik, is he there with you?" JuJu demanded in his deep dialect.

"Yes JuJu, he is with me. We got out of jail after the Police said we could go if we told them about you. We were scared mon, you left us sitting there and we didn't know what to do! What you want us to do?

Anything you say, we will do." Tion's pleading became a whisper. He knew the Obeah man could find him anywhere.

"I want you to do two things," JuJu said, "If they are not done exactly as I ask, you and your friend will be eternally damned!" I will turn you over to Legba myself and you will serve him in the eternal dark world!"

"Anything," Tion repeated. "We are at your service!"

JuJu gave his instructions to Tion. "You do as I say and then wait for my call,"

It was almost noon when JuJu placed a call to Marshall at the number Gerard gave him. "Copper Dog!" a woman's voice barked.

"Is Marshall there?" JuJu asked.

"Hold on."

He could hear the barmaid yelling out, "Marshall! Get your skinny ass over here to the phone. If this call is about money, you better pay up your bar tab right away cause I can't carry you any longer after today."

After about a minute JuJu heard a wary voice, "This is Marshall."

"This is JuJu. You got time for some work?"

"Yeah, man," the pilot answered. "What you got in mind?"

"Not over the phone," said JuJu. "You got a car?"

"I can borrow one," Marshall answered. "Where you want to meet?"

JuJu spoke carefully, not knowing if the pilot was already drunk. "Do you know where the Speedway Gas Station is in Marathon at Mile Marker 51?"

"Yeah."

"Meet me there at nine tonight. Come alone. You better be sober, understand?"

"Okay. You gonna have any money for me?"

"You show up on time, and sober, and we will see," answered JuJu.

Everything was coming together. JuJu took a long line of heroin then laid back onto the shoddy mattress using his cash-filled backpack as a pillow and closed his eyes. Two hours later, the cheap plastic alarm clock buzzed loudly, jolting him from a deep, drug-induced sleep. He awoke with half-formed memories of bizarre dreams of faceless African warriors killing and maiming people. "Obeah - give me the soul of the warrior who defeats his enemies!" he whispered over and over, each time raising his voice until he found himself almost shouting.

Refreshed, he assumed his waiting spot in the plastic chair outside his room door and swatted the bugs that swarmed over his head. From there he could see the gas station across Florida's Highway One where he would meet Marshall. The backpack rested on the concrete sidewalk beside the chair. He absently reached a hand down and patted its front pocket, feeling the outline of the 9 mm Beretta.

Shortly before nine o'clock, a beat up, brown Kia van pull into the gas station and parked on the side of the building. After watching Marshall exit the van and walk inside the station, JuJu picked up his backpack, crossed the highway, and slipped into the van's back seat.

Five minutes later, the driver's door opened and the pilot climbed in and sat behind the wheel without noticing his new passenger. "Hello, Marshall," JuJu spoke quietly, his voice startling the pilot.

"Holy shit, JuJu, don't do that to me! I almost had a frigging heart attack!" Marshall exclaimed, turning around to look at his passenger.

"You should be more aware of your surroundings, Marshall," JuJu told him. "Are you sure you have not been drinking? You have the smell of alcohol about you."

"Honest JuJu, I ain't had nothin' since I talked to you on the phone this morning. I had to borrow this ride from a guy at the bar and I'm supposed to fill up the gas tank. You got any money man?"

JuJu was silent and didn't answer right away. *Maybe this was a mistake.* "I don't want you drinking or acting in such a manner that will bring any attention to you or to me. I have money for you, but you'll get it only after we conclude our business, understand?"

The pilot nodded. "Yeah, I get it. I just came on to bad times since I seen you last. I gambled away all the money I had at the Hard Rock up in Miami. Been drinking too much. But you know I'm the best damned pilot around these parts. I can put a plane down on a dime. Remember the trip from Columbia last year? I zipped that load into the Glades and nobody ever saw us, remember that?"

"I do, Marshall," said JuJu. "That is why I wanted to find you." JuJu reached into his shirt pocket and took out some cash, "Here is two hundred dollars. Fill up the tank and keep the rest for now. Let's go for a ride."

Marshall started the van and pulled up to the gas pumps. Before he could start pumping gas, he had to go back inside and prepay. *Jeez – can't a guy even pump gas without prepaying? They don't trust anybody!* After filling the tank, the pilot pulled the van out onto the four lane highway headed south to Key West. He felt like shit and knew why. His five-foot-six inch frame was already beginning to tremble from the lack of alcohol.

He drove carefully to compensate for his trembles. Unlike other people JuJu usually encountered, Marshall wasn't afraid of him. He viewed JuJu as a way to make quick money so he could get back to his favorite hobbies; gambling and drinking. He didn't believe in any of that voodoo crap. Marshall's prowess as a pilot was well known to the drug players in South Florida. Despite his alcohol-related offenses, he managed to remain off the local law enforcement's radar where drug connections were concerned. His ratty choice of clothing and aged sixty-five year old tanned and lined face gave no visible credence to the fact that he was a very able pilot and drug transporter, and not just another retired guy living the Jimmy Buffet lifestyle.

As they were about to pass the Marathon Airport entrance, JuJu told him, "Pull over into the parking lot of the airport here." JuJu saw a number of small aircraft tethered on the other side of a high cyclone fence separating the parking lot and the planes. The lighting was dim and the lot appeared empty of people. "You have any access to a plane?" JuJu inquired.

"How big and what are we going to use it for?" Marshall answered with his own question.

"I need you to fly me to Trinidad-Tobago. This is not a drug run," he lied. "But it needs to be done very quietly."

"Well," responded Marshall, "I don't have any connections that will let me just have their plane. The Mexicans always had one of theirs for me to fly. You want me to try and rent one or something like that?" he asked.

"What about just taking a plane," JuJu asked. "Like one of those," he said pointing at the parked aircraft.

"I suppose it could be done but some of the newer ones are hard to take. We would have to find something older like a Cessna 172. But it wouldn't make it all the way to Trinidad-Tobago without refueling stops along the way. That's almost 1,700 miles," Marshall noted.

"If you want to make some serious money, you will have to come up with a plane to take me there, "JuJu stated.

A car entered the parking lot and pulled up to the driver's side where Marshall was sitting. JuJu was relieved to see that it was not a Sheriff's car, but was still wary.

"What are you guys doing here?" the man driving the car asked. "This airport is closed."

"We were just looking," Marshall answered back.

"Can you give me any information about maybe renting a plane?"

"No dude, I work here and just stopped to get some ice from the hanger. You'll have to come back tomorrow, alright?"

"Sure, no problem," replied Marshall.

JuJu watched the employee use a gate card and then proceed onto the tarmac with his car. He thought about taking the man's card but decided it was too risky to make a move until he had all of his plans in place. Do not become impatient, he reminded himself. "Let's go before he comes back."

"Good idea," the pilot agreed, and started up the van. "Where to?"

"Is the place that you frequent close to here?"

"Yeah," Marshall replied. He never could get quite used to JuJu's way of speaking. One minute the guy could sound like any native street guy and the next like he was from the upper crust of England. What did they teach them in Trinidad anyway?

"I could use a drink," JuJu said. "Let's go pay your bar bill and I will buy you a couple of drinks. Then we have to figure out how to get a plane. But first I need to contact some associates."

"Fine with me," Marshall said, turning the van right onto the four lane divided Highway One.

JuJu's cell phone rang. "Yes," he answered. "Is the task completed?"

"Yes JuJu, we have done what you have asked," Tion said. "What do you want us to do now?"

"Just wait until I call you again. It should be not much longer now, maybe another day. Remember, your lives will depend upon following my instructions!"

Marshall only went a short distance before turning left into a parking lot adjacent to a Kmart and parked the Kia van. "We're here," he said.

This was the same bar where Clyde had taken him to meet Bobby G. "This is where you go?" he asked Marshall.

"Yeah," Marshall replied, "The Copper Dog. Been here since the prohibition days. We got millionaires and homeless people sitting next to each other on barstools. People in here keep to their business and I know all of them," he boasted. "Everybody who grew up in the Keys was either a smuggler or knows one! Don't get many black guys in here though, but if you're with me it will be fine. I been coming here for thirty years. If we need to get a plane, this is the place to find one."

JuJu was apprehensive and almost said no to Marshall's offer to go in but knew it was becoming very late in the game for him. He was responsible for four murders, a major drug heist – from the Mexicans no less - and was carrying around a backpack stuffed with millions of dollars. Yes - Marshall-the-pilot was his last chip in the game and his only hope of getting back to Trinidad.

"Okay, mon." JuJu picked up his backpack and followed the pilot into the bar.

Chapter 31

T he Dog was crowded and a band played loudly – hits from the '70's. JuJu and Marshall ordered their drinks from Mary, the owner of the bar. She gave Marshall a wary look that transformed into a rough smile after he produced cash to settle his bar bill.

Every bar stool was occupied with a mix of locals as well as tourists. Three barmaids hustled between the bar and tables, letting bottle caps drop to the floor as bottles were opened. "Wait here a minute," Marshall said. JuJu watched him push through the crowd, then stop to talk to a couple men. Intent on keeping an eye on the pilot, he didn't notice the dope man, Bobby G, watching him from across the bar. The dealer had an upcoming drug case in the Monroe County Courts and had been supplying information to the authorities to avoid prison. Bobby G slipped out the bar's door to the parking lot and placed a call to his police contact.

"Detective Murphy?" he asked when his call was answered.

"Yeah, this is Larry Murphy, who is this?"

"Bobby G here Detective, remember me? I'm the guy who gave you those Cubans last month that were bringing in the bales of weed onto Sugarloaf Key."

"I remember you Bobby. That was good information.

We got your case tossed out in exchange right? Everything go okay with that?"

"Yeah, it went away just like you promised. Uh, I caught another one for possession last week in Key West. I think I might have something for you in trade to make that case go away if you're interested."

"That depends," replied the Detective, "What do you have for me?"

"I'm at the Dog and this big black guy came in with a drug pilot named Marshall. I know the black guy has heroin and a gun on him and he's carrying a backpack full of something, might be dope, I don't know for sure but he keeps a tight grip on it."

Detective Murphy had received an alert from the Miami DEA just that morning asking for any information on a person fitting that description. This might be his lucky break! He told Bobby G to hold on and placed a call to the Miami DEA office from another line.

"This is DEA Agent Morales, how can I help you?"

"Hey Morales, this is Detective Larry Murphy from the Monroe County Sheriff's Office. Are you the one who sent out the BOLO on a fugitive from Cleveland?'

"Yes," replied the agent.

"I believe the person you're looking for is in our jurisdiction."

Detective Murphy got back on the line with his informant and instructed Bobby G to "stay put" in the parking lot until he got there. Bobby G heard the excitement in the detective's voice and he knew this might work out in his favor. Inside the bar, JuJu watched as Marshall became heavily engaged in conversation with a man who looked like a tourist. He wore baggy tan pants and a loud turquoise and white flowered shirt. A blue captain's hat sat slightly askew atop a bald head the graying tufts could no longer camouflage. His face was lined and deeply tanned, identifying him as a man who was used to a leisurely lifestyle. Marshall shook the man's hand, then made his way through the bar crowd back to JuJu, giving him a "thumbs up" sign as he approached.

"The guy I talked to has a plane. He used to have money but has had some hard times lately and could use some cash, so he's agreeable to renting his plane. It's parked at the Marathon Airport and ready to go, but it's going to cost us a lot!"

"How much?" JuJu asked. He was getting very anxious and just wanted to leave.

"The guy wants $10,000 cash and a deposit of $80,000 in case we lose it or crash. It's an old C-47 Gooney Bird like I learned to fly on back in Vietnam - it's perfect for us. It may even make it to Trinidad non-stop. The plan has extra fuel tanks for longer trips. We just got to fill 'em up before we leave." This was good news to JuJu. If they could complete the flight without stopping, there was less chance of the authorities finding them.

"If I have to," Marshall continued, "I got a spot in Grenada I can drop into in an emergency. But the guy wants to speak to you first. Probably to see the money."

"Bring him over to me," JuJu instructed. Marshall made his way back to the plane's owner, whispered into his ear, and led him to JuJu. The man was obviously drunk and had trouble forming his words.

"John Archibald, former Monroe County Judge," the man said, extending his hand to JuJu. "But you can call me Judge!" He swayed a bit from the alcohol he'd already consumed and JuJu took half a step back. "I understand you need my plane for a vayyycation purpose," he said with a wink. "Did Marrrsh here explain the cost to you?" he asked, the pilot's name coming out as a long slur.

JuJu refrained from shaking the man's hand and answered, "Yes, it is no problem. When can we leave?"

Marshall interrupted them, and grabbed the former Judge's arm, "Archibald, do you have the gate key fob with you and can you get someone to the airport to top off the tanks?"

"You want to go right now?" asked the Judge. "What's your hurry? How about a couple more drinks first? I'll buy."

"Right now or it is no deal," JuJu answered for Marshall.

"Okay, if you insist. I have to call the airport's owner to get somebody to gas her up first."

"Do it," said JuJu.

Archibald went outside to use his cell phone. JuJu didn't trust the man. A former judge? "C'mon Marshall, let's go!"

"Can't we just finish our drinks?" Marshall asked,

looking at the full glass sitting on the bar. "He's just making a call – don't worry about him."

"Now!" JuJu commanded and headed toward the door into the parking lot of the bar.

After a few minutes of quiet conversation the Judge turned to JuJu and told him that Mark, the Marathon's Airport owner, was calling one of his workers to meet them. "I need cash for the gas," he said. "My credit with Mark is a little over extended at present."

"All in hundred dollar bills," JuJu assured the man. "Let's go now."

"Okay," the Judge said. "Maybe I can get back in time for a last call drink!"

"Maybe you will Judge, maybe you will," JuJu said.

Chapter 32

Silvano and Goetz left Miami before sunrise and headed south toward Homestead where the Florida turnpike ended. "Got to beat the rush hour traffic," said Goetz weaving the black Dodge Challenger through the early morning traffic. Nick's cell phone rang, belting out the theme song from Hawaii Five-O that identified the caller as one of his partners.

"You're up early," he said by way of greeting.

Frank Hartness replied, "I don't want to be, but Tina from the Captain's Quarters called the Narcotics Unit a little bit ago and asked for you. She told the office man that her barmaid Kat never showed for her shift last night." Nick sat up straighter in the car seat.

"The office man called me. He knows you're out of town on a case. I called Tina back and she wanted me to call you 'cause she saw your Honda in the Marina parking lot and she went to your boat, but no one was there. I didn't tell her you were in Florida looking for a murder suspect," he paused. "You got any ideas where Kat might be?"

"Not really," Nick answered. "Call Tina back, get Kat's address and go check on her, will you Frank? It's not like her to miss a shift or not call in."

"Will do," said Frank.

"Keep me posted."

"What was that about?" Goetz asked his comrade.

"Nothing really," said Nick. "At least I hope it's nothing."

Nick had never given much thought about his relationship with Kat. In the fifteen years since he and Cheryl divorced, Nick's Italian charm and easy-going style had attracted many women; dating was never a problem. But he never got close to any of them. He rationalized that the job kept him from having anybody in his life on a permanent basis. But Frank's call shook him. He was genuinely concerned.

Goetz exited the turnpike lanes and turned left into the Service Plaza, parking in front of a Burger King restaurant. "I gotta piss and get a cup of coffee. You want me to bring you a cup?"

"No thanks," Nick answered.

While Goetz was in Burger King, Nick dialed Kat's cell phone. No answer. He waited for the voicemail beep "Hey Kat, give me a call when you get this message."

When Goetz returned they continued the hundred mile trip to the Florida Keys just as the sun was coming up. "What's the plan, Chuck?" Nick asked.

"We start by showing JuJu's picture around at gas stations and hotels. Probably we should include cabs and buses too. Maybe he hitched a ride or rented a car to get here - if he is even here at all."

"He's got to be here," Nick said. "The Greyhound bus ticket was punched for here and from what those two Jamaican guys said, the man's on a mission to get back to Trinidad."

"I'm bothered that those two guys got out before we could talk to them," Goetz said. "Something doesn't smell right."

"Agreed," Nick said. "They had to be with JuJu on Dickens."

"Four people murdered by one dude? He'd have to be some sort of superman or something to pull that off," Goetz said.

"Yeah," Nick agreed. "I don't care how 'bad' he is – the guy had to have help. Those two are just trying to save their own asses by saying JuJu did it by himself."

The two men exited the Florida turnpike and pushed south on the two lane Florida Highway One, traversing the twenty-four miles in silence until they crossed the Jewfish Bridge. Nick contemplated what they would do when they found the fugitive. *I should just put a bullet into the prick. Should have done it two months ago at the Marina.* His thoughts kept returning to Kat. *Keep your head in the game, Silvano!*

Goetz pulled into the first gas station and showed JuJu's picture to the attendants. Nick did the same at the fast food joint. After several hours of talking to people, they had still had nothing.

"Christ, Charley," Nick said as he wiped the sweat from his brow and turned up the air conditioning in the car. "This is going to take forever!"

"Yeah," Goetz agreed. "But it's all we have at this point."

It was getting late, and the two decided to stop and

check into a hotel for the night. They settled on a nice room in the Cheeca Lodge & Spa across from the Bass Pro Shops and The Islamorada Fish Company restaurant. After a good meal at the Fish Company and a couple of drinks, they called it a day. Morning would arrive soon enough.

"Maybe something else will turn up by then," Goetz tried to assure the Cleveland Narcotics Detective.

When Nick settled into his room he called his partners to see if any news on Kat had surfaced.

"Nothing, Nick," reported Lenny Moore. "We checked her apartment in Lakewood and went back to the Captain's Quarters and got more information from Tina. Her car is in the marina parking lot. I got a bad feeling about this Nick."

"I do too," Nick confided to his partner. "Keep looking. There's nothing I can do from here. Call me the minute you hear something."

"You got it! Any leads on JuJu?" asked Lenny.

"Not yet. Lots of legwork but we just gotta keep plugging along - you know how it is." Nick thought for a moment. "You got the location of those two Jamaicans narcing JuJu out? Me and Goetz were thinking that they have lots more to answer for in the Dickens Avenue murders."

"Yeah – that's what Frank was thinking too," Lenny answered.

A loud pounding on the door startled Nick.

"What's going on?" Lenny asked.

"I don't know, hold on," Nick responded.

Nick opened the door to find Charley shaking his car keys.

"Jesus, Charley," Nick exclaimed. "I already told you I didn't have any beer in here. What do you want?"

"C'mon Nick, got a call from the Miami office. JuJu's been spotted in Marathon and a Monroe County Sheriff's Detective is on his way to grab him."

"Gotta run, Lenny," Nick spoke into the phone while gathering his things. "Might be home sooner than we thought!"

Chapter 33

Monroe County Detective Larry Murphy roared in- to the Copper Dog's parking lot in his white county Ford Taurus, not knowing what to expect other than he hoped to collar an "FBI most wanted" suspect. It would be a big feather in his cap. A full moon hung heavy over the Keys that night. Its white light slid over the cars in the bar's parking lot, casting box- shaped shadows across the asphalt. The parking lot was full, which was typical for a "Dog Band Nite" and Murphy looked for the Kia van Bobby G had described, but it was nowhere to be seen.

He continued cruising the lot with his lights off when Bobby G jumped in front of the car and pounded on the hood. "They just left, all three of them!"

Murphy reached over and unlocked the passenger door of the unmarked Ford. "Get in!" he yelled.

Bobby G jumped in and pointed north in the direction of the highway. "That way, they went that way!"

Detective Murphy pushed the gas pedal all the way to the floor. The car's tires spewed gravel and dark colored shards of broken beer bottles. The detective turned on the siren and made the flashing grill lights visible to the drivers in front of him to "get out of my way."

Marshall had the Kia maintaining the speed limit of 35 miles an hour and stayed in the right lane of Florida Highway One, still within the city limits of Marathon. It was only a couple of miles to the Marathon Airport where retired Judge John Archibald's C-47 Gooney Bird was parked.

"Judge, what is the fuel capacity of your plane?" Marshall asked.

"My plane was built in 1943 as a C-53 and later modified to a C-47," the Judge explained. He seemed to have sobered up some since they left the bar. "Normally it holds between 800 to 850 gallons of fuel but I put an extra tank on it to make a total fuel load of almost a thousand gallons. You're going to burn about fifty gallons an hour per engine."

"How far can I make it on a full fuel load?" Marshall asked.

"Maybe 1,200 miles on the regular fuel load but with the extra 200 gallon tank you might go 1,600 or 1,700 miles if you tooled around with the engines, but not at full power. Where are you taking my bird?" he asked Marshall.

Marshall looked at JuJu.

"You are going to make a lot of money, Judge. Do not ask any more questions," JuJu told the man. The tone of his voice and grave expression had the Judge second guessing the deal he had just made. The drinks he'd so heartily consumed just hours before now sought escape through the pores of his skin; the alcohol and the happy evaporating. *Holy Christ!* Maybe he'd made a mistake saying he'd rent his plane to this man. But he knew Marshall, everyone knew Marshall on Marathon. Did he let his own desperate need for cash cloud his judgment? Ha – judgment – that's a good one. He was questioning his. The trio pulled left off of Florida Highway One and into the dark entrance to the now closed Marathon Airport.

"Pull up to the gate there," the Judge said, pointing to the entrance. He pulled out a gate card from his pocket and handed it to Marshall. The pilot swiped the card through the electronic sensor and the gate rolled open, allowing the Kia entrance to the airport property.

"Where's your bird?" Marshall asked.

The Judge pointed toward a large twin engine airplane sitting on the tarmac that had "Ozark Air Lines" painted across the fuselage. "There it is. Ain't it a beauty? You got my money now?" he said to JuJu.

"Here is $10,000 now and the rest will be given to you when the plane is running and we are ready to leave," JuJu said as he counted out ten thousand dollars cash and handed it to the Judge.

Archibald quickly snatched the money from the big man. "Look, George is coming up with the fuel truck. You'll have to pay him out of your money for the extra two hundred gallons, agreed?"

"Agreed," JuJu said. He got out of the Kia van with his backpack and watched George's advance, ready to bolt if this was a trap. George pulled the fuel truck slowly up to the airplane and applied the airbrakes, causing a loud hissing sound. George got out of the truck and addressed the Judge. "Hey Mr. Archibald, isn't it a little late to be going out now?"

"I'm not going George, these guys are," he said, pointing to JuJu and Marshall.

"Oh," George responded. "Aren't you the same guys that asked me about renting a plane earlier tonight? Didn't waste any time, did you?"

"No, we got lucky," Marshall answered. "The Judge here agreed to rent his aircraft for a few hours. Just wanting to have some fun air time, you know how it is."

The airport worker replied quietly to Marshall, "The Judge looks a little under the weather. You sure he isn't going to try to fly this plane? If he is I got to call my boss and I don't think it will happen."

"No, he's not going up with us. Fill up the tanks, okay?" said Marshall.

Before George topped off the C-47's tanks he told the Judge, "I'm sorry Judge, but my boss told me that you had to pay cash, that okay?"

"Yes," Marshall answered for the Judge. "I'm paying. I fly, I buy."

"Okay then," George answered. He finished fueling the airplane and just as he was rolling the hose back onto the truck, Detective Murphy arrived at the airport gate, siren blaring and grille lights flashing violently.

The Judge started backing away from JuJu and Marshall, realizing something seemed wrong. "Stay where you are!" JuJu told the Judge and grabbed him by the arm.

JuJu pulled out the 9 mm Beretta he had bought from

Bobby G and held it to the Judge's head. "Marshall, fire this plane up right now, we're leaving!" he instructed. Marshall scrambled up the ladder and disappeared inside the C-47. After a couple of anxious moments, the engines started. Next, JuJu pointed the gun toward George. "Stay put!"

George backed up to the fuel truck, his eyes never leaving JuJu and the 9 mm that pointed alternately between him and the Judge. "You ain't gonna shoot me, you big son-of-a bitch! You hit the fuel truck and we all go up!" George yelled, once he had reached the relative safety of the door. He got into the truck and sped away. Reaching the gate, he brought the fuel truck to a lurching stop, jumped out, and ran to open the gate.

Detective Nick Silvano and Charley Goetz were just approaching the Marathon Airport and saw the Monroe County Sheriff's car go through the gate. They followed it through to the tarmac, then stopped by the idling twin engine C-47 airplane. Nick recognized JuJu standing next to the plane's boarding ladder, holding a gun to the head of an elderly man. He and Goetz exited the car, keeping their doors open to serve as a makeshift shield.

"Everybody just stay back," JuJu shouted. "We are leaving and if you try to stop us I will shoot the Judge in the head, understand me?"

Detective Murphy and the informant Bobby G, stood next to their car. "You guys with the DEA?" Murphy yelled over the engine noise.

"Yeah," Goetz yelled in return.

"Well, this is your baby," Murphy shouted. "You call the shots."

"Not them!" JuJu yelled, thumping a large hand against his broad chest. "I am calling the shots now."

Nick spoke first, "JuJu, that guy means nothing to me. You think you have the upper hand? You got nothing! I won't hesitate to put a bullet in your head." He pulled his 9 mm Smith and Wesson and aimed it at JuJu and the Judge.

"Do you believe in your God, Nick?" JuJu asked. "Come a little closer, I have something to tell you."

Keeping his gun pointed squarely at JuJu, Nick advanced to within five feet of his adversary.

"The only thing you are going to tell me JuJu is 'goodbye' cause you are within a couple of seconds of meeting your maker," Nick said.

"You know something Nick? We are a lot alike. We both have the warrior spirits in our souls. You could kill me and I could kill you and neither of us would lose a minute of sleep. My maker Ogun is with me," JuJu continued. "It is your God that allowed me to take people you care about and put them in harm's way. Your God is weak! If you want to roll the dice and test the power of my Gods, you will not like the outcome."

Nick only half-heard the words JuJu was dishing out; he was focused on finding a clear shot but the Judge's bobbing head made it difficult to retain a line of sight that didn't also go through the Judge's head and, unlike what he had told JuJu, he didn't really want to shoot the Judge. But something about JuJu's rant caught in his head and without lowering his weapon he demanded, "What do you mean by 'taking people I care about'?"

JuJu's response was to pull a cell phone from his pocket and place it into the Judge's hand. "Call this number and hand the phone to the Detective," said JuJu, pointing toward Nick while keeping the Beretta trained against the Judge's temple.

The Judge did as he was ordered and after the call was answered, he slid the phone along the ground to the Cleveland Narcotics Detective. Nick squatted down and picked up the phone with his free hand and held it up to his ear, all without taking his eyes or his gun off JuJu. "Anybody there?" he said into the mouthpiece.

"Nick, is that you?"

"Kat! Kat where are you?" he asked, not able to keep the surprise from his voice.

"I've been kidnapped! There's two of them, Jamaicans I think!" she spoke hurriedly, not sure when, or if, she'd get another chance. And there's another girl too. They said they will kill us if you don't do exactly as you are told. Nick! Where are you?"

Son of a bitch! Nick looked at JuJu, who now sported a wide grin across his broad face.

"Don't worry Kat," Nick told the terrified girl. "Who else is with you?"

"She says her name is Sydney," Kat answered. "Here, she wants to talk to you."

"Nicky, that you?"

"Holy Christ," Nick exclaimed. "You're with Kat?"

"Yes!" Sydney said. "These two Jamaicans are crazy,

Nick. I really think they are going to kill us!"

"Don't worry, Sydney," he answered. "I will get both of you out of there," he said, staring intensely at JuJu making sure that he heard every word he spoke into the phone.

"Now - end the call," JuJu instructed. "But keep the phone – I won't need it anymore."

"Sydney, just stay cool," Nick said into the phone, then reluctantly hung up.

"It appears that your situation is dire, Detective Silvano," JuJu said, emphasizing his title. "You still want to roll the dice?"

Detective Murphy spoke. "I don't think this guy is going to shoot anybody, Detective," and lifted his weapon toward JuJu. Murphy advanced three steps. JuJu took his aim off the Judge and shot Bobby G between the eyes, dropping him instantly onto the tarmac.

"What the fuck!" yelled the Judge.

"Why did you do that?" Murphy shouted.

"Two reasons," answered JuJu. "He's the reason you are all here to try to take away my freedom. If it wasn't for him calling you, I would be gone by now. And besides, he didn't bring anything to the table of life anyway," continued JuJu.

"And you do? You are a common killer JuJu, nothing more, nothing less," Silvano taunted.

"So are you, Nick," JuJu answered. "The people I killed were lowlifes that you could give a shit about. The only difference is that you do it behind a badge."

"Okay JuJu, what's next?" Charley Goetz spoke, attempting to diffuse the hostilities.

"What's next is that me and the Judge are going to get on this plane and fly out of here. Any attempts to stop me and I will dump the Judge's body into the Atlantic Ocean and those two girls back in Cleveland will die a very horrible death."

Nick spoke to JuJu. "If any harm comes to those girls, there will be no place on this earth that you will be able to hide from me. I will hunt you down and kill you, you got that?" Nick's voice was low and measured and he glared at JuJu like he was the devil himself.

JuJu knew the Detective meant every word. "Nick, I am going to keep my word with you," JuJu said as he walked the Judge up the loading ladder into the plane, the Beretta still pressed into the back of his neck. "After we leave, I will make a call from the plane and the women will go free. Wait exactly fifteen minutes then hit Redial. But if you call before I have made my call, both women will die. It is up to you. Your turn to roll the dice."

Nick instinctively knew JuJu would make good on his threat. JuJu instructed Marshall to take off and the old plane taxied to the south end of the runway. Marshall keyed the mike six times to signal the unmanned tower to remotely turn on the landing lights. The Gooney Bird raced down the runway with its engines roaring fire and the ancient plane's nose rose up into the sky. It made a lazy turn east over the ocean, becoming smaller and smaller until it was gone from the sight of the men standing on the tarmac.

JuJu watched Marshall work the aircraft controls. The cockpit lights were dim and somehow comforting and the electric glow from the Florida Keys was fading in the western sky. "I think we can make it JuJu," said Marshall. "What's going to happen to the Judge and them girls?"

"I am a man of my word, Marshall. Those women will live as long as nobody interferes with us. I do not believe the authorities will shoot us out of the sky as long as we have the Judge as our hostage. Turn off the plane's transponder and do not answer the radio," he instructed.

The Judge huddled on the floor behind the pilot's seat. The pungent odor of sweat, whiskey, and fear emanated from the frightened man's skin and hovered around him like an invisible shield. "Please Lord," he sobbed, weeping uncontrollably into his hands.

The pilot and the fugitive ignored him. "We need to stay away from the Boca Chica area," Marshall said. "We get into that airspace and we'll have the entire United States Navy on our ass. And they won't care if we have a hostage or not. Key West Naval Air Station will scramble fighter jets to take us out. Low and slow is our only option."

Nick watched helplessly from the ground as the plane took a lumbering turn away from U.S. territory and disappeared over the ocean.

Chapter 34

After the longest fifteen minutes of his life, Nick hit the redial button as JuJu had instructed. The phone rang four times before a familiar voice answered. "Who is this?"

"Sydney! This is Nick. Are you and Kat okay?"

"Yeah," she answered. "We're both fine. They never hurt us but we were plenty worried."

"Are the Jamaicans still there?" he asked.

"No. They untied us, then ran out of the door. I could hear the car tires screeching when they took off."

"Sydney. Now listen. Call 911 right now and do not leave until the police get there! And put Kat on the line!"

"Hey, that girl is something," Sydney told him. "She tried some psychology shit on those two guys and she just about had them crying for their mommies before they found their balls and gagged us. She's okay!"

"Yeah, great Sydney. Glad you like her," Nick answered wryly to break the tension. "Guess I should have run all my dates past you for your approval. Now put her on the phone!"

"Nick?" Kat asked. "Where are you?"

"I'm in Florida – Marathon Island."

"Did you get the bastard?" she asked, all traces of fear

gone from her voice.

"Almost Kat, we were that close," he said, holding his thumb and forefinger together in the air in front of him as if she could actually see the gesture.

"You'll get him Nick – I know you will," she said. "So what do we do now?"

"After the police come, you'll have to go to the station and make a statement. It might be hard right now, but the more you can remember and tell the detectives, the more they'll have to work with to nail these guys."

"Don't worry, Nick. We'll do what needs to be done. I just can't wait to see you."

"Me too," he said into the phone. "Kat," he stopped for a moment before he could get the words out. "I'm so sorry. I never thought for a moment that you'd get dragged into this mess. If anything had happened to you..." He wanted to say more but the words wouldn't come.

"It's okay Nick, I can take it," she assured him. "Besides, now I think I have the topic for my master's thesis."

"Oh yeah? What's that."

"The Psychology of Hostage Negotiations: When you're the hostage!"

Chapter 35

M arshall saw aircraft lights fast approaching his starboard side and he took the plane lower until it almost touched the eight foot ocean swells below. The plane's radio came alive with a barely controlled angry U.S. Coast Guard voice demanding a response from the renegade plane. Marshall ignored them.

He turned the plane toward the Cuban Coast and crossed into the Twelve Mile Zone claimed by the Cuban government as their sovereign airspace and maneuvered the lumbering aircraft back and forth over the forbidden line separating Cuban space from international waters. Now the radio crackled with demands from the Cuban Air Traffic controller. "You - unidentified aircraft, leave our airspace or you will be shot down!"

Marshall knew the threats were very real and his grip on the controls tightened. "This is the most dangerous part. If the Coast Guard does what I think, their attention will soon be focused on the Cuban fighters scrambling to intercept us. But if we can make it to that cloud bank ahead, we may be able to avoid being shot down by either side."

"No!" wailed the Judge. "Not my plane!"

JuJu gave him a kick and barked "Silence!"

To Marshall, he said, "Just do it!"

"Don't worry, man," Marshall said. "I learned this in 'Nam. We trained for stuff like this when we dropped the Green Berets into Cambodia."

The radio barked demands from both the U.S. Coast Guard and the Cubans but Marshall soon disappeared into the cloudy haze, skimming the water to avoid the radar pings searching for the old, but sturdy, C-47 airplane. He adjusted course for the coast of Trinidad-Tobago and Couva Airfield. A brisk tailwind pushed the plane from behind and the expert drug smuggling pilot played with the controls like an intense video gamer, coaxing the engines to use as little fuel as possible.

"We might just make it without having to drop into the ocean," Marshall said.

JuJu didn't comment; his mind was filled with "flights of ideas" and he was second guessing his actions.

Should I kill the judge?

Should I have the Jamaicans return and kill the girls?

Should I have them hunt down and kill Nick Silvano?

JuJu remembered the Proverbs of the Ogun's Okano that said, "Your dead enemy wishes the worst for you. The dead are not so dead."

His options were many but he decided to not test the power of Ogun's proverbs. A living Nick is able to be seen; a dead Nick cannot be anticipated. I am more fearful of the dead than the living, he thought and his decision was made. *All will live. I have my money and my freedom.*

The plane flew on; the pursuers no longer visible. The radio stopped squawking.

"There's Couva field," said Marshall pointing out the cockpit windshield. "We made it." The plane began its descent just as the low fuel alarms sounded. Couva was a small airfield with a single landing strip, unmanned by authorities. As Marshall dropped the old C-47 onto the concrete and taxied to a stop, JuJu saw a car driving out to meet them, his friend Gerard behind the wheel.

"What about my money?" Marshall asked.

JuJu removed a wrapped bundle of one hundred dollar bills from the backpack and handed it to Marshall. "This is payment for your services. If you wish to pay the Judge, that is your decision. The authorities saw you at the Marathon airport and I suggest you tell them you were forced to fly the plane. I see no benefit in killing the Judge as long as both of you agree to forget about me."

JuJu turned to the Judge and said, "You will be paid and you can keep your plane, just keep your mouth shut about Marshall helping me, you got it?'

Judge Archibald never knew such relief. "Yes sir, I am grateful, thank...thank you!"

Exiting the plane, he turned to Marshall and the Judge. "Remember what I said," he warned, then got into the waiting car and drove off.

Marshall turned to face his reluctant passenger. "Judge, I highly suggest you do what the man said. We're both alive – now let's fly your plane back to Marathon, agreed?"

Judge Archibald answered, "Just get us out of here and when we get back to the Dog, the drinks are on me!"

"Looks like we'll have to pool our funds to refuel," Marshall said. "How much you got?"

Chapter 36

The east Port of Spain Mayor Louis Lee Sing had been quoted in the Trinidad Express Newspaper saying that "the level of shootings, the level of banditry, the level of violence, has risen a thousand times fold."

The main source of the Mayor's troubles now stood on Nelson Street in Trinidad-Tobago watching the annual March 30 Spiritual Baptist Parade go by. JuJu was home; just meters away from the Housing Development Corporation's Nelson Street housing estate, or HDC, as it was called by the residents. Since returning to his native land, and with the help of his friend Gerard, JuJu re-established control of his old territory. As the bodies of those who had filled the vacuum of his absence began appearing in public places, the remaining competitors were now "glad to be working for the Obeah Man again," or so Gerard reported.

This is where JuJu had grown up and to the desperate, gritty, youth of Nelson Street, he was a hometown hero and the real deal. The money was pouring in.

Under his tutelage, his young students excelled at petty robbery. A tourist stuck in busy Nelson Street traffic would suddenly find their vehicle surrounded by five or six young thugs. One would attack the driver while the others would reach into the windows and grab jewelry from the women's necks and wrists and rip wallets from pockets. JuJu paid the young robbers for the merchandise, then resold the goods to the gold dealers and camera shop owners for a handy profit. It was a win-win proposition.

The annual March 30th Celebration of the Spiritual Baptist Liberation Day continued as it had since 1951 when the government officially recognized that the religion and members of JuJu's faith were able to openly practice their beliefs without fear of being arrested or harassed by the Police. Colorful dancers filled the streets, clanging bells and singing. JuJu watched as a Moko Jumbie in a colorful costume and skeleton carnival mask deftly threaded its way through the throngs of participants and on-lookers from its stilted perch.

He could almost hear his grandmother's voice relating the legend of the Jumbie to him and Moon when they were children. "A Moko is a god that originated in Africa from the Nuapa people in the Congo and Nigeria," she had told them. "He was said to be very tall and could watch over villages and foresee danger and evil. The Moko walked to Trinidad from the west coast of Africa, across the waters, enduring hardships and inhumane treatment. He lived in the hearts of the African descendants during slavery, to eventually walk the streets of Trinidad in a celebration of freedom."

The people of Trinidad adopted the Moko by adding "Jumbie" or "ghost" to the name. JuJu hated that his people no longer looked at the Moko-jumbie as a symbol of freedom for his African ancestors but just as a colorful, amusing participant in a parade.

As JuJu watched, the Moko Jumbie stopped in front of him and he tilted his head back to look up at it. Why was he stopping? The Jumbie's gaze locked upon him as the parade continued on past the large, black man and the stilted character. Blackness emanated from behind the Jumbie's mask, and JuJu squinted to clear his own vision, which had dimmed slightly. *What's going on? Why can't I move?* The Jumbie raised its arms toward JuJu, both hands extended, reaching for him. The masked head shook from side-to-side for several seconds before finally turning away to rejoin the throng of people in the street.

JuJu still didn't move. Even though it was a very hot day in east Port of Spain, he was chilled. He looked up the street, but the Jumbie had disappeared from view. JuJu willed himself to move and with one last glance up the street, he turned and retreated to his flat in the HDC.

Why did the Moko-Jumbie ghost stop and look at me? This was a sign – a very bad sign. He had been back in Trinidad for almost two months and while it was very profitable and he still had almost four million dollars in cash, he knew it was inevitable that he would be robbed or killed for his money. He had to get off of

Nelson Street. The Jumbie had warned him. JuJu summoned Gerard to his flat and told him about the Moko Jumbie.

"Gerard, mon, he looked right at me like he knew who I was! It is a warning! It is time for us to leave this place. The Spirit Ghost has sent a message – we must obey!"

Gerard answered his friend, "You be the big believer in the Orisha, JuJu. Me, not so much. But I respect your beliefs. We can go to the Hyatt Regency Hotel and stay there until you decide what to do next."

The cash from the Dickens Avenue killings and the Canadian sales of the Mexicans Cartel's stolen cocaine were safely stored in a safe deposit box in the Central Bank on Frederick Street. The daily take from his young protégés' crime sprees was more than enough to meet their daily needs for quite some time. JuJu had avoided contact with his remaining family members to ensure they would not fall prey to the Mexican Cartel; he was still a wanted man and the Cartel was known for kidnapping family members of those they needed to "persuade".

He and Gerard gathered their belongings and called for a private taxi to drive them the ten blocks from the slums of Nelson Street to the Hyatt Regency Hotel. The trip took much longer than it should have as the driver had to weave his way through the colorful crowds that filled the streets. Even the distance of a few blocks put JuJu at ease. Now, he was thinking less of the Jumbie and more about getting his heroin high, which he had been doing every day since he returned to his place of birth.

How strange that this day is a celebration of release from being persecuted for religious beliefs but I am becoming enslaved by the God named Heroin, he thought as he exited the taxi. He watched as Gerard paid the driver, then lifted their two duffle bags out of the taxi's trunk. *My use of the drug is becoming too much of a need! I must get to the altar of worship and thank Ogun for sending the Moko-Jumbie to warn me.*

JuJu turned toward the street and saw the parade had now caught up to them and was passing by his location. *No! It couldn't be!* The same stilted Moko-Jumbie was making its way toward him. JuJu watched its approach, unable to move. Gerard had already entered the hotel and the taxi driver had pulled back into the cab line, leaving JuJu alone on the sidewalk. The carnival's spiritual ghost stopped in front of the hotel, towering over JuJu, and again extended his arms toward the unmoving man. Twice now, the Jumbie had sought him out!

Suddenly, the Jumbie produced a gun from under his garb and fired six rounds into JuJu's chest, then turned and disappeared into the crowd, no longer visible despite the extended height afforded by the stilts. It was almost as if he had never been there at all.

JuJu felt several thuds pound through his chest and automatically raised his hands to search for the offending stones the Jumbie had seemed to throw at him.

I must be dreaming. Why don't I feel anything?

A figure advanced toward him, and all light seemed to be sucked from the day.

Who is there? Moon? Is that you, Moon?

The figure darkened into a massive shadow, filling his field of vision. He felt something gritty move across his forehead, and then nothing. *Obeah Man Ogun....I am going to the Home of Warriors....*

***

When interviewed by police, the hotel clerks checked their reservations. "No sir, there are no reservations for anyone under those names."

"Try Moon DeBoissiere," an officer said.

"No sir, nothing," the clerk reported.

"You've got cameras. Let's see the security footage."

The video showed a tall black man, later identified as Gerard, carrying two duffel bags enter the hotel lobby then continue past the main desk and through a hallway to the hotel's back parking lot. At one point, when it looked like the man's face was about to be shown, the picture blurred. When it cleared a second later, there was no one in the hallway. A check of the parking lot video also showed nothing but parked cars. No Gerard, no one at all.

A tourist who had been standing a few feet away from the Jumbie's victim reported what he'd heard. "He said something like, 'Obey the man with the gun.' What does that mean?"

Chapter 37

After a long lunch with Kat, Detective Nick Silvano left the Captain's Quarters and returned to the DEA Office where he had been assigned since ending his active pursuit of JuJu. He had to admit it, this case had him feeling like a Rookie again; full of possibility.

Life was good! His relationship with Kat was progressing nicely since she and Sydney had been released unharmed – thank God. Nick and his partners were unable to locate Darik and Tion; the two kidnappers seemed to have vanished, just as JuJu had. The Judge and his plane made it back to Marathon Key but since they claimed JuJu had kidnapped them and forced Marshall to fly the plane, no charges were filed. A pair of Marathon detectives responding to a report about an abandoned motorcycle in a shopping center parking lot reported that someone had used the nearby Marathon County Library computers and had signed in using the name Nicholas Silvano.

Agent-in-Charge Charley Goetz entered the large office where the agents and police met daily to receive orders and exchange information. "Hey Nick," he said excitedly. "You've got to see this! C'mon, everyone should see this!" he said and clicked on the large computer screen in the meeting room. "This is unbelievable!"

"What is it, Charlie – another porn film declared as evidence?" an officer joked.

"Aw, shut up." He brought up a YouTube video narrated by an attractive television news reporter with a Caribbean accent.

"The following video was captured by a cellphone user in front of the Hyatt Regency hotel in downtown east Port of Spain during the annual Spiritual Baptist Liberation Day parade. The video is graphic so you might want to exclude your children from viewing this," the reporter warned.

The agents and cops watched as a colorful stilt walker left his position in a parade and fired six rounds from a handgun into a bystander and then walked away as the victim fell backward into the portico of the Hyatt Regency Hotel.

The newscaster continued speaking as the coverage zoomed in on the surprised face of the dying JuJu to the world. "What is most amazing," the reporter continued, "are these marks left on the victim's body." The shaking cellphone video moved closer to the body and focused on the crudely drawn black crosses visible through the blood on the dead man's forehead and bare chest. "Anyone with information on this case is urged to contact the east Port of Spain police department...."

Nick watched in silence – his search for JuJu had come to an end. "How about that, Charley? Just goes to show you – the dice of God are always loaded!"

Epilogue

E ven though they hailed from warm climates themselves, the three men seemed uncomfortable in the Mexican resort setting of Cancun. It wasn't the warmth; they were used to the heat. It wasn't the sounds; they were used to the rhythmic crashing of waves to the shore and the ever-present tourist chatter. Maybe it was the company. For across the thatch-roof covered table anchored in the sand of one of the Zona Hotela's prime beach resorts, was Senor Marti, head of Mexico's most violent drug cartel. Four of his men stood just feet away. They were like alligators; for every one visible, many more that remained unseen.

"You have been most helpful in cleaning up this loose end," Senor Marti said as he handed an envelope to one of the men across the table. "This should be satisfactory compensation for all of you."

The man accepted the envelope without looking at its contents; he didn't want Senor Marti to think he didn't trust him.

"Gracias," Gerard said. "Let me know if I can be of further assistance to you."

"Si, si," Darik and Tion chimed in. "Gracias, gracias."

Gerard smiled at the Jamaicans. He'd deal with them later.

COMING SOON!
FROM THE AUTHORS OF
"BAD JUJU IN CLEVELAND"

Chapter 1

"Assholes!"

Joshua Ramsey looked disgustedly at the three psychiatric interns gathered around his patient seated at a table in the day area. The young black girl sat with her head in her hands and sobbed while the interns spoke to her as they waited for their instructor/mentor to show up for the mandatory morning rounds. While he could not hear what they were saying to her, he knew it was upsetting her. He moved closer to the trio of would-be medical doctors and overheard the tall one say, "Honey, why don't you tell Doctor Ativan here what is bothering you? My name is Doctor Haldol and this other fella here is Doctor Valium and we are here to help you get better."

They stood over her, arms folded over their short, white physician's coats to obscure their real name tags from being seen by the trembling patient. While the tall intern kept speaking, his companions tried, unsuccessfully, to stifle muted giggles.

Registered Nurse Joshua Ramsey had enough of the immature interns and their childish actions. He walked quickly to the young girl, took her hand in his and assisted her to her feet while adjusting the hospital gown that hung on her rail-thin frame and tightened the string ties to her neck. He glared at the interns while he gingerly walked the girl away from the day area and down the white painted hallway. Her slippered feet made small scuffling sounds on the blue carpeted floor all the way down to Room 243. Nurse Ramsey helped her sit on the edge of her bed. The room was furnished with an immovable bed and a brown dresser. The only other creature comfort was a metallic mirror screwed into the wall. The lone window to the outside world faced the parking lot one story below. Adjustable blinds affixed between the double panes of unbreakable glass assured no access by patients looking for the means to do themselves harm. The "Behavioral Health Unit" of Cleveland's Mercy Hospital was a locked unit with eighteen identical rooms housing the most violent and sickest mental health patients in Northern Ohio.

Ramsey had the mental health technician sit with his patient while he removed an injection of 2mg IM Ativan and 5mg of IM Haldol from the locked drug cabinet at the nurse's station. He returned to Room 243, swabbed the girl's left shoulder with an alcohol swab, and deftly injected the mixture of mind-calming medicine into her deltoid muscle with the familiarity of having performed this action hundreds of times during his five years of nursing mental patients at Mercy.

"It's okay, Tamara," he spoke softly as the tech laid

her back onto the bed. "I won't let those men bother you again." He watched as her clenched jaw muscles relaxed, her anxiety quickly subsiding as the medicine told hold.

"What are we going to do about this, Joshua?' asked Henry. The large, black mental health technician had worked at Mercy Psych Unit for seventeen years on the night shift. "Those fucking interns are the worst I have ever seen come through here, and I have seen a lot of them!"

Mercy was a teaching hospital located on the near west side of Cleveland, Ohio. It had five medical floors over a newly revamped Emergency Unit and was classified a Level 1 Trauma Center with a helicopter landing pad newly built just below the Behavioral Unit.

"I don't know just yet, Henry," replied the nurse. "Let's wait and see who the instructor is before we take any action."

Retaliation by doctors to the nursing staff was common at Mercy. The inner city hospital was funded by Cuyahoga County taxpayers and most of the patients had no medical coverage. "Obamacare" did little to bring money into the hospital system. Future doctors had little interest in studying in a place that they knew they would not stay. Constant turnover of medical professionals was commonplace at Mercy and the three interns Joshua had rescued his patient from were no different.

After a cursory search of her sparsely furnished room turned up no plastic cutlery that she could use to harm herself, the two men left Tamara's' room, satisfied that she would not attempt to hurt herself by "cutting." The numerous scars on both her arms revealed her history of mental illness.

Joshua saw that it was approaching 7:30 a.m., which was the end of his 12 hour 7 a.m. to 7 p.m. shift. Three twelve hour shifts per week had him receiving seventy two hours every two week pay period and kept him from any overtime which the hospital administrator opposed at all costs. He had just finished his nursing reports and signed off on the meds he had dispensed when he saw Doctor Katrina Westerly hurriedly swipe her employee card through the card reader on the locked door to the nursing station. Resident Psychiatrist "Kat" Westerly was a new graduate of Case Western University School of Psychiatry. She dropped her red, oversized, bag on the counter and plopped into one of the blue office chairs lining the nursing station counter.

"Morning Josh," she said, setting her coffee mug on the counter and dangerously close to one of the eight identical computers. "How was your night?" She reached into her bag, removed the white physician's coat and stethoscope, put the coat on over her clothes and placed the stethoscope around her neck.

Joshua looked at her admiringly before he mustered an answer. In her late 20's and almost six feet tall, "Kat" as she requested she be called, had short blond hair and bright green eyes that sparkled under the nursing station's fluorescent lights. She was the "whole package." The male employees, and even some of female employees, wondered if they had a shot with her. She had paid for her college education entirely by herself working nights as a barmaid and attending classes during the day.

Her physician's coat partially covered her maroon pants and black top. Daily workouts at the hospital's employee gym had her in top physical shape and accounted for the stares received when she entered a room. The name tag she clipped to her coat while on the behavioral unit read: "Dr. Katrina" in bold black letters over the blue "Mercy Hospital Staff" on the white plastic card.

Mercy mental health unit workers had requested and received permission from the hospital administration to utilize only first names after the unit's charge nurse had been threatened by a patient with a midnight telephone call to her home phone. The patient had called her a "devil bitch" for not believing his delusions that the government had placed a computer chip in his head. The former patient had used her last name in the online search site Spokeo to obtain her number and it was the underlying belief that a disgruntled hospital worker had released the phone number to the patient after being fired when he was caught drinking on duty.

After looking around to make sure the other nursing staff was out of earshot, Joshua leaned into her personal space. "Kat, I'm having a problem with your three interns," he said, his glance moving to the nursing station glass windows through which the offending men could be seen sitting quietly at a table reading patient charts. "I caught them taunting my patient, Tamara, from Room 243. I want them to stop their childish behavior! My patients are very sick and cannot tolerate the emotional stimulation being placed on them."

"Josh," answered Dr. Westerly. "We both know you are the best advocate for your patients and I absolutely will take care of it. As a new doctor mentoring medical students in the psych rotation, my situation is touchy. The veteran docs all squeezed out of teaching this rotation and I got stuck with it. Trust me, it will be dealt with and I guarantee it will not happen again."

She rose to her feet and taking her coffee cup in one hand and a patient census sheet in the other, stood over Josh waiting for his response.

"I know you will, Doc. I just get really pissed off when my patients get abused. I trust you and will keep this between you, me, and my aide Henry. None of the other staff here seems to give a shit. Night shift robots. That's all they are. Gotta go punch out before I get a minute of overtime and get points on my personnel jacket," he said sarcastically.

Dr. Kat Westerly made a mental note, "Joshua Ramsey seems to be getting some nurse burnout." Little did she know that he was beyond "burnout" and into the "angry" part of his nursing career.

Chapter Two

"I can't move! Nick, I can't fucking move!" Detective

Richie Allen moaned.

"C'mon, Richie, I know these chairs are uncomfortable but stop messing around," replied Cleveland Police Homicide Detective Nicholas Silvano, Badge #124. "We've got a murder scene to get back to." Nick stood just inside the door to the small Police Report adjacent to Mercy Hospital's Emergency Room intake desk. The room held a small metal desk, three wooden chairs and two tan plastic phones with "Police Only" scribbled on the receivers in black magic marker.

"What the hell?" His young partner was shaking, arms crossed rigidly over his chest, and his eyes were glassy. Nick waved a hand in front of Richie's face. No response. He could hear the young detective's teeth grinding in his mouth as he fought to remove himself from the chair.

Nick went to the door and yelled out to the nurse bent over one of the many computers on wheels affectionately nicknamed COWS behind the intake counter. "Get me a doctor in here quick!" he yelled. She looked up, annoyed that the detective would interrupt her pounding on the keys.

"What do you need, Detective?" she asked impatiently looking over the top of her black rimmed glasses affixed low on her face.

"I'm not sure," answered Nick, "Just get somebody in here quick!"

Nick returned to Richie and pulled up one of the chairs and sat down facing the still unmoving police officer.

"Richie, what is it, what's wrong?' Nick asked nervously.

"I just can't get up, Nick. I want to but my body won't work," Richie said through gritted teeth.

The attending Emergency Room Doctor entered the report room. Doctor George Saradakis had just pronounced the Homicide Detectives' murder victims, "deceased". The mother and her infant son were killed by her husband, the boy's father. Both were stabbed to death with a large butcher knife. Dr. Saradakis had pulled the serrated blade from the mother's abdomen and it was now encased in a clear, plastic evidence bag on the desk in front of the two cops. You could still see the blood. "Detective, what is it?" asked the doctor as he waved his pen light into the detective's eyes.

"I don't know, Doc," Richie grimaced. The doctor grabbed his arm and tried to move it away from his chest.

"Damn!" muttered "Doctor George" as he was called by his patients and staff. "Get me a cart and an IV kit," he ordered to the ER staff assembled in the doorway.

In a matter of minutes the skilled ER employees had an IV inserted into the detective's right ante cubicle and had piggybacked the ordered valium mixing with the 1000 cc's of normal saline bag flowing through the tubing into Richie's arm. The IV pump was affixed to a pole placed next to the still unmoving detective.

"Let's give him a couple of minutes. And get that frigging knife out of here," ordered Doctor George.

Nick picked up the evidence bag containing the

bloody knife and put it inside his jacket, out of sight of his partner but still in his possession, being careful to not disturb the chain of evidence that could have it thrown out of court at a later date.

Doctor George was busy taking Richie's vital signs and after a few minutes, he was able to pry his arms away from his chest. "Let's get up on the cart, Detective," he said calmly. "You're going to be just fine now."

Richie allowed the two male paramedics gently assist him to stand and turn and then help him to lie back onto the gurney while the nurse kept the IV tubing intact, positioning the pole next to the wheeled cart.

"Put him into ER 12 for now," Doctor George said.

After Richie was taken from the report room, Nick asked, "What the hell was that Doc?"

Doctor George closed the door and turned to face Nick. "I'm not sure, but I think your young partner had a psychotic episode of sorts. What happened to you guys back at the house where the mom and son were murdered?"

"Aw, it was bad Doc, real bad," Nick said, shaking his head. "The uniforms were sent to the apartment on Detroit Avenue by 65th Street. A neighbor had called 911 on a 'female screaming' and all kinds of crashing sounds coming from the upstairs residence. Zone Car 112 responded and found the female dead on the floor with the knife sticking out of her stomach and the husband in the kitchen cooking something in a big aluminum pot. He had gospel music blaring and acted like nothing was wrong. After they cuffed him they called for an ambulance and a boss. You know the drill, the boss calls radio for Homicide and CSI. We get there pretty quick and the neighbor tells us that they had a newborn baby boy just home from the hospital last week.

"Me and Richie start looking and I find the baby – dead – wrapped in a blanket inside his crib. Before I could do anything else, Richie yelled from the kitchen and I ran in there to see him puking into the sink."

Nick paused and took a long, deep breath before continuing.

"Richie had looked into the pot and found the baby's head floating in the boiling water. The father had decapitated the little kid and was cooking him on the stove. The dad was asked what he had done and he calmly said that 'Jesus told him to do it' and that the mom and baby were possessed by the devil. What would make this guy do something like that Doc?" asked Nick, his voice quavering and gaze directed at the floor as if the answer to his question were scribbled on one of the dirty tiles.

"Nick," said Dr. George. "You, more than anyone, know this world if full of awful things. You cops see it all and you bring it into my Emergency Room for the rest of the world to see. The terrible things people do to each other and to themselves is never ending. This is one of the worst and most senseless things I have ever seen in my twenty some years of emergency doctoring."

"Doc, I've been a Cleveland cop for twenty-one years and this is the worst incident I have ever seen. And I've seen it all: killings, suicides, dead kids that went missing and later found suffocated in abandoned refrigerators, and all sorts of terrible things. This is at the top of the list. Just unbelievable misery."

Both men stood quietly engrossed in their own thoughts until Nick straightened up and asked, "What about Richie, Doc. You think he's gonna be okay?"

Doctor Saradakis took Nick by the arm, steering him out of the Police Report room and into the ER's main lobby. "I've seen this before Nick. In Afghanistan. I'm still a member of the National Guard and did a tour in the Middle East a few years back. It's a form of 'shell shock'. Your young partner witnessed a tragedy that sent him into a state of mind that caused his physical body to just shut down. I think he will be fine, given some time. Let's go check on him."

The two men entered the curtained ER-12 room to find Richie sitting up on the side of the hospital bed. He hopped off and stood sheepishly in front of the ER Doctor and his partner. The IV line was still imbedded into his arm and kept him tethered to the shiny aluminum pole.

"I'm sorry, Nicky," he said quietly. "I don't know why I acted like that. I just kept thinking about my two little boys at home with my wife and what my life would be without them. You're not gonna say anything about this to Lieutenant Fratello, are you?" he asked, referring to his commanding officer in the Homicide Unit. "I don't want him thinking I can't do my job."

"Not if you don't want me to but maybe we should ask the Doc here if you are going to be okay.' Nick turned to Doctor George and asked him, "You think this can stay 'in house' Doc?

Dr. Saradakis spoke quietly to both Detectives. "Detective Allen, I can't allow you to be on active duty until a complete evaluation is made. Once we treated you as a patient, you are in the system and reports were generated. Too many people saw what happened and I can't jeopardize the ER Department's staff by ignoring the incident. But, I think a couple of weeks on what you guys call light duty and a follow up with a licensed shrink will make you whole again. Physically you are fine but your mental state was compromised by what you saw and until you are given a return to duty slip by the assigned doctor, I suggest you take it easy for a few days. You going to be okay with that?"

"I guess I am going to have to be, Doc. I feel fine now, just a little woozy from the valium."

"Good," the Emergency Room physician said. "Let's make a referral for a follow-up with a mental health professional and we can get you out of here now." He turned to Detective Silvano and said, "Nick, you still seeing Dr. Katrina Westerly? Any problem with me referring Richie to see her since she is a psychiatrist in-house here at Mercy?"

"No problem at all," Nick answered.

"Good." He turned back to Richie. "Dr. Westerly's office is in the Medical Building next door. If you're okay with that, let's get you discharged."

"Sure, Doc. Whatever you say," Richie answered quickly before the Doc could change his mind.

Nick had his own thoughts but kept them to himself. He didn't like Kat knowing too much about his job. Mixing work with pleasure was never a good idea. But Richie was his partner and he knew Kat never blabbed about her patients.

ABOUT THE AUTHORS

KARL BORT was a United States Air Force jet mechanic in Texas and Georgia before joining the Cleveland, Ohio Police Department. During his 27-year police career, he worked Patrol, Auto Theft, and spent 11 years as a Narcotics Detective. He worked closely with the DEA, including a two-year assignment on national cases, often in an undercover role. As the elected president of the Cleveland Police Patrolmen's Association, Karl was responsible for negotiating contracts and protecting the rights of all Cleveland Police Officers. Following retirement, he returned to school, became a Licensed Practical Nurse, and worked 15 years as a medical surgical nurse and psychiatric nurse for the Cleveland Clinic. Karl now spends his second "retirement" in Ohio with his wife, children and grandchildren, indulging in his new career – writing police thrillers.

THEKLA MADSEN is a corporate business analyst, technical writer, and marketing consultant. She has worked for cooperative and corporate businesses in the agriculture, medical, and banking and financial services industries, was executive editor, writer and photographer for a regional women's magazine, and has published articles in national trade magazines. Thekla and her husband live in Wisconsin on the family's century farm.

Visit the authors' website at: www.bortmadsen.com